MW00585718

FIGHTER

S. MASSERY

This book is a work of fiction. Any references to historical events, real people, or real places are used fictitiously. Other names, characters, places, and events are products of the author's imagination, and any resemblance to actual events or places or persons living or dead is entirely coincidental.

Copyright © 2022 by S. Massery

All rights reserved.

Editing by Studio ENP

Proofreading by Paige Sayer Proofreading

Cover Design by Qamber Designs

Cover Photo by Wander Aguiar

No part of this book may be reproduced in any form or by any electronic or mechanical means, including information storage and retrieval systems, without written permission from the author, except for the use of brief quotations in a book review.

introduction &
warning

Dear reader,

Thank you for joining me! If you are unfamiliar with my work, fair warning: my stories run dark (violence, explicit content, etc.). Sterling Falls is no different.
Reader discretion is advised.

xoxo,

Sara

Prequel: THRILL
(download at smassery.com/thrill)
#1: THIEF
#2: FIGHTER
#3: REBEL
#4: QUEEN

wolfe

I peer over the edge of the cliff. The skies are angry today, the clouds low and dark. The waves crash into the rock below. There are more whitecaps than usual, the wind catching the spray and catapulting it up. The cold breeze buffs my frozen face.

We seemed to have skipped fall and gone straight to winter.

"This would be a nice place to die, don't you think?" I turn my back to the cliff.

The man on the ground lets out a noise, muffled by the ball of fabric shoved in his mouth. The whites of his eyes are yellowish, matching his nicotine-stained teeth. His dull brown irises keep rolling around, hunting for an escape.

"It's peaceful up here." I dig my toe into his ribs, and the whimpers get louder. "The taste of saltwater in the air. The view."

He finally jerks away from me, as much as he's able, and I laugh.

I crouch and grip his hair, ripping his face back. His arms are bound behind his back, and rope cinches his legs together from ankle to hip. If I pushed him over the edge—which he's no doubt envisioning—he would either sink or float. And if he floats, the waves smashing into the rocks would do the rest. Unless he can swim like a mermaid...

"Do you know why you're here?"

He shakes his head as much as he can.

I tsk. "You're *here* because you own a trucking company that doesn't go through us. I get it. I'm all for entrepreneurs. But when you come into my territory, encroach on my business, and then spit in my face by working with my enemies? That's a death wish."

The man goes still, and what little light was in his eyes extinguishes.

I release him. He sags back into the grass, facedown, and stays like that. He owns the truck that hit my Jeep. Whether he was there or not, it doesn't fucking matter. His truck was never reported stolen. In fact, it's still sitting in a lot in South Falls. The tires are blown out, and the engine has been stripped, but that's another matter.

"Tell you what, Marv. I'll remove your gag. If you tell me everything I need to know, I won't gut you and shove you into the ocean."

He lifts his head and nods frantically.

I pull my knife and ignore his flinch. I saw through the rope that's been holding the wad of fabric in his mouth for the last four hours. He spits it out as soon as he can and works his jaw. There's a deep, twisted imprint on his cheeks, cutting straight to his mouth. I drop the rope to the ground in front of his face. I flip my knife, and the handle makes a satisfying noise as it smacks into my palm. I picked up that habit from Apollo, and now I can't seem to stop.

The weight of my blade is familiar. It's been my faithful

companion, especially for the last few days. I've seen and done things that pushed me past the point of redemption.

I'm not sorry for it, either.

"Don't kill me, man."

I sneer. "You're in no fucking position to barter."

Blood rushes to his face. I grab his hair again and lift him by it. He yells, wriggling, but he can't get away. I force him off his belly and to his knees, and he sags there. He's already defeated. And why shouldn't he be? He was screwed the moment he came to Sterling Falls.

I pull the video of Kora being taken, the clear view of *his* truck smashing into my Jeep, and shove it under his nose. That damn video circulated for almost a day before it was taken down. The hastily stitched-together auction video garnered enough attention.

Still, it wasn't a lot to go on. It took too long to find him.

The auction started yesterday. It ends today. But before that, we went through five days of agony, searching down any lead. I hovered in between hopefulness and doubt. The thought that constantly replayed in my head was that we could've missed the auction and she was simply... gone.

There was just no trace of Kora or Kronos. No clue as to where he took her.

Saint was finally able to locate the missing truck and its owner. It wasn't like he was stupid enough to put his logo on it—or if he was, Kronos thought ahead and removed it. The license plate on the back was covered.

"I'm sorry," Marv moans. "I had no choice."

We don't have time for this.

In the back of my head, the clock is running down on ever being able to find Kora again. And in my irrational anger, I slice my blade across his chest. His shirt splits, falling open like a curtain parting. His skin is pockmarked, creased and tan with a distinct weathered-leather look. I nick his skin, and beads of bright-red blood well to the surface.

Adrenaline flushes through my system, louder than my anger for a moment. I crack my neck to relieve the pressure. "Where did you take her? I won't ask a second time."

Saint couldn't get access to the West Falls traffic cams. We tracked the truck after the attack up from South Falls, past SFU, and directly into Titan territory. And then he vanished. It took us three days to figure out that the truck had circled back to South Falls that afternoon. And another day to find where it had parked.

Another twelve hours to find where Marvin Kyler, the squirming man in front of me, was hiding.

And now we're here, on day six. I haven't slept through the night in over a week. Kora doesn't need me to sleep. She needs me to find her.

"Okay, okay." He blinks rapidly, shifting from one side to the other. "There was an old chapel by the reservoir. It appeared to be under construction, and I didn't ask any questions. He said he'd kill me if I did."

"They took her there?"

He nods sharply.

I saw that chapel when I was a kid. It's technically outside of Sterling Falls, and therefore neutral ground. Supposedly. Apparently, Kronos has been taking liberties.

My phone vibrates in my hand, and I answer the call from Saint.

"It's over," he says.

I swear. Our time just officially ran out. He's been watching the auction for me, jumping servers with our tech guy to avoid getting kicked out. The bids that came in were coded, but they cracked that with relative ease. So we were able to tell *who* was bidding–and how much. It quickly went from heart-wrenching to heart-*stopping*. Too much fucking money. God only knows what these bastards would want from her.

"Who got her?"

He pauses. The weight of it is heavy. So fucking heavy.

"Saint. *Who got her?*"

"Your father," Saint finally admits. "They put in a last-minute bid and beat out everyone."

I hang up on him and stare down at Marvin. "Sorry, Marv. Your time has run out."

"But—"

I move behind him and pull his head back. His breath stutters in shock, his eyes rolling back. The fear pours off of him, and then a sour smell fills the air. I wrinkle my nose and slide the knife across his throat.

There's a spray of blood, and I tighten my hold on his hair as he wheezes his last few breaths. The blood slows, gushing down his front. It takes a minute, maybe two. I keep my gaze on his face the whole time, letting some of my anger go with his death. I attach it to him—because if not him, I'd go south to my father's clubhouse and murder every last one of them.

He goes limp, dying a pitiful death. Poor bastard. I drag him to the cliff and push him over. His body crashes into the water, and then the waves swallow him whole.

I stare down for a moment at the spot where he vanished.

Nothing has changed. Kora is still gone, and the rage still simmers under my skin like a living thing.

At least he died with a good view.

kora

I *don't want to die.*

The folded knife the sheriff gave me is tucked into the waistband of my underwear—the only hiding place I had at the time. My head spins, but I manage to shift my hips toward one of my hands. Flames sear my skin, but it's still mostly at the other side of the room.

If I think about burning, I might lose it.

So I focus on the ceiling, gritting my teeth as I manage to locate the knife. My arms are tied to the chair, and my ankles, and my fall backward didn't do me any good. It takes too long for me to flip open the knife and work out how to cut the zip tie. I can't think straight, but I can't afford *not* to think straight.

And above it all, a pressing fear that if I move slower, I will die.

Kronos will win.

The smoke is descending. It curls along the ceiling, dark and thick. The air is getting hotter, harder to breathe. The fire has reached this side now, fueled by the gasoline. Flames lick at the walls, the boxes. So many freaking boxes, stacked all the way to the top. The cardboard curls and blackens.

With a *snap*, the zip tie breaks.

I grab the front of my shirt and yank it over my nose and mouth, then cut the rest of my limbs free. My heart is beating out of my chest.

I roll away from the fallen metal chair and scramble for the stairs. Kronos left only minutes ago—he might still be outside.

But even that fear can't deter me from gripping the doorknob and shoving it open.

Well. I *try* to shove it open.

It doesn't budge.

The smoke is worse up here. It burns my eyes. I keep my shirt up, but it doesn't help much. I can still taste the ash on my tongue with every inhale.

You've got to be kidding me. An extra precaution? Lock the tied-up girl in the on-fire basement?

I pound on the door. "Help! I'm down here!"

I don't know who will find me. This place seems to be a party spot and nothing more. I throw my shoulder into the door, and it shudders but doesn't move.

So I repeat. I slam my fists against the painted wood, but a wave of dizziness hits me.

This is stupid–I can't get out this way. What I should do is stay away from the smoke, go back lower. I don't know what I'd rather take a chance with–the smoke or the flames. Vague memories of fire safety comes back to me, but besides *stop, drop, and roll,* I can't remember much.

Lower on the staircase is safer, I reason. Better to not suffocate...

I turn and go down a step, then freeze.

It's too late.

The fire has caught on the bottom steps. I sit heavily and put my head between my knees. The panic is ebbing, and defeat floods through me. I *almost* made it. I grip the closed knife and cough weakly, trying to stay calm. My lungs are burning, my body aches, but I try to keep breathing. To stop is to give in.

Any hope of thinking straight is gone. Between the lack of oxygen and the hit I took when I fell, my vision is blurred and spotted. My mind runs sluggishly, and I can't help but acknowledge that this is it.

The end of the line.

I lie on the step and cover my face with my arms, making myself as small as possible. Maybe it won't hurt as badly as I envision. Maybe it'll be over quick.

There's a *whoosh*, and smoke floods past me.

Cool air touches the back of my neck.

And then hands grab at me, hauling me up. I'm tossed over someone's shoulder, and the jolt loosens my hold on the sheriff's knife. It slips from my hand and clatters down the stairs. Into the flames.

My rescuer steps over a something, and I blink a few times to bring it into focus.

A body.

The Titan who brought me here with Kronos, from the looks of him.

There's a hole between his eyes.

I gasp, and it triggers a coughing fit. And then we're outside. My rescuer–maybe abductor–sets me down and roughly pats my back. I hunch over, expelling the smoke from my lungs, trying to get a decent breath. The grass is cut short, bald in some places. My knees lock and keep me from falling down, but the world spins.

When I turn toward my rescuer, they grip my chin and

9

force my head the other way. I stare down at the neighboring backyard. My eyes water. I can't believe I'm outside. A few feet away, heat pours off the building. The fire has spread upward, and black smoke belches out from the open doorway, the windows. It's going up like a house made of matchsticks.

"Who are you?" I force out. My voice rasps.

The smoke, the screaming.

The *week* I've had.

"No one you need to concern yourself with." A man's voice. Deep and smooth.

It's no one I recognize off the bat, but that doesn't mean much. Still, I burn it into my mind. I need to know who rescued me. Who killed to get me out. And maybe, if I get out of here, I'll find out.

He still has my chin in his fingers, but now he slowly releases me.

The next second, something comes at me out of the corner of my eye. And I only have a moment to realize it's the butt of a gun.

It smashes into my temple. There's a flash of pain, then nothing.

kora

"Kora Sinclair."

I shift. My eyelids are heavy, but I drag them open.

Hospital. There's just something about them that all looks the same. The walls, the lighting, the quiet beeping.

I swallow, but there's something in the way. I immediately gag and raise my hand, but it's restrained. I jerk against the padded cuff circling my wrists and try to figure out what the hell is going on.

It takes me too long to work out that there's a tube protruding between my lips.

Panic seizes me, and I try to suck in air—only to realize I can't. My lungs expand and contract on their own. The hum of a machine forces air in and out. It's hard to override my panic, to stop trying to swallow and breathe, and some of my fight-or-flight lessens.

After I absorb that, my focus lifts.

A man stands at the foot of the bed, his hands in his pockets. He reminds me of someone I know, but my brain is sluggish.

"Cerberus James," he introduces, and my heart sinks. "Kronos did quite the number on you."

"Ah, ah." He frowns. "They've kept you sedated while your lungs heal. Something about hot, toxic air. That tube is breathing for you. I will admit, it wasn't strictly necessary. You could've been out of here days ago. But I insisted."

My eyes widen.

The contract.

Of course Cerberus James ended up being the one to buy it.

Buy *me*. How much power does that give him?

He pats my foot.

He's too smug, with his salt-and-pepper hair and matching trim goatee. For the first time, I take in more of his appearance. The crisp navy-blue collared shirt, the black jacket folded over his arm. His dark jeans. He has tattoos creeping up his neck.

"I'll keep you here until you're all healed up. However long that takes." He makes a show of glancing around. "Hospitals are a safe place, aren't they, Kora? So many people trying to *help*. The problem is, most of the workers are woefully underpaid. It makes it easy for them to follow my orders. Everyone has a price."

I shake my head, trying to make sense of what the hell is happening. My mind is slow to catch up, to realize that he ordered them to keep me sedated–and they did it. He has the power here–but he can't keep me like this, with a machine inflating and deflating my lungs. It's invasive. Like he's reached inside my body and is controlling my breath.

He wouldn't keep me here... Right?

From the Titans into the possession of the Hell Hounds leader.

I shudder. An alarm beside my head goes off, a quick

beeping that matches my heart. My focus swings around the room, and I gag again on the tube. I can feel it go all the way down my throat. My chest rises and falls against my will.

It needs to come out.

Right.

Now.

A nurse rushes in. She has a syringe in her hand, and she puts a hand on my arm to steady me.

No. I can't let this happen.

I thrash, trying to dislodge her. The needle goes into a port attached to the IV, and my eyes roll back. I choke on the tube again.

"Kora? You need to calm down. It's okay, honey." She strokes my hair, trying to ease my wild eyes.

Fucking hell.

Ice spreads through my veins. It's like cold water inching higher and higher. I fight the sedation, even as it numbs my muscles. I direct all my hatred toward the man at the foot of the bed. Through it all, he hasn't moved. He seems curious, watching like he's never seen anything quite so odd.

And then the drugs win, and I slip back under the sea.

The next time I resurface, I'm alone. My head rolls to the side, and I lick my lips. The tube is gone, but my mouth is drier than the desert. Even my tongue is scratchy. I try to touch my face, but my arm is held fast.

I blink slowly and try to make sense of the wide, padded cuff on my arms.

Nicer than the zip ties, but a restraint nonetheless. I

vaguely remember them from when I first woke up, but it's hazy. Like a dream.

I shift on the bed and swallow again. My throat aches.

My other arm is similarly restrained to the railings of the bed. I pull on it senselessly for a moment, until my muscles ache. Although, to be frank, it doesn't take long for me to tire.

I'm obviously still in the hospital, but now that I'm alone–and not in a panic–I take a look around. There's a window to my left, and the curtain around my bed on the right, hiding the rest of the room. I sit up more, ignoring the stabbing pain behind my eyes.

Now would be a great time to get out of here—if I wasn't chained to the freaking bed like a dog. The sky is lightening.

The curtain moves, and it's my only warning. I slump back and close my eyes to slits. I can barely see through my eyelashes.

It isn't Cerberus, though. A nurse moves around the room, checking monitors and glancing down at me.

"Your elevated heart rate means you're most likely awake," the nurse says quietly. "Which means I need to notify Cerberus."

I let out a slow exhale and open my eyes fully. She reminds me of my mother. Same dark, curled hair caught back in a low ponytail, same kind softening around her eyes when she meets my gaze. My chest squeezes.

I never should've left Emerald Cove.

She slips her hand into mine. "I also need to remove your catheter."

I hold fast, digging my nails into her skin. I can't make a sound, but I want her to help me. I don't know how she'd even do that. Smuggle me out? Fake my death? I'd take

16

fresh clothes and her car keys and call it a day... But those are impossible asks.

The nurse is on *his* side. The Hell Hounds haven't messed with me since I got to Sterling Falls. My issue was with Kronos and my guys. Cerberus James had nothing to do with it... but now he has everything to do with *me*.

Why?

I close my eyes as she removes the catheter–I pretend I can't feel it, because my other option is too embarrassing to admit–and ball my hands into fists. I breathe out slowly, and she smooths my blankets back over my legs.

"Apollo Madden," the nurse says. "Familiar?"

I cringe and reach for her again. She knows him? Is he here? Alive? My expression must give me away.

Her lips twist, and she just nods slowly to herself. "Good luck with everything, Kora."

She leaves. I don't know what it means, and the unknown might kill me more than anything else. Jace is gone. Apollo had been shot... and I don't know what happened to Wolfe.

A tear slides down my cheek.

The curtain moves, and Wolfe's father comes in. He seems smug again—maybe it's his permanent face. Some of us are graced with resting bitch faces, and he has *that*. Resting smug asshole face.

I know which I would prefer.

The same nurse follows him back in, stopping behind him.

"You're being discharged," Cerberus says.

"That was fast." I swallow. My voice sounds *terrible*. Like my vocal cords were hit by a bus and dragged for miles across the asphalt. It's the first time I've spoken since the fire...

I'd kill for water, but on the other hand, I'd rather die than ask *him* for anything. All of Wolfe's warnings about his treacherous father come roaring back. How he raised the three of them, how they got free from his grip.

How their childhoods were nonexistent thanks to this man.

Cerberus raises his eyebrow. "Fast? You've been out for a week."

I choke. "*What?*"

"A medically induced coma," the nurse mumbles.

I stare at them. A week. A WEEK? A helpless cold crashes over my head. He didn't even have to fucking snap his fingers, and he put me to sleep for a week.

Why? That damn word keeps bouncing around my head.

Cerberus tosses a bag on the foot of the bed. "Get dressed."

He strides out, and the nurse doesn't hesitate to undo the restraints. I take a moment to rub each of my wrists and take deep breaths. Slow and controlled. I count to five for each inhale and exhale.

The brand on my wrist leers at me, shiny silver against my pale skin. It's still raised, the flesh around it slightly puckered. It isn't pretty—it's a badge of courage. Something I got through... I just have to believe I can get through this.

In the brown paper bag is a t-shirt, leather jacket, jeans, socks. Underwear, much to my horror, sit at the bottom.

"He didn't buy that stuff." The nurse helps me undo the ties of the hospital gown. "He had it delivered by a woman." She pauses, watches my face, and then her expression turns to sympathy. "Your throat. I'm sorry. This is an abnormal situation..."

I watch her leave. My back is bare, and only my arm keeps the gown covering my chest. I wait a beat, then reach for the t-shirt. But she returns before I can get it on, and in her hand is a Styrofoam cup with a lid and straw.

She offers it to me. I sip, and cool water fills my mouth.

My eyes close of their own accord.

It's the balm my throat needs. I get a few gulps down, and then she's pulling it away.

"Too much, too fast will make you sick," she warns. "Let's get you dressed, then you can have more."

My brain can't decide what the hell to focus on. The aches and pains, this current situation, the texture of the clothes, the fact that I was out for a week. I haven't eaten real food in more than a week, then. She helps me put the clothes on, and the jacket is the last straw.

No, seeing the *back* is the last straw.

It has the *Hell Hounds* logo on it with the three-headed dog. The white stitched into the black leather.

The nurse eyes me, but I can't put that on. Even if it's five degrees outside, I'm not walking out wearing it. She sighs and grabs a wheelchair from behind the curtain. She helps me transfer to it, and I quickly fold the jacket so the logo isn't visible.

I don't know how I'm going to do this. The fear of the unknown is building in my chest, threatening to burst free. I didn't used to be this terrified. I didn't think fear could be this potent.

She pushes me out into the hall, and I lift my hand to block the light. It's a lot brighter out here, and my eyes burn. There's more bustle, too, as we get closer to the nurses' station. I didn't realize it, but the quiet was due to room location: the end of the hall. There's a tall man with a similar Hell Hounds jacket standing at the nurses' station, his gaze moving from person to person. His stance says, *Don't mess with me.*

A guard dog?

He follows us down the hall.

Another waits at the elevator. They could be brothers, both with dark-brown hair and square jaws. Mid-thirties, if I had to guess. The elevator one has a mustache. He hits the button.

Neither seem inclined to look at me.

I glance back at the nurse, and she gives me a tight smile. She rolls me into the elevator and turns so I can face out, and the two Hell Hound guards step in with us. Normally, I'd have some sort of quip. But my words are stuck in my throat behind a painful lump.

From one prison to another.

I never should've signed that contract with Kronos—it was designed for me to fail.

We get off on the first floor. The guards trail us down another hall, then another. We pass rooms, and my breathing quickens. My heart thumps painfully, and an ache starts behind my ribcage. The closer we get to the door, the more anxiety roots in my chest.

"Stop!"

I grab the wheels, and we jerk to a halt.

I know that voice.

And I think the nurse does, too, because she doesn't try to force me to keep going. Instead, she rotates me so I can see him.

Apollo.

His gaze is glued to me, and he rushes down the hall. He has gray sweatpants on under his hospital gown, and he drags a wheeling pole with a hanging drip bag with him.

"Stop him." Cerberus steps up beside me, coming out of nowhere, and his lackeys spring into action.

They block Apollo before he has any chance of reaching me.

"Get your fucking hands off me." He shoves at them, but his attention never leaves me. Even when they grab at him again and keep him back. "Kora. Are you okay?"

"Physically?" My voice sounds rough even in my own ears–it's no wonder when he winces.

One of the guys blocks him again, slowly trying to shuffle him back.

"We're coming for you," Apollo vows.

Cerberus chuckles. "And you know what's waiting for you if you do." His hand touches the back of my neck, his fingers hooked like claws. His nails dig into my skin. "This is all perfectly legal, Apollo. It's time you start respecting the order of things."

Apollo scoffs. "Fuck off, old man. We left because the *order* of things needs to change."

Cerberus shrugs. "You've been trying for five years without success. I think I like my odds."

Chills rush down my spine. The guards manhandle Apollo, but he's having none of it. He swings, ignoring the fact that he's still attached to an IV, that he's in a hospital gown, that he's more than likely still recovering from his gunshot wound...

I squeak.

His fist crashes into a Hell Hound's face, and the guy staggers back. The other one is on Apollo in an instant. He kicks out Apollo's knees, forcing him to the floor. The IV pole clatters down beside him. My heart stops when Apollo's cheek presses to the tile.

21

And Cerberus tightens his grip on my neck, keeping me seated.

"Please stop." I squeeze the armrests of the chair hard enough that my knuckles go white. "This is insane. He's injured."

The Hell Hound presses his knee into Apollo's back.

It's painstakingly familiar to how the Titan controlled me before putting me in the truck.

We've drawn a little audience around us, but no one intervenes. No one stops the Hell Hound from leaning down and pinching Apollo's cheek and whispering something in his ear.

Like they know each other.

They probably do.

My heart sinks when the Hell Hound rises and Apollo doesn't move.

"No." I struggle, but I'm still weak. "Someone help him–"

"Quiet," Cerberus snaps. He had pushed the nurse away from my chair, and now he gestures to someone.

The second guard, the one who took the punch, lifts me easily out of the seat. I guess a wheelchair is too damn slow for them.

He carries me out, followed by Cerberus and the third.

And my heart stays with Apollo on the floor.

THREE

kora

I sit on a stool at the bar and watch the Hell Hounds in the clubhouse this evening. They've been shuffling inside for the last twenty minutes, some in pairs and groups, others on their own. They fill the tables. One of the younger ones rushes back and forth between the bar and the tables, dropping off drinks. Some of the men scowl in my direction. Some ignore me. But no one has said anything, and that probably has to do with my shadow.

The big guy at my shoulder leans on the bar, his arms crossed. His biceps bulge, straining against the short sleeves of his t-shirt. He's at least double the size of some of the guys in here—which is why they're keeping comments to themselves. He wasn't the one who carried me out of the hospital—that one, with a dark bruise forming on his cheek, plus the lookalike with the mustache, disappeared shortly after we arrived.

I'm no stranger to the thoughts that run through a man's head–and part of me thinks Cerberus has to be aware of the variety of men under his leadership. That's why he assigned the big guy to watch me like a hawk.

So we sit. In silence.

I'm like a museum feature for them to gawk at, to look but not touch.

My mind turns over what I know about Cerberus James, and I have to conclude that my knowledge is painfully limited. I never met him until the hospital, although I'm pretty sure he was one of the men outside Olympus when Apollo stabbed someone.

I just have the conversation Wolfe and I had at the diner.

He sees the world one way. I see it another.

How does he see it? I had asked him.

As something to manipulate.

I suppress my shiver. Is that what I am? A piece used to manipulate his son?

A million-dollar pawn.

"What the fuck are you gawking at?" One of the men glares at me. He has a gun stuffed in the front of his pants, and his leather vest hangs open. He leaves the table of his buddies and inches closer. His eyes are wide, his pupils blown out and obscuring the color.

The stench of booze pours off of him, and my skin crawls.

Big Guy does nothing.

The man stops right in front of me, his gaze going up and down my body. "Breaking in a new little club whore, Malik? You know the rules."

Rules? *Club whore?*

He leers at me. "No cunts at meetings."

Big Guy—Malik, apparently—pushes off the counter. His attention flicks up, to the door, then back to the man in front of me. Malik towers over the drunk Hell Hound, who stands his ground. My guess? He's too far gone to feel the sudden chill in the air emanating from behind him.

I feel it.

Malik grabs him by the front of the throat and walks him backward with ease. The guy doesn't even fight it– more like he knew it was coming. He leers at me even as Malik moves to intercept the line of sight. Malik slams him down on top of the table he just left.

I jolt in my seat, and the rest of the room abruptly silences.

The only sound is the man's harsh breathing and a single pair of footsteps.

Cerberus has arrived.

Just in time, it would seem.

He pauses next to Malik and chuckles. My heart pounds hard enough that it feels like it might burst. They brought me here straight from the hospital and made me sit on the bar stool with nothing more than a glass of water beside me. The leather Hell Hounds jacket sits folded on the seat beside me.

"I'm glad you're aware of the rules, Percy. Seeing as how you're so fond of breaking them." Cerberus nods at Malik, and the latter releases Percy. "Do you think Malik was... what? Flagrantly disregarding my orders?"

Percy blanches. "N-no, sir."

Malik has to have a position of authority. Or Cerberus' favor. I watch half in fascination, half in terror. How much power can one man wield? It was easy to ignore Kronos' power. I saw him in an office, sometimes with that guard. Never in a room full of his gang, commanding their attention just by arriving.

Cerberus watches the younger Hell Hound for a

moment, then nods. His attention turns to me, and he motions for me to join him. "Kora."

I automatically stiffen. The attention in the room switches to me, and I can't move. My throat is suddenly dry, and every little trauma comes alive. I'm under the microscope. Throat, bruises, soreness.

Malik strides over and grips my arm, pulling me off the stool and to the front of the room. Cerberus doesn't have to do much more than raise his hand to capture the silence he desires. It's so quiet, I'm suddenly very aware of my breathing. I let Malik hold most of my weight, because otherwise I'd fall right through the floor.

"This is Kora Sinclair." Cerberus waves a hand at me. "She's officially under our protection. So get a good fucking look at her, and know that if any of you touch her, you'll be dealing with me."

My stomach bottoms out, and I mouth, *What?* I can't even fucking speak.

It isn't the first time my voice has been taken from me. It *has* to be the last.

He smiles and drapes the leather jacket–that I hadn't even noticed him take–over my shoulders. The thing weighs a million pounds, but somehow I keep my knees from buckling.

I hate that he can shuffle me around like his property. That one bad decision, to take money from Kronos, led me *here*. Okay, maybe a few more bad decisions helped, but still. In a normal town, I'd have gone into debt. Or had every door slammed in my face. I can almost see who that girl is: the one who returned to Emerald Cove instead of trying to exist here.

And for what? How much school have you missed?

The one reason I *wanted* to remain in Sterling Falls was

for an education. I've practically thrown that away at this rate.

"You protect her like one of your own. You kill anyone who tries to take her from us." He winks at me. "Welcome to the Hell Hounds, sweetheart."

Malik hauls me away.

I'M A PRISONER AGAIN.

I pace in front of the window, keeping watch for something–*anything*. My mind keeps jumping back to Apollo, forced to the hospital floor yesterday morning. To Jace, who may or may not be alive. To Wolfe.

They're keeping me in a small apartment above the bar, although I was too nervous to get much sleep last night. The regular occupant has moved out, leaving behind a fully stocked kitchen, clean sheets on the bed, and an assortment of mystery items. Nothing personal, but... maybe meaningful? Taped to the inside one of the cabinet doors is a photo of a young girl. There are a few spy books in the drawers of the coffee table. A set of dumbbells in the bedroom closet under some hanging shirts.

While I couldn't sleep, I explored. Obviously. I did the same thing at the guys' house.

I hunted for a way out, but it was futile. There were always Hell Hounds lingering outside, coming in and out of the bar. In fact, the later it got, the more of them showed up. I thought Cerberus had called an all-hands-on-deck meeting to introduce me, but I think I met a quarter of them.

Every roar of the motorcycles pulled me back to my impossible reality.

My eyes burn, even though I can't make myself relax. I've been on high alert for too long. Maybe I've been sleeping for too long, too. My throat aches from the tubes, my muscles are sore from being trapped in bed for over a week. I'm restless and exhausted.

Cerberus James had me sedated for a *week* just because he could. Intubated for the hell of it. I didn't inhale *that* much smoke. And even then, I'm pretty sure regular patients that come in for smoke inhalation aren't intubated unless it's severe. So, him snapping his fingers and making it happen seems to be the definition of power.

Yet, he hasn't laid a finger on me. No one came for me last night, even with the ruckus downstairs. Whether there was a guard or a locked door...

I'm filling up with too many questions, and sooner or later I'm going to explode.

Movement at the top of the driveway catches my eye.

The security doesn't look new–everyone moves like an oiled machine, and that doesn't strike me as an overnight thing–but they do seem on high alert today. A tall fence blocks in the back of the clubhouse. The front is left open. There's a long, narrow driveway off the main road and opens up into a square parking lot in front of the clubhouse. The whole property is framed in by the forest—no one wanders this way by accident.

There are only a few bikes out front right now, as we approach lunchtime, and I've seen some Hell Hounds patrolling the perimeter. They walk around in pairs, their assault rifles slung over their shoulders.

I don't know if everyone lives here or just a few. I don't know what the clubhouse contains beyond the main level, which had the bar-slash-meeting area and a few offices in the back, and the stairs that came directly up here.

Everything I *don't* know is going to get me killed.

Now, a bike coasts down the driveway. Someone moves to intercept him, and it seems like everything tenses. The air, the people, even the trees seem to stiffen and lean away.

Outsider.

I step closer to the glass.

The rider removes his helmet, and my stomach flips. Wolfe sets the helmet on the handle, the engine noise fading away, and holds his hands up.

Please, don't hurt him. My stomach twists, and I can hardly breathe as I watch them.

A Hell Hound strides forward and grips his shoulder, nearly ripping him off the bike.

Wolfe keeps his hands raised in surrender. The Hell Hound steers him toward the clubhouse. He has Wolfe's jacket fisted in his grip at the back of the neck. My heart is in my throat when I catch the gun the Hell Hound has pointed at the small of Wolfe's back. I press my hands to the window, trying to get closer.

Before they disappear under the porch roof, Wolfe's gaze flicks up to me. Like he knew I was there all along.

He winks.

He fucking *winks.*

I stumble back, sitting heavily on the couch. It only lasts a minute, though, before I'm up and pacing again.

Wolfe is here.

Did he actually surrender?

Or come to talk to his dad?

To negotiate?

I go to the door and press my ear to the wood. I've been able to hear some conversation in the main room if it's loud enough, and I hope their voices carry. But I get nothing until footsteps pound up the stairs.

I hurry back to the couch in an attempt to pretend I wasn't eavesdropping–pointless eavesdropping, but probably punishable nonetheless–when the door swings inward.

"See? She's fine." Cerberus steps out of the way.

Wolfe rushes in, and I'm on my feet in an instant. He stops in front of me, hesitating for a second as his gaze sweeps up and down my body. And then he hauls me into him, hugging me tightly.

I let out a ragged exhale and squeeze him back.

He's real.

He's solid.

"Are you okay?" Wolfe's lips brush my ear.

I swallow. "All things considered? Yeah."

He nods and slowly loosens his hold. He looks back toward the door. "Can you give us a minute?"

Cerberus snorts. "You can have five."

The door closes, and then Wolfe and I are alone.

I grab his hands. "Please tell me you're here to get me out of this place."

"I'm trying."

"Apollo–" God, I still feel sick over what happened at the hospital.

Did he tell Wolfe what happened?

"Is fine," Wolfe finishes. "Angry at himself but fine. Dad's henchman didn't do irreparable damage, and he was discharged later that morning. Jace–"

"Oh god." How did I forget *Jace*? In the midst of everything. The fact that he was shot was put to the *far* back of my mind. I don't want the confirmation, but now, I need to know. "He's dead, isn't he? He got shot–"

Wolfe's expression stops me. "He's not dead. He probably wishes he is, after letting the Titans get their hands on you, but he's his normal, grouchy self."

I stare at him and try to let his words sink in. *Not dead.* Even though I heard the gunshot. But... maybe it was a trick.

I leap into Wolfe's arms and slam my lips to his. He doesn't hesitate to respond. His fingers wind into my hair, angling my head as he deepens the kiss. Our bodies press together. I grip his jeans, my thumbs hooked through his belt loops.

This is a balm I didn't know I needed. My anxiety melts away, and even if it's temporary, I can breathe again. The taste of him is familiar and sweet, and he cups the back of my head in a way that makes me feel *safe*.

And I'm addicted to him.

I slip my hand down and cup him through his jeans–but that only seems to snap some sense into him. With a groan, he moves my hand away.

His lips go to my ear. "Listen carefully, Kora. You can't trust my father with anything. Not cheap childhood stories, no stray details. Don't give him a millimeter, because he'll find a way to twist it and take a mile."

"I—"

"Everything is going to be okay." He leans back to meet my gaze, his eyes soft. "I know we failed you, and I'm so fucking sorry. But no one is going to get their hands on you again."

My laugh sounds mean, even to my own ears. "Except your father."

He scowls. "Not even him."

"He has me, Wolfe. Did you miss where we are?" I shake my head. "Unless you plan on taking me out of here right now?"

33

He exhales, but he doesn't look away. I'll give him that: he's never been purposefully deceptive.

"It's his game. We all need to play it. But I'm serious, Kora. No details. Nothing."

I shiver, and he's immediately pulling me back into his embrace. He kisses my forehead, and I shut my eyes. Wolfe accepting this seems to push it forward in my mind, out of a nightmare and into reality. A chill sweeps through me.

I fist his shirt again and give voice to one of my fears. "Will he hurt me?"

"No." His voice is fierce. "If anyone touches you–"

"Because you're in a position to make demands," his father says behind me.

I cringe, but Wolfe holds me fast. He kisses the top of my head one last time, and then he releases me. And I have to carefully release him, too. Unlock my fingers, let the fabric slip away. The loss is immediate.

He strides to the door and out, ignoring his father. Cerberus watches me for a moment, and I have the uncanny sensation of being flayed open. Like he can see everything he needs to in just a glance, and I have no guard against it.

When it comes to his son? Apollo? Jace?

I have a feeling I'm a trump card.

apollo

"No." Jace glares at Wolfe across the kitchen island. "Are you fucking insane?"

Wolfe shrugs, picking at the piece of bread on his plate. "Probably."

He got back from the Hell Hounds' clubhouse looking grim. Once Jace returned home, Wolfe laid out his plan for us. It isn't just terrible–it's the worst fucking plan I've ever heard. But I'm keeping my mouth shut, because for once, I think Wolfe is right. Yep, it's the most god-awful plan in the history of plans, so much so that it shouldn't even be called one, and I'm agreeing with him.

Cerberus has us by the balls, and the smug bastard knows it. This is our only option.

"All this time," Jace mutters to himself. "Wasted. You really want to fuck this up for us?"

"Not wasted." Wolfe drops the bread and folds his arms over his chest. "It's temporary. You know that."

"Fuck." I rub my eyes. My wound has barely healed, the stitches removed from my abdomen at the hospital this morning. I'm sore, bruised, but other than that? Just dandy.

Except, when I went into surgery, everything was fine. Jace had Kora. Wolfe and I got out of West Falls. Even though we failed to get the contract, we made it out.

And then Kronos ambushed them.

Seeing her yesterday morning was torture. The nurse managed to get me a message about which hallway to be in, but those Hell Hounds... I should've had a weapon. I should've shot them for standing next to her.

I was fucking unprepared, and I *know* better.

I force myself to take long, slow breaths, but my anger doesn't subside. I'm pissed at myself. At letting them manhandle me and cart her away.

"I know," Wolfe says. "I know it sucks. I want to gouge my eyes out. But what else is there? He could turn around and sell her. He could let his guys have her. Right now, he's being strategic."

And we all know what happens when that fails.

"You already know I agree," I say quietly. "I don't *like* it, but I'll do it if we get our girl back."

Our girl. Some part of me hates calling her that. She's *my* girl. But she's Wolfe's, too. And Jace... well, he's a little late to the party. But he had his own moments with her, and I think he likes her more than he wants to admit. I'm not ready to pry that particular secret loose.

Jace slams his hand on the counter. He glares down at it and seems to think about it. Maybe he's trying to come up with something a little less... drastic.

But in the end, there's nothing else.

He slowly nods. "Fine. Set it up."

Wolfe grimaces. "There's no setting up. We just... go."

"We're really doing this?" I look from Jace to Wolfe, suddenly apprehensive. Yes, I'd do anything to keep Kora safe. "I was sort of envisioning a smash and grab."

"That can be plan C," Wolfe offers.

I groan. "What's plan B?"

"Not getting shot."

"I fucked that one up already." I slide off the stool and leave them in the kitchen.

Nearly six years ago, we left the Hell Hounds. Negotiated our way out. It was a little bloody, but we did what we had to. We dreamt of change, of cleaning up Sterling Falls. We were being suffocated under Cerberus, under expectation.

And look at us now.

We can still do it. Part of me believes we still *will* do it. This is a setback.

The gangs grease the wheels of Sterling Falls. They keep everything running smoothly. Take them away, and something else has to fill it. Something just as dark and as willing to get as dirty as them—or something worse.

I go down to the basement, where we keep one of our weapon caches. I quickly type in the code and scan my thumb. Once I'm in, I load up on weapons. Everything that can fit on my body. I've had years to get creative with it.

Wolfe and Jace leave me alone, although Jace comes down and passes by, casting a glance in before disappearing into the gym. Better that we don't show up on the Hell Hounds' doorstep looking for a fight.

Well. That's not quite right, is it?

The key is to be prepared for a fight—thus the weapons I'm concealing on my body—but to try not to, you know, *actually* fight.

Wolfe and Jace have differing opinions on that front.

I sigh. There's only so many magazines a person can stow in their pockets before it becomes obvious. Even with the cargo pants giving me many, *many* pocket options.

39

"Guys," Wolfe yells from the top of the stairs. "Get up here!"

I beat Jace to the stairs, barely, and he grumbles the whole time I climb. I have to resist the urge to donkey kick him.

We find Wolfe in the den, staring at the television.

And on the screen, what looks like an outdoor press conference. The mayor stands at a podium planted on a sidewalk, Sheriff Bradshaw beside him. And on his other side... Kora.

"What the fuck?" Jace snatches the remote and turns up the volume.

Behind them is what remains of a burnt building.

"...could've been a tragic death was prevented, thanks to the fine civil servants of Sterling Falls." Mayor Thompson glances down, then back to the crowd in front of him.

He continues on, but I tune him out and focus on Kora. She seems to be a blank slate, bundled in a navy peacoat. Her dark-red hair is pulled away from her face, and her nose ring is gone. Her makeup is minimal, making her the picture of innocence.

"That's their angle?" Wolfe rolls his eyes. "Cracking down on the college district?"

"Because the fire took place in a frat house." Jace shrugs. "What do you expect?"

"Please welcome our head of this new operation, Cerberus James." The mayor steps away, and the camera pans back.

We had missed it.

So zoomed in, he wasn't in the frame–but now Wolfe's father leaves his place beside Kora and steps up to the mayor. They shake hands, and Cerberus takes the podium.

My stomach flops, and nausea rolls through me.

How the fuck is Kora keeping a straight face?

"Thank you, Mayor Thompson," Cerberus says. "I plan to make this city safer, and that starts with protecting the young college students who, frankly, don't know any better."

"Absolute bullshit." Wolfe's hands shake. "How the fuck did he get in with the mayor? And Kora—"

"Shut up," Jace snaps.

We stand in front of the television and wait, tense seconds passing as Cerberus seems to be perusing the crowd. He glances back at Kora, then motions for her to join him.

"Kora Sinclair almost died. She was only released from the hospital yesterday for her injuries in this fire... a fire that could've been prevented." Cerberus puts his arm around her shoulders, cinching her to his side.

Her expression never changes. But her lips tremble the slightest bit before she presses them firmer together. I ball my fists.

"Starting tonight, we'll be patrolling the streets around Sterling Falls University. If there's trouble, we'll be there to end it. You have my word."

"He's taken over the neutral zone." I turn away sharply, unable to watch anymore. Of course—of *course* he sees this as an opportunity.

"Kronos is probably kicking himself." Jace shakes his head. "Brad doesn't seem too happy by this turn of events."

Sheriff Bradshaw's expression, while neutral, hints at disgusted. He stands immobile beside Kora, stiff and at attention. Cerberus inserted his Hell Hounds in *police* duties. He might not have even had to try very hard, since the mayor just handed it to him on a silver platter. Limiting police activity in the neutral zone will enforce the Hell Hounds' power.

Not good.

The press conference ends shortly after that, and Jace hits the power button.

He looks at me, then Wolfe. "You both good?"

Wolfe nods.

"Still want to go through with this?" I ask him.

He grunts. "No, but I don't think we have a choice."

Jace sighs. "Well, let's go. No time like the present."

FIVE

kora

"All set." The mayor's aide guides him past us. They ignore the questions from the gathering of reporters.

Cerberus, still at the podium, leans into the cluster of microphones. "Thank you for joining us today. No more questions."

And then he has a hand on my back, propelling me after the mayor. The sheriff follows. A few of his men block the reporters from giving chase, and our little group comes to a stop behind one of the large, black SUVs. I try not to make eye contact with any of them, keeping my gaze trained on my shoes.

"Well, that went as expected," the mayor says. He flashes a smile at Cerberus and extends his hand. "Happy to be in business with you, my friend."

"Likewise," Cerberus answers.

"And you must be Kora." Mayor Thompson smiles at me. "Are you from Sterling Falls?"

"No. Emerald Cove." I shift. "I was originally going to attend SFU on a scholarship…"

"Oh?"

Why did I say that? I lift a shoulder, trying to play it off. "That part didn't end up working out, but I was happy to still be able to make things work and continue my education." *Lie.*

Cerberus, beside me, stiffens.

The mayor's focus remains on me. "You poor girl. Hearing that one of our own college students was caught in that blaze is one thing, but seeing the remnants is quite another. Tell me, how did you get out?"

A question I had been expecting. I swallow past the lump in my throat. "I'm so sorry, I don't remember."

If they ask you anything, tell them you don't remember. No one can question that. I forget where I picked up that piece of advice, but I hold my breath and hope it works. Sure enough, his brow furrows. His expression turns quizzical.

He must be in his sixties, with mostly silver hair and wrinkles around his eyes. His blue eyes, which seemed kind a moment ago, sharpen. It reminds me that he's a politician.

"Someone must've pulled you out, wouldn't you agree?"

"Girl said she doesn't remember," the sheriff says.

The mayor scoffs. "And you believe her?"

Bradshaw shrugs. "Not sure why she'd lie."

I latch on to that—and his defense. It conflicts with what I know about the sheriff—the listening device he planted in my bag, his involvement with Kronos. But he tried to help me, too.

Maybe he rescued me.

Waited until the Titans had left and...

Oh god.

There was a body. When my savior carried me out, he

stepped over the fallen Titans guard. And yet, no one has mentioned a body. A death. I'm sure that would've been something Cerberus would exploit–not just me, a survivor.

I open my mouth and promptly close it. On the way here, Cerberus showed me the glass bottle he had in his pocket, and a waiting syringe. A sedative. Seems I'm only of use to him when I'm quiet and docile–but he couldn't have me drooling on camera. His words, not mine.

So fear keeps me quiet now, knowing what might come next.

"She's still processing the trauma," Cerberus says.

No kidding. Just not the trauma they think.

"That's why it's so important to monitor this district, Jeff. These kids are fresh out of their parents' houses. They're not used to the responsibility that comes with being an adult and making wise decisions. Someone needs to watch them."

Mayor Thompson smiles. "You're quite right."

"Sir," the aide urges.

"Right, right. Sorry, gentlemen. I have an unavoidable meeting across town." The mayor shakes Cerberus' hand again, then the sheriff's. "Let's meet for lunch next week. My assistant will be in touch."

We watch them go, and the sheriff casts one more look at me. His expression is back to being blank, like he never stepped up for me.

I let out a small breath, but the danger isn't over. A Hell Hound opens the car door for me and then scurries around and opens the other for his boss. We both get into the back seat and wait for the mayor's vehicle to leave. Once we're back on the road, Cerberus turns to me.

"Emerald Cove?"

I jump. Cerberus watches me blandly. Making... small

47

talk? It's not a secret that I came from Emerald Cove. The town is an hour away, and I haven't hidden it.

"Yes," I answer carefully.

"And you had a scholarship to Sterling Falls University?"

"Right. But it was revoked, which is how I ended up with a loan through Kronos. And that's why I'm here." Again... common knowledge. I assumed it was.

He hums, glancing away. His fingers tap on his thigh, then still. "Interesting."

My stomach knots. Did I say too much? Did I give him something new to chew on? Wolfe *told* me not to give him any more information. No cheap throwaway childhood stories–nothing. And here I am, opening my big fat mouth.

But he doesn't continue, and we lapse into silence.

I hunch in my seat as we drive back toward the club-house. The longer the silence gets, the more nervous I become. I drum my fingers on my thigh and suck in shallow breaths. I just need to not panic, right?

Nothing is going according to plan. I'm so far off-kilter, I don't even *have* a plan.

At some point, Cerberus retrieves the small glass vial from his pocket, the capped syringe in his other hand.

"Please don't." My nerves are rioting against me, twisting in my abdomen and spreading ice through my veins. "I did what you asked."

He inserts the needle and pulls back the lever, loading it with clear liquid. "You were remarkable. Better than expected."

Because of *that*. The syringe, the sedative. The threat of it hanging over my head.

After Wolfe left this morning, a woman came in and ordered that I shower and dress. She gave me clothes, makeup. Once I was presentable, I was brought to the car. If I spoke, if I made a face, if I did *anything* against him, he wouldn't punish me. He would put me right back to sleep... for as long as he chose.

A day, a week, a year.

Something to manipulate.

He took my reaction to waking up intubated and twisted my fear to suit him.

To use against me.

"I did what you asked." I lean away from him.

He sighs. "Yes, you did."

"Sir," the driver calls. "We have a problem."

Cerberus grunts and caps the syringe, stowing it and the vial in his pocket. He leans forward to see around the driver, and then he chuckles. "Wolfe delivered."

I bolt upright.

Ahead of us, blocking the winding road that will bring us to the clubhouse, is a familiar black Mercedes. The driver door opens, and Wolfe climbs out. The passenger side doors both open, and Jace and Apollo round the hood to stand beside their friend.

They seem like they're prepared for war. Apollo is strapped with weapons. Jace has a handgun in a shoulder holster and another at his hip. And Wolfe... Wolfe has nothing visible on him. But I know that doesn't mean anything.

Seeing them together...

They've come for me.

I unbuckle my seatbelt and lunge for the door. Cerberus grabs my hair and hauls me backward. My fingers slide off the lever, and I cry out at the sharp pain at my scalp. The gleam of the needle, newly uncapped, reappears. He injects it into my neck before I can escape his grip. A searing sensation pours under my skin and spreads up my neck.

Above me, Cerberus tsks. He angles my head back so I can see his face. "You do not get to see them without my approval. Do you understand?"

I shudder and nod, and he pushes me back upright. I fall back against my door and stay there, afraid to even breathe. Afraid of how fast the sedative will kick in and how much it'll affect me.

"Stay," he orders.

Like a dog. I remember making that exact same retort to Jace.

Funny, coming from a man who embodies a mythological three-headed dog.

My mouth opens and closes, but there's a lump in my throat that keeps me from speaking. The fear of what he injected me with is greater than my imagination. The fear balloons in front of me. Is my throat going to close completely? Will I fall asleep?

He chuckles to himself and pushes his door open, casting one last curious look at me before getting out. "Watch her," he orders the driver. "Make sure she doesn't choke on her own saliva."

The door slams shut behind him, and we're encased in silence. My muscles are relaxing, my body slackening. I feel like my mind has become untethered. The floating sensation is odd—and not entirely unpleasant.

My eyes go to the driver. I can feel my control on my conscious state slipping through my fingers, but I need to know what's happening. If Cerberus is going to let me go...

The driver seems torn between keeping an eye on his boss and watching me. Which is why he doesn't notice my hand inch toward the handle again.

He glances forward again, and I yank it. The door swings open quickly under my weight, and I fall out of the car.

Yep. I tumble without balance, and my reflexes are too slow for me to catch myself.

My shoulder and forearm take the brunt of the fall. My teeth clack together, my molars catching the inside of my cheek. Blood fills my mouth. My reaction time was *abysmal*.

The pain wakes me up, though. Adrenaline shoots through me, kicking up my heart rate.

I don't think he gave me enough of the sedative to truly knock me out. That's my only hope as I push myself up with both hands. It's either going to be that, or I'm about to face-plant on the asphalt.

Someone hauls me up, easily swinging me into their arms. I belatedly look up and meet Jace's gaze.

"Sedated me," I mumble. "I don't like him."

Safe now, a voice in my head whispers.

He doesn't laugh. His hold tightens on me, and I let my head fall on his chest. His heartbeat is loud in my ear, quick and steady. He might be acting calm, but his heart tells another story.

My mind works sluggishly as Jace carries me. Someone brushes the hair back from my face. His grip on me tightens, and he maneuvers us into a vehicle. I open my eyes belatedly and jerk back.

We're in the Hell Hound vehicle. Cerberus is back in his position behind the driver. I'm still in Jace's arms, cradled on his lap, and he's taken my seat. I face Cerberus—a view I could definitely do without, but I'd rather keep him in my sights.

I ball the front of Jace's shirt my fists. My eyes close, and Jace absentmindedly rubs my arm.

"You can put her down," Cerberus says.

"I'm good."

"So, to what do I owe this pleasure?"

Jace is quiet for a moment, then sighs. "Do you hate us that much?"

"Hate?" Cerberus seems surprised. "I don't hate you."

"Then why did you *buy* Kora?"

So they didn't know. Some part of me figured they—or Wolfe, at the very least—had to know what his father had planned. Or even that they asked him to do it.

"Shall I assume, since you've come to me, you're willing to discuss terms?" Wolfe's father's voice is light, like he doesn't give a shit why Jace is in his car. But there's an underlying tension to it.

"Obviously," Jace answers.

"And they decided you were their spokesperson."

"They're too attached."

To me.

Cerberus snorts. "And you're the one holding her like she might float away. You know what I want, Jace. You, Apollo, and my son. Back in the Hell Hounds—for good this time."

I force my eyes open. He wants them back? After all they did to leave?

No. That doesn't seem right.

"I know." Jace's voice stays steady. He expected this.

"That's why you're here, of course." Cerberus exhales. "But I don't expect the transition to be easy. You've been living on your own for a while. Independence is a hard thing to scrub away."

They seem like ordinary people. Sitting in a car, conversing about their lives like this is a regular day. Like they do this often, bargaining for freedoms.

My mind turns that over. *Independence is a hard thing to scrub away.* Like it's a callus that's grown over their skin to protect them. Something that was hard-won and came from time. Effort. But they're talking about giving that up? Going back to the Hell Hounds?

The loss of freedom would gut me, so why is Jace acting like this isn't the craziest thing he's ever heard? This sort of thing is a typical day for them?

Even the gun at Jace's hip seems normal.

If it was me, I'd be rebelling—ah, wait. It *is* me. And my life is intertwined right along with him. So why am I not doing just that? Acting for myself for once?

Fight, Kora. But how?

Ah, wait.

My fingers inch to the side, and I find one of the soft leather straps of Jace's shoulder holster. The handgun is secured with a strap across the handle.

"Come home." Cerberus is still trying to talk Jace into a peaceful surrender. "Kora will remain with you. She'll be protected by the Hell Hounds. By *you.*"

If Jace feels what I'm doing, he doesn't try to stop me. Cerberus is watching the road pass, his attention misplaced. He isn't worried about either of us—and maybe it's a fair assumption of Jace, who came into the car willingly. But he should be worried about *me.*

I sit up straighter, using his shoulder to propel myself.

"No." My voice is surprisingly clear. I slide the gun from the Jace's holster smoothly. I don't know much about guns, but this one seems relatively easy. I spot the safety on the side, pull the slide back to check that it's loaded, and a brass cartridge gleams back at me. "None of this is okay."

Cerberus eyes me, then laughs. He spares a glance from

the weapon to Jace, whose only response is to tighten his grip on my hips. "Get her under control."

"No," I repeat. I meet Jace's gaze. The anxiety and panic I *should* feel are repressed, and I have to be thankful for it. "Do you trust me?"

He inclines his chin.

"We're not going with you," I declare. "Let us out."

Cerberus laughs. The driver checks back, and his grip tightens on the wheel. But the bastard doesn't so much as slow.

I peek out the rearview mirror and catch a glimpse of the black Mercedes.

"I can't do this." My admission is for Jace's ears only. "I won't be a prisoner again."

"Are you going to shoot me?" Cerberus asks. He's fully focused on me now, and the gun in my grasp. We're in close quarters–I think the only thing that's stopping him from reaching out and snatching it is *Jace*. That's a sobering thought. The girl with a gun isn't a threat, but the unarmed man is.

Jace is all coiled energy. My words seemed to wind him tighter, and his gaze bounces from Cerberus to me. He hasn't so much as flinched since I yanked the gun from the holster.

But this isn't personal. Not for me or him.

It's clinical.

I shake my head at Cerberus. "I can't kill you. Pretty sure your whole club would come after me. And I'm not that stupid."

He smirks.

But there is another way out of this. My whole body numbs at the thought, but my desperation wins out. It's a slow-moving feeling, inching through my veins like lead. It weighs me down, makes my limbs heavy. Maybe it's slowed by the sedative still wreaking havoc in my system. But if I have to live with this feeling anymore, I might never find myself again.

So I swing the gun toward the driver, and this time my hesitation evaporates.

I pull the trigger.

kora

Death has been on my radar for too long. Truthfully, I think that's what causes my bouts of insomnia. When Death ventures too close, that's when my hackles rise. I felt it with my ex, lying next to him in bed and wondering what temper tantrum was going to end with an injury I couldn't come back from. I felt it with Kronos, and every night I tried to sleep in my apartment wondering if a Titan was going to bust down my door because I couldn't afford to pay my debts.

So I've had a lot of time to think about what happens when someone dies. To mull over the light fading from someone's eyes. I've seen someone die before. That guy in Kronos' office, of course—that was traumatic. My grandmother on my mom's side. And maybe I've seen death as a child.

I don't know that. But I do know that I've been haunted by dreams of dying for far too long. Long enough for it to be normal. To twist and turn the concept, to explore every variation of what could happen *after*.

There's a large part of me that hopes its just lights out. Boom, gone. Our consciousness dies with our bodies.

That's the only way to free ourselves of the trauma we go through in life, isn't it? Because I can't picture a man in the sky absolving me of my sins and me *letting it go*. No, if there is life after death, then all the sins I've committed will haunt me for eternity.

That's what flashes through my mind in the split second between squeezing the trigger and the explosive noise that rips out of the gun.

Bang.

My arm jerks with the force of the kickback. Blood splatters the front windshield, and I don't react. Everyone else does, though. Jace grabs me tighter. The driver slumps forward against the steering wheel.

Cerberus stares at me with a new expression: *shock*. At least his smirk is gone.

The car drifts to the side, then swerves.

"One too many car accidents, princess," Jace says in my ear. And then our door is opening, and he drags me out.

We hit the ground hard and roll off the side of the road. We tumble down a short embankment. My bones rattle with the impact, but I barely feel it. Jace cradles my head to his chest, protecting what he can, and we finally stop against a tree. My body thrums with adrenaline, and it's enough to block out the pain. Not that I'd feel it anyway.

Jace groans.

We're on our sides, my cheek smashed to his pec. His heart still hammers, a wilder tempo than I've heard it. He releases me and pushes himself up, then extends his hands. He doesn't waste time trying to brush himself off or check himself for injuries. Just his hands hovering in the space between us.

I stare at them for a moment and lick my lips. I taste blood and dirt and immediately spit it out. Horror fills me. Death as a concept is one thing–being the one to pull the trigger is another entirely.

"Don't get lost in your head," he warns. "Get up."

I take his hands, and he lifts me to my feet. He briskly pats me down, hands running down my sides, my legs, my arms. More care than he gave himself, I note dully.

And then he takes my hand again.

The Mercedes skids to a halt at the top of the embankment.

Jace propels me up and yanks the back door open.

I only have a moment to see what happened to the Hell Hound vehicle. It's on its side in the middle of the road, broken glass all over the asphalt. Smoke comes out of the hood.

I'm stuffed into the Mercedes and quickly slide across the leather. Jace piles in behind me and slams the door shut. I grip the handle as Wolfe whips the car around in a tight U-turn. We speed away from the wreckage.

Panic constricts my lungs. I try to gulp in air, but it isn't working. It's like my body has forgotten how to take a deep breath.

Apollo cranes around, reaching for me. I grip his hand and clench my eyes shut.

I just killed someone.

Shot them in the back of the head. The side of the head? Does it even fucking matter?

Was I aiming for their head? *No*. It just happened. Like a video game or target practice. Aim and squeeze. Too easy–except for the guilt that seems to be attached to my skin. Shock accompanies it. Dulls the razor-sharp edge a little... or maybe the sedative is still there. Still making me feel *less*.

"What the hell did you do?" Wolfe snaps at Jace. "We had a plan. You—"

"Wolfe." Jace hesitates. He doesn't continue.

And then their attention switches to me.

"Kora?" Jace reaches out and touches my arm.

I flinch away from him, pressing myself against the far window.

I killed someone.

His eyes in the rearview mirror, the blood on the glass.

The flash of his life leaving him, the kick of the gun and the ringing crack of noise. I stare at the back of Wolfe's seat, unable to make eye contact with any of them.

In a quiet tone, Jace explains what happened. I try not to listen. God, what an absolute nightmare. And what am I supposed to do?

"I should turn myself in." I wipe my eyes, ignoring the warm tears that come away on my fingers. "Wolfe, go to the police station."

"Fuck, no." Wolfe scoffs. "No offense, Kora, but if you go to the police, you'd probably end up back to square one. Or arrested."

"I killed someone. I deserve to go to jail."

Jace grimaces. "You don't. Cerberus will cover it up."

I face him. He looks as beat up as I feel, bits of dirt and leaves all over his clothes, a few scratches on his face. His jeans have a rip in them at the knee, and blood soaks the edges.

"You don't know that. He could easily call the sheriff and hang the whole thing on me—"

"He won't," Wolfe interrupts.

I glance out the window when we slow, surprised that we're already entering the guys' familiar neighborhood. The spread-out homes are unmistakable—as is the large gate that rolls open as we get closer. He pulls into the drive-way, letting the gate close behind him before parking in the garage.

They all hop out, and Wolfe opens my door. He spreads his arms, and he doesn't have to ask twice. I leap into his embrace. He rocks back, hugging me tightly. His hand comes up and cups the back of my head, and his lips press into my hair.

"You're okay."

"I just killed someone."

He grunts. "It happens sometimes."

A laugh slips out, more disbelief than anything, and I lean back. "It just happens?"

He shrugs. "Yeah, sometimes you have to go there."

Not for the first time, I wonder how the hell these three didn't murder me in the woods—it clearly would've been an option for them. And how many people have they murdered? More than their fair share, I would guess.

Wolfe extends his hand to me, and I take it. I need to get a better look at Apollo. And Jace. My brain still feels foggy, but not nearly as bad as when Cerberus injected me. We get into the house, and I let out an unexpected breath.

Last time I was here... Wolfe and I had sex. And then Apollo was shot trying to save me from Kronos.

I'm bad luck.

But it feels like months ago, and simultaneously, like no time at all has passed. The house is the same, plus a few more weapons on a side table. My shoulders inch higher. There's another shoe dropping soon.

What's to stop Cerberus from busting in and taking me back?

We go into the den, where Apollo and Jace wait. Jace has a cloth that he rubs over his face and neck, and he

61

hands me another one when we join them. I run the damp towel over my mouth, then ball it in my fist. I need a scald-ing-hot shower to get the crawling sensation off my skin. A hand towel isn't going to cut it.

"Sore?" Apollo leans forward from his spot on the couch, trying to catch my eye.

I can only glance at him, then away. I have the urge to climb into his lap and hug him. He tried to get to me in the hospital, and the Hell Hounds manhandled him. Shame fills me that he was put through that on my account, and it keeps me immobile.

I shake my head slowly. "He injected me with some-thing, so I think that might be numbing the pain."

Wolfe sucks in a breath. He hasn't moved from my side, still close to the doorway.

Why? Am I subconsciously planning an escape?

"I shouldn't stay here." I force myself to turn to Jace. "I'm not sure why the hell you guys would risk going against the Hell Hounds for me—"

"Not against," Wolfe says.

"You... were going to join them?" Of course. Of course they'd be stupid enough to give themselves back to Cerberus after working so hard to get free. Of *course* they would throw away everything for a rash decision. And honestly? That pisses me off even more. I wheel around and smack Wolfe's chest. "Stupid, idiotic jerks. That's the dumbest thing I've ever heard—"

Arms wrap around me from behind, pulling me against a chest.

"Breathe," Apollo says in my ear.

"I don't want to breathe. I just want to..." I let out a sob.

His touch unravels me, and my knees buckle. We both sink to the floor, him behind me, and I clutch his forearms while I completely come apart. He rocks me back, adjusting me until I'm sitting on his lap. I wrap my arms around his neck and bury my face in his chest.

I can't go home. I won't put my parents in the middle of this, not when I know how dirty the gangs fight. I can't go back to my shitty little apartment. I'm not even sure the landlord would let me back into the building. School, Marley... all that normalcy has gone up in flames. I've missed two weeks of classes, so even if I wanted to go back...

"When's the last time you ate?" Apollo's thumb skates along the bare skin just above the waistband of my pants.

Goosebumps crawl up my arms, and heat shoots straight to my core. Now is not the time for my body to be reacting like I want to jump his bones.

My stomach growls, and embarrassment flushes through me. "Um..."

I'm not about to tell him that I can't think when he's touching me like that. Because it seems innocent enough– my mind is freaking *dirty*.

"Cerb dosed her with something," Jace says. "Food should help. And water."

I shiver, but his tone brooks no argument. Apollo lifts me off him and transfers me to the couch. My gaze lingers on him and the slight limp in his walk as he ducks out of the room. I sit gingerly, pulling my legs up, while Wolfe and Jace both watch me.

They exchange a look. Jace sits on the other section of the L-shaped couch and rests his elbows on his knees. Wolfe takes a blanket from the back and offers it to me but remains standing.

"Where did he take you this morning?" Wolfe asks. "After I saw you at the clubhouse."

I swallow. "Um, to the house. The one Kronos tried to…"

"Burn down with you still inside it," Jace finishes. "Did he tell you why?"

"I didn't know where we were going until we got there."

It was surreal, seeing the charred house. If that man hadn't saved me…

My eyes well up, and I press the heels of my palms against them. I don't want to cry again. It feels like all I've been doing is going with the flow and crying, letting myself be hurt. My control was shredded the moment Jace's Jeep was attacked and I was taken.

Speaking of…

"How did you not die?" I drop my hands and stare at Jace, trying to see if I can determine his injuries. Wolfe had said he was grouchy but okay… he doesn't seem grouchy *or* okay. Worry lines crease his face. He dragged me out of a moving car less than an hour ago. Yeah, it was to save us from the crash that was coming… but still. The echo of the gunshots I heard while Kronos' men put me in the truck rings in my ears. "They *shot* you."

He runs his hand down his face. "They didn't. I kicked out the front windshield while you were putting up a fight, but I didn't get out in time. I dropped them, but by then, you were in the truck. I tried to get to you, Kora." He meets my gaze. "I'm so fucking sorry."

"I sat in a locked room for five days thinking you were dead."

I'm not sure where my anger comes from, but it's swift. I'm angry that I spent so much time worrying about them. Mad at Kronos for letting me think they killed him. In the back of my mind, I know it's misplaced. It wasn't Jace's fault. I could've held faith that he was alive, but I didn't. No, instead, I grieved as much as I could.

My hands tremble, and I shake them out. Emotionally, I'm a fucking mess. I need sleep and food and to not feel like demons are chasing me.

"And Apollo. He was shot because of *me*. You both were. And you still come after me?"

"Gunshot wound can't stop me." Apollo carries a bright-yellow bag of chips and a plate with an array of sandwiches on it. He sets the plate down on the cushion next to me. There are eight peanut butter and jelly halves. "A little surgery, stitched me up just fine."

"You didn't look fine yesterday." I cross my arms and ignore the cramps in my stomach. "I'm not worth the risk. Any of it."

"It isn't your fault." Apollo kneels in front of me and takes my hand. "We weren't going to abandon you. Okay? So put that thought right out of your head. It was a joint decision. Now, please, Kora. Eat."

As if to make a point, he takes a half for himself and bites into it.

Joint decision. I don't know if that makes me feel better or worse.

I sigh and lift one. A PB&J is one of those things that I can eat a million times—and when I was on a tight budget, I *did*—but not get sick of it. A water bottle magically appears at my side, and after I've finished my half, I guzzle down most of the water. My throat still hurts, residual pains from the intubation.

What I did... it was the right thing. I had to get away from the Hell Hounds.

Right?

I mean, I guess I can either rationalize it or self-destruct. *Good choices.*

"We have a few problems." Apollo holds up his hand

and starts ticking off fingers. "We need to figure out what Cerberus wants with Kora. Plus, he has that new role with the mayor's office. How did he get in the mayor's ear in the first place?"

"And why he dragged Kora to that press conference," Jace adds.

I straighten and suddenly remember that I haven't seen them in a while. *Duh*. But... I have problems of my own that I need help solving. "Um, so you know I was in that fire."

Apollo narrows his eyes. His hands return to my thighs. He hasn't moved from his position in front of me. He doesn't seem surprised, exactly. Someone had to slip that I was in the hospital for smoke inhalation. That nurse maybe. Or even Cerberus. He could've bragged to the guys...

"Right. Because Kronos tried to kill me." I laugh nervously and pick at one of the sandwich wedges. "But I didn't make it out by myself... Someone pulled me out."

Jace turns away and rubs his face.

"Say again?" Wolfe lowers the sandwich half that he had grabbed, his eyebrows almost in his hair. "Who?"

My face is probably scarlet right now. "Um, I don't know."

Jace sighs. "Okay, we're going to get back to that in a second. We also have the Jeep issue."

It's my turn to be confused. "Huh?"

Apollo sits beside me and opens the bag of chips. He offers them to me, which I shake my head at, then pops one in his mouth. "The Titans planted drugs on the car after they took you. Coupled with some dead bodies Jace left behind... It wasn't a priority over the last week or so, but the DEA has been sniffing around."

"The Jeep was under a throwaway LLC," Wolfe says. "Most of the valuable stuff is."

I tilt my head. "Like a shell company?"

"Yeah, except we're not laundering money. Just using it to protect our assets," Jace says. "We have contacts in the sheriff's office that are trying to make it go away. And the company masks our identities. But if it's the Drug Enforcement Agency, we have to assume that they'll discover us eventually." His expression darkens. "And then we'll make that go away, too. But it's not as urgent as your story, so let's hear it. From the beginning."

I swallow another gulp of water, then screw the cap on the bottle and set it aside. This shouldn't be hard. I just need to tell them the facts.

So I do. How Kronos kept me in a room for days, feeding me dosed food until the auction. The bright lights, the camera.

Sheriff Bradshaw.

"Bastard." Wolfe rises and paces in front of us. "He was there? He saw you?"

I suck my lower lip between my teeth. "He wasn't concerned that I was there until the auction was over. Then he gave me the knife that helped..."

That draws their attention again. Not that I ever really lost it. Apollo next to me, Jace adjacent on the opposite side of the couch. Wolfe in front of me. I had forgotten how intense they all are together, but that intensity is what makes telling them... manageable.

They're not going to burst into tears because of the pain I endured. My eyes still burn from my earlier breakdown, and I use the hem of my shirt to blot at my nose.

I swallow past the sudden lump in my throat.

"Kronos kept me outside of town." I rub the brand on my wrist, tracing the shape with my thumb. It's quickly becoming a bad habit. To touch it when I'm nervous, as a sort of morbid reminder. Lest I forget what I went through. "Once the transaction, if you can call it that, was complete, he said we were going to a neutral location for the trade."

"And they took you to that frat house?" Jace asks.

I glance from him to Wolfe, still pacing, to Apollo. They seem to be struggling with this. Not Jace, though. He's analytical, trying to make sense of the past two weeks. Two. Weeks. One of which I spent... asleep.

Against my will.

I start. "It's November."

Apollo frowns. "Yeah."

I shiver. How did I miss that? I guess it wouldn't have been a big shift. Leaves changing color, falling. The temperature dropping. I missed Halloween—and that makes me wonder if the guys missed it, too. If they paused in their search for me to celebrate the dark holiday.

Time has slipped through my fingers, and I ache to go back. To experience the precious minutes and seconds that I was robbed of.

I must keep talking or else the words will rust in my mouth. "They tied me to a chair in the basement, and that's where Kronos told me that Cerberus had won the auction. And he said... He said there was only one person he hated more than the three of you. Something snapped, and he poured gasoline along the back wall. I think maybe he wanted to kill me... painfully. As payback."

Apollo's hand slips into mine, and he squeezes tightly. I squeeze back.

"Keep going," Jace urges.

I have to remind myself that I'm not there. That I *can* breathe now. If I inhale deep enough, sometimes I imagine that I can still smell the smoke clinging to my hair, my skin. Maybe that's a trick in my mind. The smoke might still be there. The heat is a memory hiding right under my skin. But taking a few deep breaths doesn't calm my racing heart, and neither does Apollo's hand in mine.

The panic ebbs through me, and I can't do anything but let it. Still, I continue. "The sheriff had given me that knife, and I used it to cut myself free. But the door at the top of the stairs was locked, and there was so much smoke. I couldn't get out, and I accepted that I was going to die."

That's an ugly truth.

"Then the door opened, and I was carried out..." My voice trails off. "I don't know. The guy didn't let me look at him, and then he knocked me out. Next thing I know, I'm waking up in a hospital. Intubated. And Cerberus is telling me he has control over my life. The contract was transferred to him from Kronos. I think he made them put me under for another day or two..."

I shudder. "I never want someone to have that sort of power over me again. Do you understand? That's why I pulled your gun, Jace." I meet his gaze. "I didn't want to kill anyone, but that beat the alternative–all four of us under his thumb? No."

Wolfe growls. "He kept you sedated on purpose? I'm going to fucking kill him."

"You won't," Jace says quietly. "There are too many eyes on him."

"Your long-range rifle would do." Wolfe raises his eyebrows. "What, you don't think he deserves a bullet between his eyes? Pick him off from a distance, and no one would be any the wiser."

"Right, there's no way anyone would suspect *us*." Apollo rolls his eyes. "Think smarter, man."

"But..." I look around the room. "I'm not safe here. Especially after what just happened, and I killed–"

"They won't," Jace interrupts.

I narrow my eyes. "I killed a Hell Hound," I finish. I have to say it out loud. And it doesn't pass me that Jace winces just the slightest. Even he doesn't know how Cerberus is going to react. If he'll change his mind about me, if he'll drag me back to hell and sedate me until...

Forever seems like an awfully long time.

"You're safe here," Jace says. "They will not come onto our property."

I scoff. "They already did, don't you remember?" That day when the Titans followed Wolfe and I back up the driveway. The breached security–which has since been doubled, but *still*. The lingering feeling of being watched has been impossible to shake.

"He's right," Wolfe says. "My father is a supreme asshole, but he wouldn't ruin our truce to take you. He's not that..."

Apollo sighs. "He'd rather make it be your decision."

They can't be serious. My gaze bounces from Apollo to Jace, and finally to Wolfe.

"Is that how it's going to be? Manipulation?"

My father sees the world as something to manipulate. He warned me as such.

"Yes." Wolfe rubs his hand over his face. "But it might take him some time to come up with a clever enough ploy. We have time. They won't snatch you out of the blue."

"And Kronos?"

Jace grunts. "He's in hiding after his stunt backfired. I doubt we'll see him for a while."

I let out a breath. That makes me feel better.

Apollo keeps my hand in his and stands. He tugs me to my feet. "Come on, Kora."

I go with him. The tips of Wolfe's ears are red, and he

turns away as we pass. He doesn't seem like himself. Not really. It took too long for me to notice that something's off, but concern settles on my shoulders. I almost stop and ask him what's wrong.

I don't have time to question it, though, because Apollo whisks me upstairs.

"Where are we going?"

He doesn't answer. Instead, we end up on the second floor. He leads me to my bedroom, through the familiar room, except the green is gone. Just when I was starting to get used to the obnoxious colors and floral print.

I skid to a halt. "What happened here?"

He shrugs. "Little makeover, nothing to worry about."

Cream, blush pink, charcoal gray. A *little makeover* has changed the whole color scheme of the room. And I have no idea why, unless they wanted to erase me from their memories.

Then they wouldn't have come back for you.

"Do you like it?"

I meet his gaze and nod slowly. "I do."

"Good." He tips his head toward the bathroom, closing the main door behind me.

I step into the bathroom and spin around just in time for him to shut this door, too.

He locks it and winks at me.

We regard each other in silence as the water heats. Soon enough, steam billows from the shower. It fogs the mirror. Only then do I feel safe enough to turn and brace my hands on the counter. I can't face the blood on my skin or the bruises. I've avoided looking at myself in the mirror at all since I left the hospital.

Isn't that sad?

I couldn't bear to face what the fire did to me, or my

71

week with Kronos, or my week unconscious. They've said I'm brave, but I feel anything but. I hide from my fears. Shrink before them. Apollo's motorcycle blew up, and I stopped going to school. I left my hometown to escape my abusive boyfriend. I shot someone to avoid dealing with Cerberus.

So instead of eyeing my blurry shape in the steam-covered mirror, my gaze drops to the counter. My makeup is still here. My hairbrush. Toothbrush and toothpaste, deodorant. Everything is exactly where I left it, but I can't help but feel disconnected from it.

Like I'm not quite the *me* who was here before.

But who am I supposed to be now?

Apollo comes up behind me and carefully frees my hair from its tie. He runs his fingers through the tangled strands, carefully picking out pieces of leaves and pine needles. He drops them on the counter next to my hand.

"You know what I like most about you, Kora Sinclair?"

I lift one shoulder.

"You're resilient."

"Yeah, right." I roll my eyes. "I think I'm the opposite."

He picks up the brush and slowly works it through the ends, then higher. My eyes drift closed, and I let my weight rest against the counter. I don't remember the last time someone's *nicely* brushed my hair. Not like the girl forced into the Titan marriage, or the woman who came in before we left for the press conference and roughly scraped my hair back into a low ponytail.

His nails skate across my scalp, and I let out a hum of appreciation. It just slips out.

But he does it again, and I can't help the same sort of half-moan.

"You keep making those noises, baby, and my self-control will go out the window." His voice curls in my ear.

I tilt my head back. "But what if I want you to lose control?"

"Shirt." He lifts the hem, and I raise my arms. He pulls it off and tosses it behind him. He pushes down my pants, and I kick those away, too, until I'm in my underwear.

I rotate around. He's right in front of me, inches away. Yet I won't touch him. Not even if I want to–and I do. I really, really want to fucking touch him.

"What are you doing?" I ask.

"Putting you in the shower."

"Uh-huh."

He smiles and yanks his shirt off. His stomach... there's a jagged, pink scar across his abdomen. "Stitches came out yesterday. That's why I was there."

"You had an IV."

"I was dehydrated."

Right. I gnaw at my lower lip and reach out tentatively. My finger ghosts along right under the line. "I expected a round scar."

"Surgery–they had to open me up. There was some internal... issues. But hey, it's nothing to worry about." He catches my hand and brings it up to his lips, kissing my fingers. "The doctor said to lie low, but that I'd survive. Sounds like fine odds to me."

I hang my head. "Everything is so fucked up."

"I know. But it won't be that way forever." He opens the shower door, and a wave of warm air hits me.

I reach behind me and unclasp the bra. It slips down my arms to the floor. I ignore the way Apollo's gaze heats, lingering on my breasts. My panties join the bra, and I don't feel like a freak for baring myself to him. Maybe I'm trying

73

to scare him away. My ribs are visible again. If I had to guess, there's shadows under my eyes.

"You're beautiful," Apollo says. It's the opposite of what I want but exactly what I need.

I have nothing to lose. I don't know why that thought comes on so strongly, but it nearly knocks me off balance. And I'm sick of being scared, defenseless, *helpless*. For once, I just want to reach out and take what I want.

And right now, that's Apollo.

My cheeks flush. A memory bubbles back up: he had held my throat while Wolfe...

I press my thighs together and point to his pants. "You're taking those off, right? Or do you usually shower clothed?"

"You want me to join you?" His voice is husky.

I tip my chin up. "Unless you want someone else to take your place..."

An empty threat, but his eyes darken anyway. He unbuttons his jeans and shoves them down. He kicks them away and steps into me, using his body to back me into the shower.

The steam envelopes us first. The water is hot, on the border of too much, but it relaxes my muscles. Until Apollo's hand wraps around my throat. I start, but his grip never tightens. His palm is cool against my skin, and I swallow.

"You want someone else in here with you? Wolfe maybe?"

My shoulder blades touch the cool tile, and I meet his gaze. "No."

"What do you want, Kora?"

I smirk. "Isn't it obvious?"

"Tell me anyway."

"I want *you*. I want you inside me, on me." These words don't feel like mine. My brain doesn't have time to process them, because there's a pulse between my legs that's taken over. I grab his wrist, his hand still light on my throat, and drag it down. Between my breasts, over my stomach and down to my hot core. Together, our fingers find my wetness.

He lets out a groan. "We just got you back. I watched you and Jace jump out of a moving vehicle an hour ago." His other hand glides up my side, over sore spots that will darken into bruises by tomorrow.

I don't care about that. "Please."

He curls his fingers, ghosting over my clit, and brings his hand back up. He inspects his index finger and then sticks it in his mouth. I watch, rapt, as his tongue works over his digit. Tasting *me*.

"You're just as sweet as I remember. And I'm going to taste you again..."

"Later." I step into him and reach for his cock. He's already hard, and it jumps under my touch. I stroke him, and he lets out another groan.

"You're destroying my restraint."

I squeeze and tug, like I can use his dick to make him come closer. There's too much distance between us right now. He takes another step toward me. It's just us in this space, and I wouldn't want it any other way. The steam cocoons us, muffles the outside world. There's no one beyond this room.

He removes my hand, then slides his down my sides. He grips my ass and hoists me up, grunting slightly. My back hits the wall, and I wrap my legs around his hips. The slight pain, my muscles burning, is worth it. It makes sure I'm in the present with him.

He braces one hand under my arm and the other beside my head.

"Do it," I plead.

The tip of his cock slides through my folds, and I suck in a breath. He teases me like that a few times, back and forth, until I dig my nails into his shoulders.

"I like it when you beg," he admits. "I like watching your face when you're turned on, and when I do *this*." He makes the same motion, hitting my clit, and my eyelashes flutter. His lips touch my ear. "So beg."

For once, my words come easily. "Apollo. God, please, stop torturing me." I grip him tighter, turning my face toward his. My lips part when he inches inside me and withdraws. "Please fuck me. Fill me up–give me everything and make me forget the last two weeks."

He kisses the corner of my mouth. "You have a filthy mouth."

His thumb presses down on my lower lip. I open for him, letting him see my tongue, my teeth. He seems to examine all of it, even as I pant and grip him. I roll my hips, trying to take him deeper, and he chuckles.

"Please," I whisper, "I'll–"

"Don't make me promises." He ducks down and nips my throat. A reprimand maybe.

Heat floods through me, going straight to my cunt.

"You like that. A little pain with your pleasure." He's speaking against my throat. Without warning, he pushes all the way inside me.

I scream. I don't try to muffle the sound, don't care about anyone else hearing. My nerves are shredded, and it's the unexpected fullness that shoves me toward the edge. But he doesn't move. He just stays there, and his hands glide up and down my torso. He kisses a trail up the side of my neck, to my ear. He sucks my earlobe into his mouth, nipping my flesh. I let him continue his assault on my skin. I say unintelligible things. A babble of *please* and *oh god*.

He palms my breasts, his fingers pinching my nipples.

I arch into him, gasping.

This isn't sex–this is beautiful agony.

"Enough torture," I whisper.

He lifts his head and analyzes my face. He nods once and wraps his arms around me. He cinches me tight to him as he begins to move, pulling out slowly and slamming back in. The force of it jolts my body, but I don't release him–and he doesn't let go of me, either.

My head falls back against the tile. He fucks me like he's been waiting to do this for weeks. The slap of our skin connecting fills the air. I'm overloaded with stimulation.

"Fuck, you feel too good." He leans down and sucks my nipple into his mouth.

My lips part, electric zaps going from my sensitive nubs straight to my core. I clench around him. His teeth graze my nipples next, biting and tugging. I let my hands travel up, threading my fingers through his hair and holding him there. The sensation builds and builds. My heart is keeping time with his pounding.

And then his hand dives between us, and his finger presses on my clit. He pinches and twists–again, using the pain to amp up my pleasure–and that's all it takes for me to lose it.

I scream again. I tip over the edge, senseless. Every muscle in my body tenses. He keeps going, relentless, until he gasps and stills. His cock pulses inside me. It matches the spasms of my pussy, and he comes with his teeth in my shoulder.

"Holy shit," I whisper. I wiggle against him, unable to ignore that he's still fully seated inside me. Still hard.

We're both breathing like we ran a marathon.

He carefully grips the backs of my thighs and lifts me, sliding out of me. As soon as I'm back on my own two feet, leaning against the wall, an emptiness hits me.

All that, and we didn't even kiss.

After the shower–in which Apollo washed every inch of my body–he bundles me in a robe and slips out of my room. He only has a towel around his waist, and he goes off in search of his clothes.

I flop back onto the bed. The dusky-pink color really is quite pretty. I finger one of the accent pillows above my head and then I pause. Front and center on the otherwise-bare bookshelves is the flower mask.

The colors of the mask perfectly match the room's new aesthetic.

I hoist myself back up and walk toward it, unable to tear my eyes away. It's in a glass box, pinned to a charcoal velvet backing. The flowers are drying out slowly, but they still look as delicate and fragile as when they first gave it to me.

Persephone's mask.

I've changed since then.

The girl who put on *that* mask was afraid, in a lot of ways. Of death, of Kronos, of the future. But she was hopeful, too. That her guys would get her out of that situation. That they'd stop the auction, end Kronos and the Titans, free her once and for all.

What a daydreamer she was.

My fingers itch to break the glass and put the mask back on, to see if I can still see her way of the world. Hopeful and fearful all at once, and incredibly naive.

Now, what am I?

A murderer.

Apollo made sure to get any blood off my skin. Truth be told, I'm not sure if any got on me to begin with. I only know that I thought I tasted it on my lips. My fingers remember the weight of the trigger. My arm knows the kickback after it went off. And my eyes can't get the sight of the driver slumped forward against the steering wheel out of my mind.

The next mask I wear should be shades of black, because that's where my soul is heading.

I take a deep breath and turn away from it. No good will come from looking backward. It's so obvious that I'm not her anymore. It's been two weeks, but it may as well have been a lifetime.

I change into sweats and a t-shirt, then pause again. The outfit I wore to my first Olympus with the guys hangs in the closet. The orange-hued cream colors, the skirt and matching top. I had let it go, but now I want answers.

So I take it off the hanger and carry it with me downstairs.

Apollo and Jace are in the kitchen, opening takeout boxes. Apollo meets my gaze and grins. My co-conspirator.

Jace's brows are pulled down in a permanent scowl.

"Hungry?" Apollo asks.

Jace jerks, and he glances at me. Then at the fabric in my hands. "What are you doing?"

I set it on the counter. "I didn't ask that night, but I want to know who bought this."

Apollo chuckles. "You wore it to Olympus, didn't you?"

"Yes, but I didn't buy it. Did you? As a..." I shrug. "I don't know. I assumed it was a present. You guys got me the mask, after all."

Jace picks up the cropped shirt. It's been laundered, but there's a smudge of red in the hem that didn't come out. "Why do you think we got it for you?"

"Because I didn't." I plant my hands on my hips. "Obviously."

"Obviously," Jace echoes. "I don't think any of us would think to get you this, Kora."

I snort. "Well, then why was it in my closet with tags? *Way* out of my price range, by the way. Everything else in my closet is from my apartment."

Apollo's smile drops. "You're sure you didn't buy it?"

Oh my god. "I thought *you* did," I shout.

They both stare at me like I've grown a second head. And honestly, I probably should've just come out and asked...

"Why are you yelling?"

I whirl around. Wolfe is a foot away. He scowls over my head at his friends, and then his gaze lasers into me. He seems angrier. The version of him that I know has been scraped away, leaving this man in his place. I can practically *feel* his demons emanating off his skin.

What did he spend the last two weeks doing?

"Did you buy me the outfit I wore to Olympus?"

He tilts his head, then inches to the side to see the

offending fabric. He stares at it for a long moment. Remembering, maybe.

"No," he finally answers. "Why?"

I swallow. "It was... in my closet? With tags on it."

"And you're just telling us about this now?" Wolfe's scowl deepens. "Why the fuck did you think we'd buy you that?"

"Really?" I shake my head. "Because you three gave me a fucking mask. You brought me here and fed me and got stuff from my apartment. You actually *did* buy me clothes. How the fuck was I supposed to know what was and wasn't from you?"

Wolfe shrugs.

I roll my eyes. The mystery is going to nag at me, but they're not nearly as concerned as I am. "Let's not forget that someone set off the alarms in the middle of the night. And another time, they managed to get an envelope to your doorstep. I don't know why I'm trying so hard to convince you–"

"You're right," Jace interrupts. He rounds the kitchen island. "Someone snuck in here to give you expensive clothes."

He's... *sarcastic*.

That's my last straw. I lunge at him. My palm strikes his cheek, the *smack* loud in my ears. My palm stings, but it isn't enough. I hit his chest, his arms. Open-handed slaps that probably hurt me more than him. He gives me a moment, then easily snatches my wrists. He whirls us around and walks me backward, slamming me into the wall.

My fight flees.

"Giving up so easily?" He leans down, a sneer firmly planted on his lips. "Where's your courage?"

"Stop." I tug at my wrists, pinned at eye level, but I don't budge. "Jace."

"Let's get one thing straight. We protect you. And you seem to have some... attraction going on between yourself and my two friends. But make no mistake. When it comes to me? There's no us. There's no camaraderie. You slap me, you fight me, and you'll get the full force of my retaliation." His face inches closer to mine until his breath hits my cheek. His cheek is red, a handprint blossoming into view. "And I don't think you can handle that."

I lift my chin. "Give me your worst. We'll see who ends up standing."

He laughs.

In my face.

So... I do the only rational thing I can think of.

I knee him.

Well, I try.

He blocks it easily, pushing me back against the wall again.

"I'm not sure how you go from nice to biggest asshole in the universe like *that*." I snap my fingers.

"It's a skill."

"It's annoying."

His eyes flash, and his head moves to the side. "Leave us."

There's movement behind him, and I catch Wolfe storming away. Apollo hesitates, his brows furrowed.

"*Leave*," Jace snaps.

"Big bad leader." I scoff. "Ordering his little minions away so they don't think less of you?"

His smile is slow. "It's not my dignity I'm trying to protect, princess. You know, you're still stacking up the debt."

My stomach swoops. "What the hell does that mean?"

"We took you in, but it doesn't mean I've forgotten. I felt *bad* for you and your shitty decision-making skills. But now we've saved you a handful of times, and what have you done for us?" His eyes gleam, like he's enjoying this cruelty. It's another side of him—the kind of attitude more similar to Hades than Jace.

Weird, how I can separate the two. And weird how I miss *Jace*. The one who held me, who kept me company at night... But I'm oddly attracted to this version of him, too. His body pressed against mine, all hard lines and restrained anger. It makes me want to push and push, just to see how far we both can go before we break.

Danger.

His face is still close to mine, my wrists still in his grip on either side of my head. His hips pin mine to the wall.

Yet, I find myself relaxing into his hold. "You're lucky I haven't clawed your eyes out while you slept."

His lips brush the corner of my lips, then back. His hot breath whispers across my ear. "You had plenty of chances."

I jerk my wrists down, and he releases me. I push him away and step to the side.

Act cool. I straighten my shirt, even though that's the least frazzled thing about me, and grab a plate. I take my time peering into the takeout containers and serving myself. Jace taps away on his phone, unbothered—and completely ignoring me.

It's fine. I hide my trembling, my annoyance, by snatching the offending crop top and skirt. I open the trash and drop both in. They seem out of place, and part of me is hit with guilt at the waste. But I can't look at them anymore.

And they clearly don't believe me.

I take my plate and at the last second hunt in the fridge for something to drink. Something stronger than water. I wrap my fingers around a beer bottle and tuck it under my arm.

And then I beeline for a safe haven away from Jace King.

wolfe

My phone has been ringing nonstop for the last three hours. My father, other Hell Hounds. My car idles in the driveway, because that's as far as I made it. I couldn't just up and *leave*–not with everything going on. So I threw it into park ten feet from where I started, went back inside to grab a drink, and went back to sulk in relative quiet.

The radio is on, just low enough for me to pick up the words. The mayor's announcement this morning caused a mild uproar–not with us, but with most of West Falls.

It feels too ominous. Ever since this morning, the pressure has been building and building, and sooner or later it's going to explode.

It buzzes again, rattling in the cupholder.

I take a sip of beer and close my eyes. What I want to do and what I need are two different things. My first urge is to go find Kora, but my thoughts run dark tonight. Her and Apollo in the fucking shower–or rather, fucking in the shower–was too much. The tightness in my chest is too constricting. I'm being squeezed to death by an emotion I refuse to name.

I need to answer my phone.

And yet, I don't really want to do that, either.

I brokered a deal with my father, not for the first time in my life, and we broke it.

Not him, not Kora. *Us.* Jace and Apollo knew what we were going to do, and they knew the risks. I knew the risks. We could've stayed with him, helped him out of the stupid wreckage. Fulfilled the duties I had agreed to. But instead, we helped Kora get away.

Now she's somewhere in the large house, her presence like a balm for Apollo. Even Jace seems to be breathing easier. But me? I can't breathe anymore. Her back home, after what Kronos and my father did to her, is a guilt trip I wasn't prepared to handle.

My phone buzzes again, and I snatch it. I'm ready to chuck it out of the fucking window, but the name scrolling across the screen gives me pause. Malik Barlow is my father's right-hand man. He didn't rise through the ranks like a normal Hell Hound–he used me, Jace, and Apollo to get there. There was a lot of bloodshed involved, but I don't hold it against him.

We were friends once upon a time.

And oddly, I find myself curious about what he has to say.

I answer the call and wait, remaining silent.

A low chuckle fills my ear. "Always playing games. I used to like that about you, Wolfie."

I suppress my eyeroll. He can't see me, but I don't want to give him the satisfaction. "Used to? I'm hurt."

"Your father is raging."

Alive, then. Only a mild disappointment twinges in my chest.

"Of course." I take another sip of the beer, which is quickly warming in my grip. "I figured you'd call to tell me something I *don't* know."

"Three of our men were found dead in the neutral zone."

I sigh and rub my eyes. "Yeah?"

"They were part of the transport today from the press conference."

"And...?" I have the sudden hankering to move this conversation away from the house. I keep the phone pinched between my ear and shoulder as I hop out of the car. I take a side path around the garage that leads to the backyard.

There are neglected gardens at the edge of our property, and I head in that direction.

Malik sighs. Noisily. The man can be silent as a ghost when he wants to be, but... he's not naturally quiet. I grew up with him huffing, scoffing, gasping. Snoring. Everything got a loud, non-verbal reaction from him, until my father beat it out of him.

And then the silence came.

But apparently, talking to me brings out old habits.

"Out with it."

"The Titans have been silent on the matter. You know Kronos likes to brag. He claims his kills." Malik pauses. "And the deaths..."

"It's the neutral zone. They're not going to brag about breaking the truce." The college district, the schools them-selves. They're supposed to be safe. Until Cerberus stepped in and made himself the protector of the area–so to speak. *Of course* the Titans are going to get angry and retaliate, but

91

they wouldn't be foolish enough to admit it. "My father should've seen this coming."

"You're not listening to me." Malik makes another noise, some sort of groan that slips through his teeth.

I can imagine how he's standing right now, jaw clenched and hand over his eyes. The way he used to pose when Cerberus caught us doing something against his wishes. Like... like he'd rather not see the punishment coming.

It's his only downfall. A rare weakness.

"This wasn't Titan retaliation. This was... Have you ever seen a Titan decapitate someone?"

"What the fuck are you talking about?"

Decapitation? Never mind that Kronos is supposed to be licking his wounds in private. He's out here severing heads?

"The only way we identified them was from their tattoos." Malik sighs *again*. "It was fucking gruesome."

"So you're calling me."

"Because your father is in a rage, and I'm not sure what he's going to do. First he loses Kora and you three, plus his driver, and now three of his men. They were lieutenants, although you did *not* hear that from me."

Fucking hell. Decapitated Hell Hound lieutenants in the neutral zone? It sounds laughable. Something made up to scare children at night, to keep them safe in their beds.

"I'm just giving you a heads-up that there might be something worse in Sterling Falls than Cerberus and Kronos. This bought you a day or two respite while his attention is diverted—but that's it. I've got to go." He hangs up.

Great.

I shove the phone into my pocket and step into the gardens. The entrance is narrow, the path leading between two giant marble pillars. It probably used to be spacious at one point, but overgrowth has given it a wild feel. The leaves pull at my jacket as I move into the space.

A stone wall obstructs the view from the house, but it feels different back here. I can actually take a breath.

The path continues past reaching bushes and trees. Everything is starting to go dormant, their vibrant green changing to oranges and reds, yellows and browns. Leaves are scattered across the ground.

Toward the back is a gazebo.

I tilt my head, eyeing the dark thing. It's encased in shadow, but there's a glow coming from inside it. The thing is encased in ivy–nature's way of trying to reclaim the wood, the space. In a trance, I find the entrance and take the few steps up and in. The gazebo is an octagon shape, the white painted railings chipping in some places. It's missing some vertical balusters. But the bench that rounds it seems intact.

My attention goes to the candle on the bench. The flame waves in the slight breeze.

And beside it, the girl who drew me here without even knowing.

Her face is hidden in her bare arms, her knees drawn up. She's made herself as small as possible. She isn't crying, as far as I can tell. She might be barely breathing.

She certainly hasn't realized I'm here.

I wonder what Jace did to make her fold like this, and another spike of anger washes through me. Dead Hell Hounds? Fuck them. Kora hurt? Suddenly I'm ready to beat my best friend bloody.

I ball my fists and take a shallow breath. Unlike Malik, the silence my father beat into me never leaves. It's not something I can switch off–I didn't learn how to become a ghost. Or, in a way, a wolf. I was born one.

School kids teased me about my name, my hair, the leather vest I wore even in middle school. It's hard not to pick up on facts about my namesake.

Dad sure did think he was clever. The three-headed dog and his son, the wolf.

Sometimes I feel like one. Feral. Hungry. Violent. And I don't know if that's because of me or because of my father.

Kora doesn't move for a long moment. But when she does, it's only to shrink again. She takes a heaving, rasping breath and readjusts her grip. A tighter hold on her legs. Her face buried.

I hate it.

Whatever happened between her and Jace, whatever went down between her and Kronos, and then my father– dark hatred swirls through me. The need for violence is right under my skin, ready to break free. It's always there, but it's been more lately. More because I killed that truck driver and a few Titans. I've been giving in to the urges instead of suppressing them, and wouldn't you know it? That just makes everything worse.

She made herself small because of them.

"We do not bend for them."

Kora lurches at the low tone of my voice.

I stalk forward and grab her arm, pulling her up. The flickering candle is the only light penetrating this dark space, but it's enough to see her tear-streaked cheeks. The glimmer of more in her eyes.

"Stop crying. You hear me?" I shake her once, willing the fight to find her again. "We do. Not. Bend. And we certainly don't break."

She stares at me. I can't figure out if she doesn't recognize this person I've become or she's just… lost.

Guess what, flower? I'm lost, too.

I pull my gun and flip it around. It takes some maneuvering to get her fingers around it, to rest her index finger along the side. I keep both hands over hers and lift the gun. I press the muzzle to my heart.

"W-what are you doing?" She tries to jerk back, but I hold strong.

I hate this rage in my heart. I hate and hate and hate, and it doesn't do any of us good.

"Teaching both of us a lesson. Do you want to leave? Do you want to run home to your mommy and daddy?" The words are acidic on my tongue, but I'm out for blood. Hers, mine. I don't know yet.

She narrows her eyes.

"Come on, Kora. You're out here all alone, crying your eyes out. It isn't symbolic. It isn't cute. You've had a few terrible days." I carefully release her hand with one of mine, the other holding fast, and lift my keys from my pocket. "Shoot me. Take the keys. Run and never look back."

"I don't understand how this is a lesson." Her eyes bore into mine.

Such pretty eyes. A pretty face. It's no wonder Apollo is attracted to her. She's got the look about her that begs for a savior.

But *he* can't do that for her.

And I'm pretty sure I can't, either.

Neither of us is built to save, no matter how hard we try.

"There is no one in this goddamn sick world who will have your back more than yourself." I yank her forward.

Her elbows bend, the gun between us keeping some

distance. Barely. The muzzle digs into my chest. Her attention bounces between my face and it.

"And that means not being afraid to fucking *shoot* when you have to."

"I did! Don't you think I know this?" Her struggle intensifies, but her finger doesn't inch toward the trigger. Even upset, her face reddening, she isn't swayed. "Don't you think I wanted to shoot your father when he leered at me, practically dared me to do it? I did pull the trigger. I was just aiming at the wrong person." Her voice breaks at the end.

"You did what you had to do. And guess what? It worked. And now you've got the gun pointed at me. So, flower, what are you going to do now?" I take a breath. The gunshot might kill me—no, it would definitely fucking kill me. And that sort of peace will have been hard-won.

She snarls. Her teeth bared. Her fear morphs into anger, and all my blood rushes south. *Damn*, she's pretty when she's sad, but she's fucking beautiful when she's pissed.

"Pull the trigger," I goad. Because I have a death wish, and I think her face is the last thing I'd like to see. "Come on, Kora."

She rips away, and I let her go. Her fingers slide through mine, leaving the gun in my hand and the keys in my other. I drop the keys and flip the gun around, aiming for one of the wood supports.

I squeeze the trigger and unload four shots in rapid succession. Every bullet finds its mark, the wood splintering with the impact. The noise echoes around us for a moment, ringing in my ears. I relish that sound.

Kora's eyes go wide a split second, her mind whirling as she takes in what just happened. She rushes me, screeching.

"I could've fucking killed you!" Her fists connect with my arms, my shoulders. She gets a good punch in on my jaw, then immediately reels backward. She clutches her fist to her chest.

Yeah, jaws are significantly harder than arms. And the hit actually smarts.

Still, it's her fight that I want to draw out of her–the fight that Jace seems determined to squash. I take a step toward her, and she glowers at me.

"Fuck this." She storms past me, then skids to a halt a few feet from the stairs. "What the hell is wrong with you?"

"You." I laugh and shake my head, although she doesn't see it. I step right up behind her and fight the urge to touch her. "Do you know what I did while you were gone?"

She doesn't respond–but she isn't running anymore, either.

I lean down. My lips touch her ear, eliciting a wonderful shiver up her spine. My tongue flicks out, tasting her skin. "I killed people. Tortured them for information then discarded them like they were nothing."

I say it like that's nothing–and maybe it is. Or maybe it isn't.

Either way, I'm too fucked up to care.

"Who?"

I exhale. Why am I admitting my sins to her? Maybe to explain the stains on my soul. I took the name Ares at Olympus because I never heard a good story about him. He was a seducer. The angry god drew people into battle, into death. Secretly, I think him and Hades might've been in on it together. The keeper of the underworld and the one who sends souls to their grave decades too soon.

"I started with the Titans who got in my way while I searched for you–and Kronos. Then the truck's owner." I can't quite see his face anymore. Just the weight of his body as I pushed him over the cliff. "One of the firemen who delayed arriving to the scene. A cop. An orderly who had instructions to kill you."

Dark days.

My father had no idea–or, if he did, he didn't fucking care. I don't know how far his plans go to take over Sterling Falls, but they must've begun well before that stupid press conference. Getting in with the mayor, the sheriff. Taking over the neutral zone.

So maybe he did know that Kronos wouldn't let Kora go so easily. Not after finding someone so valuable, both father and son are left on the hook.

"I have a list," she says.

My brows lower. "A list."

"Of... people. Who had a hand in this."

Ah. My heart pumps a little faster at her admission. "Tell me."

"The Titans who were there that night, who put me in the truck. One named Brody, who set up the auction." Her sweet voice becomes hard. "The sheriff. Kronos. And now, Cerberus." She turns around and presses her hand to my chest.

The action is so surprising, I stiffen and very nearly jerk away.

I haven't been touched in two weeks, up until I got to touch her at the clubhouse. And that felt like... relief. That she was alive and okay. But this is her anchor lodging in my heart, cutting through bone and armor. She's going to rip it out with her smile one of these days and have it for her own.

I'm not sure if I'm looking forward to that day or dreading it.

"Wolfe, I want you to help me. They need to pay."

A stark difference from the girl who is still dealing with her first kill. But, I'm already nodding my agreement. She wants revenge, and I can deliver on that. I've let my demons out of their cages while she was gone, and wrestling them back under control is harder than I expected. I'm half out of control right now.

Her hand slides up, up, up. The side of my neck, cupping my jaw. She pulls my face down and stares me in the eyes.

Does she see it? That I've become someone significantly worse than the person she left?

"I want your help–but I want to kill them." She stares at me. "I know. I know what it means and what it might do to me. That driver might not have deserved it, but *they* do. The thought of hurting them was the only thing that kept me sane in that little room."

My mouth falls open, but damn it if I'm not even more turned on than I was thirty seconds ago. I mean, *fuck yeah*, I see her reasoning. She's drawn a line in the sand–and who am I to argue with it? I've got my own lines.

Before I can answer, a light hits us.

"What the fuck, Wolfe?"

I groan and lift my head, squinting at Jace and Apollo. "Took you fools long enough. I fired my weapon at least a minute ago."

Probably longer.

"No one comes out here," Apollo snaps.

"And yet." I step back from Kora, although it pains me to do it. I will my erection to subside, too. It strains against my zipper, drawing most of my focus. Her hand falls away from me, and she can't look at either of them.

Well, well.

99

"Why is your jaw red?" Jace climbs up into the gazebo, bringing that bright-as-shit light closer to my face.

I shrug. "Dunno. Maybe I'm fucking embarrassed."

Kora snorts. She's moved away, back to the candle. She grabs it from the bench. The little flame is alive and well, flickering like mad.

"We should get inside," Jace finally says. "Saint has news."

"About the three Titans?"

He winces. His gaze cuts to Kora, then back to me. "I'm not discussing this in front of her."

Fucking Jace and his trust issues. I roll my eyes. "She could find it on the news. On a damn Google search, even. You wanted her here, so fucking man up and swallow the consequences."

Kora flinches. "He has a funny way of acting like he wants me here."

He glares at her. "Go back inside."

"Fuck off."

I grin at her angry tone. I'm taking credit for that. Whenever Jace tries to stomp out her fire, I'll reignite it. That's my silent promise to her–and myself.

Jace grumbles and turns away sharply. "Fine. *Come* the fuck inside whenever you're damn well ready. Or stay outside all night. Your choice."

She brushes past him, flipping her hair over her shoulder. "I think I'm ready now."

kora

I don't know where I'm going until I'm on the third floor.

I've only been up here once, clearing the area with Apollo. The moonlight filters in through the glass wall in the back. I step up and stare out, beyond the backyard and into the grove of trees.

Before, it was beautiful. Even when I was scared, gripping Apollo's shirt as he cleared the space. Now, alone, my skin prickles. The hairs on the back of my neck rise. I step away from the glass, and my thoughts are pulled in other directions.

My fingers and forearms ache from holding the gun to Wolfe's chest. While the gun felt solid, my grip on reality... not so much. I had gone outside seeking quiet, to find some answers in my head. But instead, Wolfe found me.

And I ended up telling him about the list.

I even told him his *dad* was on it.

"Kora."

I whirl around.

Wolfe leans on the doorframe, his arms folded over his

chest. I let my attention wander up and down his body, and the ache between my legs gets more insistent.

"Do you care that I killed someone?" I cringe.

"Do you care that I've killed several?"

I pause. He knows I don't care—it hasn't changed between now and the first time I met him. But he's waiting for that answer to lead me to his, and that makes me feel slightly better. "You know I don't."

He inclines his chin and saunters forward. He touches my wrist and then lets out a breath when he reaches my hand. The one still clutching the candle. My fingers are covered in drying wax. It hurt at first. Little streaks of hot liquid dripping down my skin.

"Does this hurt?"

"It was a good distraction."

"Hmm..." He wets his index finger and thumb, then pinches the flame.

I jump at the little hiss as it's extinguished. He takes the candle from me, uncurling my fingers and dislodging some of the wax. Then he flips my arm, pulls it out in front of me, and holds the candle above it.

The first drop of wax has my eyes fluttering. There's been a burning sensation under my skin, and the wax inexplicably ignites it. I step forward and take Wolfe's face in my hands. He doesn't resist me dragging him down to me.

Our lips touch.

He remains frozen, but the candle falls out of his grip. There's a dull *thunk* of it hitting the floor.

My lips slide against his immobile ones, and I'm about to give up when he comes back to life. He grips the back of my head and winds his fingers through my hair. He tugs, angling me, and suddenly takes over.

I keep my hold on his face. My nails dig lightly into his

hair, and he groans. I lick the seam of his lips. His other arm winds around my back, cinching us together. He tastes my mouth, then tears himself away.

"Tell me to stop."

I scoff. "No fucking way, Wolfe. I want you to devour me."

His eyes come back to mine. His gaze is as hot as I feel, and he slowly releases me. "Okay, then, flower. Strip for me."

Goosebumps rise on my arms, and an insane idea comes over me. Something that might pull him back from whatever cliff edge he's standing on.

I lick my lips and shake my head. "Not yet."

His brow raises, and caution enters his expression. Especially when I step forward and slip my fingers into the waistband of his jeans. I tug him toward me and undo the button. Drag the zipper down inch by inch. And when I pull the fabric down, his briefs with it, he sucks in a sharp breath.

I go down to my knees. I've done *this* before... but I've never wanted to do it. Not until I met him. I meet his gaze and grab his cock, running my hand up and down the length. It jerks in my grip. I fist it tighter, my strokes rougher, until I hear him exhale. His lips part, and his hands ball into fists at his sides.

"I misspoke." I lick his tip. Just a taste. He has a beautiful dick–in a scary way. My ex was on the smaller side. I force my gaze up to meet his. "I don't want you to devour me, Wolfe. *I* want to devour *you*."

"Fuck." He shakes his head. "My self-control isn't all there these days, flower."

Apollo had said something similar–it seems I'm on a roll breaking their restraint.

"Good."

I take his hands and put them on my head. His fingers flex against my scalp, then tighten when my mouth closes around him. My tongue moves, and I take him deeper. I adjust my stance, using my hand to help guide him. The tip hits the back of my throat, and I fight the urge to gag.

I keep going, sucking hard, until his hips rock. He pulls my head back sharply, meeting my gaze again as he takes control. He thrusts into me hard, forcing himself deeper. Tears spring into my eyes at the intrusion, but I don't try to stop him. Even when I gag around him. Even when I choke, my breath cut off for a long moment.

It's all I can do to keep staring up at him.

"Keep your mouth open." His voice is rough. His movements quicken, and he jerks his hips twice.

And then he groans, and his hot seed spills down my throat. I swallow, not even tasting it because he's so far in. But he pulls out, and I suck in a breath through my nose. His cum fills my mouth.

"Fucking perfect." He runs his thumb along my lower lip, smearing it.

We're a mess.

"Swallow, flower."

I do. Carefully. My tongue sweeps my lips, collecting every last drop that I can reach. Part of me revels that I'm able to do this to Wolfe. That my mouth, my lips, my tongue all carried him over the edge.

He watches me with dark eyes, still above me. His dick twitches again. I sit back on my heels and smile up at him. My core throbs, but I stay silent. We've shifted again, and he's back in control. He leans down and takes the collar of my shirt in both hands. He rips the fabric apart easily, but the noise is loud. He groans and shucks the fabric off me, then motions to the bra.

"Take that off."

I reach behind me and unclip it, letting the straps slide down my arms. I toss it away and lean back slightly, giving him an eyeful.

"Turn over. Hands and knees." He hesitates. "If you want to stop this, leave now."

Do I want to stop? *No.* Can't say that I do. So, I bite my lip and do as he says. He kneels beside me and hooks his thumbs in my sweatpants, dragging the material down. And then his lips are on my ass cheek.

I suck in a breath and glance back. He bites. His teeth scrape my skin, digging in—a true bite. The dose of pain goes straight to my cunt, mixing with my lust. Making it... *more.* In this regard, I trust him not to hurt me.

Not truly, anyway.

He licks and bites my ass, down the curve. I groan at the odd sensation, but he doesn't let me escape. He grips my thighs and spreads them suddenly. His hand comes down on my spine. The gentle pressure guides me from my hands to my forearms. My cheek touches the rug.

I dig my fingers into the floor helplessly. He's so freaking close to touching me exactly where I need, but he doesn't. He skates around it, touching my thighs, my ass. He holds my hips for a moment, and my breath hitches.

My need burns through me, but something keeps me silent.

And then his palm strikes my ass.

I yelp and scoot forward, but he catches me easily. Hooks his arm under my hips, keeping me on my knees. He does it again, twice more in succession. I let out another moan, desire sweeping through me. My cunt is throbbing, but he doesn't touch it. His fingers stroke carefully over the sensitive skin he struck.

"Apollo in the shower," he mutters. "And then you broke our rule, flower."

I shiver. "What rule?"

"That you come first." His voice is dark. "Punishment, then."

"Punishment?"

He stills at the tremor in my voice. His hand rubs my ass cheek again. My body feels hot all over, and all I can focus on is his hand–and his voice.

"I lied a minute ago. If you want to stop this, you just say the word. But I'm taking you here because I don't think you want to stop. You don't want to go back down to your room and finish yourself off with your fingers. You don't want to go to Apollo, because then he'd see the marks I've left on you."

I squeeze my eyes shut.

He's right–I *don't* want any of that.

"You want this. Me." His finger swipes over my clit, then slides into me. "Ah, you're clenching around me. I love that feeling, flower. Your throat working around me... that almost won as my favorite feeling, but I can't wait until you're clenching around my cock."

He flips me over, and my back hits the floor. He climbs over me, aligning our faces. "Do you want to stop?"

"No."

He smiles. It's a quick flash, then gone.

We're not supposed to be gentle–that's why we're on the floor and not a bed. That's why I still have the taste of his cum on my tongue and an ache between my legs.

"Wolfe."

"No need to beg, flower. I'm right there with you." He

slams inside me in one brutal move. My body jolts from the force, and I reach up to grip the back of his neck. He leans down and recaptures my lips.

I open for him. Every thrust inside me eases some of the ache—but amps up the torment. I love this feeling. His forearms are braced on either side of my head. We're about as close as we can get and still have movement between us. He moves hard and slow, and I drag my teeth along his lower lip.

He groans, then tears his lips away. He shifts, attention going to my throat.

"He marked you."

I shiver. Apollo was paying special attention to my neck, my breasts... but I try not to look at myself in the mirror too much these days. He presses his thumb into one, and it's the same sensation as touching a bruise. A dull pain, but not in a bad way.

"What are you going to do about it?" My fingers slide into his hair.

"Besides punch Apollo in the nuts?" He grins. "Let's see..."

He shifts his weight to the other side, stilling inside me. He's fully seated and unmoving. I squirm as his lips touch the other side of my neck. Heat floods through me at his first kiss. Suck. *Bite.*

He makes a humming noise against my skin. "You're getting wetter, flower."

I tip my head to the side to give him more room. Their marks... I should've realized what Apollo was doing. Isn't this the same thing as the paint, the last time we went to Olympus? Apollo and I start something, and Wolfe inevitably finishes it. The gold streak, the red handprint.

I whimper when he gets to my breast. There must be a

trail of bite marks down my neck and chest, but he keeps going. He licks my nipple, and my eyes roll back.

"Wolfe, please."

His chuckle is rasping. "Trust me, this is just as much torture for me as it is for you."

"Then fuck me."

"Not until everyone in Sterling Falls knows you're *mine*."

Including Apollo.

And Jace.

But I can't stand that. I don't want to be owned–aren't I already? Isn't that what got us into this mess?

I shove myself upright, bringing him with me. Nose to nose, I narrow my eyes at his expression. Turned on, angry.

Well, I guess I'm fucking angry now, too.

I push him to the side and roll with him, landing on top. He huffs when his back hits the floor, but his eyes gleam. He wouldn't have let me do that if he didn't want it.

I take his wrists and put them on the floor. His fingers flex, and his gaze is lustful. His control seems to be hanging by a thread. But for now, I'll take what I can get. I brace my hands on his chest and sit up.

His cock slides out of me almost all the way. I push back down, and it hits a whole new spot. Different angle, better... deeper, almost. I never got to be on top with my ex. He liked to fuck me from behind, my hands pinned behind my back. There was never any relief for the ache those times left me with, until I found escape in the shower and took myself there. Pitifully. Shamefully.

There's nothing shameful about this.

Wolfe watches me, but it doesn't take long for his patience to break apart. He sits up and wraps his arms around me.

"You bouncing on my fucking cock is the biggest turn-on in my life. And the only reason I haven't already come is because you took me in your mouth." He grips the back of my neck and kisses me again. His other hand slides between us.

He strokes my clit, flicking and rubbing it until I'm panting against his lips.

"Come for me, baby."

Another thrust, another twist of his fingers against my clit, and I am a goner. The sensations beat over me, and I squeeze my eyes shut. My muscles clamp down, my cunt spasming around him.

He lets out an animalistic growl and flips us before I've come down from my high. He takes my wrists and traps them above my head. Our bodies are aligned, stretched out together, as he pummels into me.

Chasing his own release.

Moments later, he stills. He drops his head to my neck and comes inside me.

"Punishment," he mutters.

I still. "What?"

He lifts himself slowly. As soon as his weight is gone, I miss it. But he gives me a lazy smirk and slowly withdraws. "For not coming on my tongue."

I swallow. "Um..."

"It's okay, flower. I think you might enjoy this punishment." He hops up and gathers our clothes, then heads to the stairs. "I'll be in the den if you need me."

I sit in the silence for a moment, wondering if he's coming back. But... nope. My skin prickles, the hair on the back of my neck standing up. I glance around, toward the window–but that's ridiculous. Out there is only the backyard and the grove of trees beyond it.

Finally, I hoist myself up. When I realize that he literally took *everything*, I swear. I'm about to make a very naked walk of shame back to my room. His cum seeps out, dripping down my thigh. I clench them together and make quick work getting back to the second floor.

My heart hammers at the thought of getting caught.

No one is on the second floor, though. The hall is empty. I tiptoe as fast as I can down to my room and grab the doorknob. But it doesn't budge.

I step back quickly, making sure... I don't know. That I got the right room. I try the door again and confirm: it's locked.

"Son of a bitch." I kick the door and turn away.

His room is locked, too.

And Apollo's.

I hesitate outside Jace's, then try the door handle.

Locked.

Fucking fuck. Mortification burns my cheeks at what I'm about to do.

Even their bathroom is locked.

I let out a harsh sigh and look over myself. I appear exactly how I feel: thoroughly fucked over.

The hickeys and bite marks are dark-reddish purple against my pale skin. They'll take one look at me and know exactly what Wolfe and I were up to. Assuming Wolfe has the key.

I push my shoulders back and take a deep breath. What other choice do I have?

Still, Wolfe is definitely going to pay for this... somehow.

I tread lightly down the stairs, my cheeks getting hotter by the minute. I shouldn't–Apollo has seen me naked. And Wolfe, of course.

But Jace...

Yeah, no.

Their voices drift out from the den. They're sprawled out on the couch, video game controllers in hand. They have drinks near them, a beer for Apollo and amber-colored liquor for Jace and Wolfe.

They fall silent when they notice me in the doorway.

Wolfe smirks.

Apollo's eyes bug out of his head.

And Jace... well, his reaction isn't as big as I would've expected. The muscle in his jaw jumps, and his gaze sweeps me from head to toe, but other than that? Nothing. "Lose your clothes?"

"Locked out of my room, actually," I grit out.

"Shame," Wolfe manages.

I cross my arms over my chest. "Don't suppose you have a key, do you?"

"Me?" Wolfe raises his eyebrows. "Nah."

My focus jumps to Apollo. "Do you?"

He presses his fist to his mouth. "What did you do to deserve this, Kora?"

"Yeah, Kora?" Wolfe leans back, spreading his arms. "What did you do—"

"Enough of this," Jace snaps. He rises, tossing the controller to the cushion. "Fucking immature assholes. Nice choice you made, sweetheart." He brushes past me.

My mouth drops open, but he strides away without a backward glance.

"Ignore him," Apollo murmurs. "So?"

I swallow. "Um..."

Now all I can imagine is the last time I was naked around the two of them.

"She broke our rule," Wolfe says.

I narrow my eyes at him.

Apollo rises slowly and steps toward me. "Which one?"

"There's only one, as far as I'm concerned." Wolfe shrugs. "The one where she comes first."

"Uh-oh." Apollo circles me.

I stay still, unsure. New lust blooms through me, and I have to admit: I sort of walked into this. "The key, Wolfe."

He appraises me. "Did Apollo taste your pretty little pussy?"

I glance behind me, then back to Wolfe. "N-no."

Apollo touches one of Wolfe's bite marks, tracing it with his nail. Goosebumps rise on my skin, and I fight the chill sweeping down my spine.

"Two, then?" Apollo directs his words to Wolfe.

"Or until she can't stay awake anymore."

Apollo hums. "Well, we can carry her to bed. If we find that key."

"Right," Wolfe agrees.

I keep my gaze on Wolfe, still reclined on the couch. Apollo hasn't moved into my line of sight, besides his fingers inching along Wolfe's handiwork.

"What do you think, Kora?" Apollo's chest brushes my arm. "Here?"

I tip my head back to get a good look at him. My lungs are tight with anticipation, and my mouth opens and closes. Truthfully... not a bad way to go. Although my legs tremble at the thought of another orgasm... or two. Or more.

"Well, both of you deny having a key to my room."

Apollo winks. "We do."

I press my palms to my thighs, trying to hide my reaction. Apollo guides me to the couch, sitting me in the corner of the L shape. He sits beside me and runs his hand up the inside of my leg, starting at my ankle.

Wolfe stays where he is.

My attention goes to him and the way he watches Apollo's hand inching up my leg. Apollo opens my legs more, running his fingers in a looping pattern over my inner thigh. I can't stop watching Wolfe, though. He's spread out, his arms along the tops of the cushions. His fingers dig into them, and his hips shift.

He's hard from watching this.

Apollo swipes his finger through my center, and my eyelashes flutter. I let my head fall back as he thrusts his fingers in me. I'm slick from both my own body reacting to this situation and Wolfe's cum. Apollo doesn't seem to mind, though. His thumb rubs small circles on my clit.

"Faster," Wolfe whispers.

Apollo's pace quickens, and I let out a harsh exhale at the shift. His other hand palms my breast. He pinches my nipple, rolling it between his fingers. I reach for him, but Apollo tuts.

He glances over his shoulder at Wolfe, then hops off the couch. He lifts my leg, bending my knee and pushing it wider. He kneels before me and descends. He licks me, and my core pulses.

He's not only tasting *me* but Wolfe. Fucking hell, that's hot.

"Oh my god." I dig my fingers into my thighs.

Wolfe makes a pained noise. He's undone his pants, his cock in his grasp. He tugs it almost violently, and I can't look away. His hand jerks up and down, and his gaze is locked on where Apollo is feasting on me.

It's too much.

"I'm going to—"

"Keep count," Wolfe orders me.

Apollo's tongue spears into me at the same time that he rubs my clit, and I scream. My climax takes me by surprise, and my back arches. But he doesn't stop. If anything, it just amps him up. His vigor renews, sucking my clit like he's trying to pull my soul out.

He might at this rate.

"Kora." Wolfe's gaze moves to my face.

I swallow. *Keep count.* "One."

"Good girl," Apollo growls, his lips moving against my sensitive center. "So fucking pretty."

He continues until he wrenches another orgasm from me. My muscles burn, and I grasp his hair. I yank him away, panting for breath.

"Two," I manage. "That's enough—"

"You say *stop*, and we stop." Wolfe's hand on his cock moves faster, harder. "Anything else is just words."

I press my lips together.

Wolfe smirks and drops his hand away. He shifts toward me and lifts me onto my knees. Apollo braces my hips, and the only warning I get from either of them is Wolfe's attention going over my shoulder.

Wolfe leans down and sucks my nipple into his mouth, his teeth scraping the sensitive skin, at the same time that Apollo pushes his wet finger into my asshole. I yelp at the forbidden feeling, but all I get is a slap on the thigh. Apollo wraps his arm around my waist and pushes his finger deeper.

"God," I groan. My head falls back on Apollo's shoulder. "This is too much."

"Punishment," Apollo reminds me, his lips against my ear. "And fuck if I'm not harder than I've ever been, seeing you come apart under me while he watches."

I swallow.

Their slow assault continues. The word *stop* bangs around my head, reminding me that I can end this at any time—and I do actually believe they would listen. And when another slow orgasm creeps up on me, with Apollo's finger in my ass and Wolfe's tongue, teeth, and fingers on my breasts, no one is more surprised than me.

Wolfe grins like the cat that ate the canary. He wraps his hand around the back of my neck and pulls me off of Apollo, kissing me soundly. I grip his biceps. Lips touch my shoulder, inching up my neck.

I'm not sure I'll ever get used to them with me... together. Like this.

And my mind must be fraying, because the backs of my eyes burn. I can't seem to open them, either.

"Kora," Apollo prods.

It takes me a second to realize what he wants. "Right. Four."

"Three," he corrects, chuckling.

"Oops."

"Set her back," Wolfe says.

I slow-blink at them. "Is three my limit?"

"Technically, five for the day. Unless this idiot didn't make you come at all."

Apollo snorts. "As if."

My body has officially betrayed me. Exhaustion pulls me down. They've done it. Fucked me to sleep. And it's probably right that they did it this way—I don't know if I could've closed my eyes any other way.

Fingers press into my cheeks, and I force one eye open. Wolfe looms over me, concern crinkling his brow. "Don't go there, flower. Don't let your mind take you to places that will keep you awake."

I shrug. How am I supposed to control my brain?

One of them scoops me up. I cuddle in closer, pressing my palm to their chest. *Apollo*, I guess. From his scent and the way he moves. I crack my eye open to confirm my guess, and warmth swirls through me that I was right.

Naked, satiated, and right.

But my slim window of vision lets me see something I think I would've rather not: Jace, watching from the shadows.

Apollo breezes past him without a word, and if I hadn't seen him? I never would've known he was there.

kora

The first floor is empty. I check each room, mug of coffee in hand, just to make sure I'm not crazy. The house is silent.

It took me too long to realize it was, in fact, empty. I woke up in my bed alone, surprised to have slept through the whole night. That's due largely in part to Apollo and Wolfe... and the fact that I don't think I let go of Apollo once he put me to bed.

Oh, and my door?

Mysteriously unlocked by the time we came up.

Anyway, I woke up, took a hot shower, and pulled on sweatpants and a t-shirt, found coffee... but no guys.

I consider calling out but then suck my lower lip between my teeth.

In the garage, Wolfe's Mercedes is gone.

So is one of the bikes.

Did they leave me completely alone?

I sip my coffee and go back the way I came, winding through the wide hallways toward the kitchen. And then I pause.

The door to the basement is cracked.

Avoiding basements hasn't been an active thing, but... I'm not eager to go down into one after being trapped and nearly set on fire. Looking at the crisp hub of the building Kronos tried to kill me in was traumatic enough.

Still, curiosity tugs at me. And I've searched the rest of the house.

The door opens on silent hinges, and I quickly go down the steps before I lose my nerve. Part of me fears getting trapped down here, but the basement is a lot more spacious than I thought. I take a deep breath and try to calm my nerves.

I'm fine.

They have what looks like a whole freaking armory down here, locked behind a metal cage door. Beyond that is another door–also cracked. I can hear grunting, and a dull smack every few seconds.

I step through that doorway, and my mouth falls open. A home gym, sure, but an *impressive* one. It could rival a professional gym, minus the rows of duplicate machines. There are two treadmills off to the side. A mirrored wall. A row of free weights.

The floor is covered in thick black mats.

On the far left is training equipment. Bags, gear for fighting.

And Jace.

I suck in a breath. His knuckles are wrapped, and he jabs at the large punching bag hanging from the ceiling. It sways under his assault. He wears only black shorts. His back muscles scrunch before every strike, his whole body strung tight.

Lethal is the only word that comes to mind to describe him.

Never mind that he usually carries a gun or two–his whole freaking body is the weapon right now.

He's covered in a shimmer of sweat, and I wonder just how long he's been down here.

"I can feel your stare from here." Jab. Jab. He doesn't stop moving, doesn't lift his head or break his freaking concentration. "Go back upstairs."

I wrinkle my nose. "Why? The show is down here."

He stops, his spine snapping straight. He glances over his shoulder at me. He loves it when I pick at him, I think. It lights a fire under his ass. That's what I tell myself anyway, since he wears such a sour expression all the time. Like right now. His expression looks like he sucked a lemon between his teeth.

I give him my best smile.

"If you stay, you train."

Huh. I narrow my eyes. "Train for what? To hit that bag?"

He shrugs. He uses the back of his hand to wipe his brow. "For whatever I damn well decide."

Interesting. And... maybe it'll help me. I've got to start getting better at defending myself, after all. I've got to start doing a lot of things–but this seems to be a good item to top the list.

"Okay."

He pauses. Maybe he expected me to run back upstairs, to occupy myself with something else until Wolfe and Apollo come home. From... wherever they went. I'm not going to ask him, because he'd probably just take pleasure in me not knowing.

I should ask him about school. There's a slim chance my professors will be forgiving about what happened, and then

I can finish out the semester strong. So it–and my stupid debt–won't be a complete waste.

"Lose the coffee."

I set it down by the door and walk across the padded floor to him.

He appraises me, his gaze cold. "You're on lockdown."

"No shit, Sherlock."

"You've got a lot of people hunting for you."

I roll my eyes. "Yeah, got it. Did you think I forgot from my many orgasms last night? I mean, I wish. That would be a solid way to black out the last four months of my life."

He shakes his head, his lips twisting. "On the mat, Sinclair."

"You want your way with me, Jace?" I wink at him, my courage rising. I reach out to poke his arm. "Or maybe you just prefer to watch–*oof*."

I have a weird moment of weightlessness for a split second, upside down, before I slam to the floor. I blink up at him from my back, gasping for air. My hand didn't even connect with his arm, but he... he just flipped me. Panic holds my chest hostage, worse than having the air knocked out of my lungs.

"Get up."

I inhale sharply. My face is hot, and I brush hair out of my eyes. I climb to my feet and glare at him. "What the fuck was that?"

"Your first defense lesson." He sneers. "Don't touch."

"Oh, fuck off." I turn away from him and stomp back to the door–and my coffee.

Except, I don't make it more than two steps before he's on me. His arms hook around my torso, yanking my body into his and pinning my upper arms to my sides. I flail–my automatic response–but he's unbothered by the weak hits to his forearms.

"Get out of my hold." His voice is right in my ear. "Stop panicking and use your brain."

"You're infuriating."

"All the more reason to hit me, princess." He leans back, taking me with him. My feet leave the floor.

I squeal and grab his arms, kicking out and not connecting with anything.

"I could do anything with you right now."

How the fuck is he so calm?

He moves backward, taking me with him. I throw my head back, but he easily dodges it. My heel connects with his shin, but beyond the slightest grunt, it does... nothing.

"Come on, Kora. Think. Where am I vulnerable? Where can you reach?"

"I don't know!" I pitch my weight to the side, and it takes both of us off balance for a moment. My left foot touches the mat again. I throw my head back and somehow connect with his face.

It hurts like hell, but a second later, his grip slackens.

I rip free and stumble forward, whirling around once I put some distance between us.

He presses the back of his fingers under his nose, blood trickling out.

And he's smiling. "That was a lucky hit."

"Don't you think I would have to be lucky to get out of that? You had me off the floor."

"And you had multiple opportunities to get free." He shakes his head and drops his hand. "Relying on luck is the easiest way to get yourself killed. And you've been lucky a lot these past few months. I'm not saying luck is a bad thing. Quite the opposite. But you've got to depend on skill, and *hope* for luck. Not the other way around."

I stare at him. "You're joking. I've been the opposite of lucky ever since I met you."

"Then how have you survived?" He strides forward.

I back away from him quickly.

"How did you make it out of Olympus the first night? Or after Kronos shot that other guy? When you failed to pay, why didn't he just kill you outright? In the fire–"

"Someone pulled me out of the fire," I snap.

His eyes narrow. "You mentioned that before. Who was it?"

"I don't know."

"A Hell Hound?"

"I don't *know*." I scowl. "Well, coming down here has been a lot of fun. Nice chatting with you, Jace."

I rush to the exit, hoping he won't stop me in some lame attempt to teach me how to defend myself. Do I want to learn? Yes. Is ambushing me a good style? Probably not. Apollo or Wolfe would be better suited for it anyway. They at least *like* me.

At the door, I spin back around. Jace is in the same spot I left him, his wrapped hands planted on his hips.

"Where are they anyway?"

"Away." He lifts a brow. "Scared to be alone with me?"

I scoff. "No."

"Just looking for an itch to be scratched?"

My face heats. "Something you wouldn't know anything about. When's the last time you got your dick wet with something other than lotion, King?"

I don't wait for an answer–really, I don't need to know the last time he fucked someone. I can't get a read on him, whether he's more celibate than a nun or the biggest player in Sterling Falls. He's a mystery that I'm intent on *not* solving.

To add emphasis to my annoyance, I slam the basement door and hurry back to my room. I need to change—stupid of me to wander around in sweatpants. I need clothing that feels like armor. I pick out white jeans, heavy black leather boots that come up mid-calf, and a white sweater. I add a chunky black stone necklace that I find in one of my makeup bags and take my time applying winged eyeliner and mascara. Deep-red lipstick, bold enough to match my hair.

And I carefully flip my nose ring back down. Sometimes I keep it hidden, and I think the nurses might've tucked it up to avoid messing with the intubation.

I shiver at that reminder, pressing my fingers to my throat. It's been through so much in the last few... weeks, I guess, but really it feels like days. Minutes.

How did I lose an entire week?

I lost my phone somewhere along the way, too. My memory is hazy—I don't know if I had it with me when Wolfe and I went to rescue Apollo and Jace. If I did, it could've got lost in the wreckage of the crash or dumped by Kronos.

Either way, I haven't seen it.

I blot my lipstick on a tissue and toss it, flipping my hair forward over my shoulders. I don't know what I'm going to do, but I think I just want to be prepared for anything.

But I don't expect the front door to open as I'm coming down the stairs.

It takes me a moment to place the girl who saunters in like she owns the place. Her dark-brown hair is braided over one shoulder, and large sunglasses obscure half her face. A bright-yellow slouchy bag is slung over her shoulder.

She glances around and finds me on the stairs, and it isn't until she swipes the glasses off her face that recognition dawns.

"Artemis."

She grins. "Friends call me Tem."

I come down the rest of the way, raising my eyebrow. "Am I a friend?"

She lifts a shoulder. "You're a curiosity."

That's... just what I wanted to hear.

"Apollo called, said you might want someone to talk to who isn't a dick." She folds her sunglasses and stuffs them in her bag, then drops it on the side table. "Or have one."

I snort and follow her into the kitchen.

She opens the fridge and rummages through, pulling out a flavored seltzer. "You?"

"Sure."

She tosses me one—literally—and then cracks hers. I feel like I'm a lost little puppy in my own house, following her into the room off the kitchen. We go outside, and she tips her head back. Her eyes close, and she just seems to breathe in the sunshine.

And... I'm jealous of that.

My muscles are tight, my senses on high alert. It's just the backyard, but the hairs on the back of my neck rise again. It keeps happening, like a set of eyes has found me, and something in my subconscious knows I'm the prey.

Does she know the whole story?

Does she know any of the story?

I shift, even as she takes a seat at the patio dining set. I don't know the last time the guys used it, but it's spotless. A housekeeper I haven't seen, I guess, must come in and take care of the place. The guys cleaning? Can't see it.

Although I think I would want to see it. Especially in a little maid outfit–

"You know, I was just getting used to the idea that they'd be alone forever."

I jump and glance over at Artemis. "What?"

"They've been more fixated on their mission than anything else. And Olympus. *God*." She leans forward, planting her elbows on the glass surface. "You should've seen them in the beginning. Moody plotters, threatening to take down the whole damn city. Every corrupt officer, gang member–all of it."

I blink at her. "What?"

I think, on some level, I knew they had a deeper mission than just running Olympus. It's easy to see how they got off track. Holding the line between the gangs seems like a full-time job, let alone dismantling all of them. But the thought that they *want* to do that, to make the city better, both hurts and doesn't at the same time.

Of course they want it.

Of course they're failing.

The city is made of bullets and blood–it would take a lot more than three guys to change it.

She chuckles under her breath. "Just like them to keep you in the dark."

I shake my head. "I don't know what you're talking about."

"Exactly. *Sit*. Let's chat. Or..." She shoots me a look. "We can put some hair on the guys' chests."

"Oh?"

"Yeah. Sneak out with me. An innocent joyride never hurt anyone."

I wince, and the last time I was out in the wild comes back to me. It didn't end well. "Oh. Um, no–"

"Shit–I forgot about the Jeep incident." She looks away and fiddles with the seltzer can, spinning it in her hands. "I'm not implying that something like that would happen again. That was obviously a targeted thing. This is... spontaneous."

Right.

Anxiety knots my stomach, and that reaction alone is unsettling. I don't want to be afraid to leave their house. I don't want to get in a routine where I'm happy to stay home while they do whatever it is they're doing. Out there. Without me.

School used to be the most important thing to me. My driving force.

I let that go in the last two weeks. Didn't even ask, even though I wanted to.

So, I should do it. I should just go for a quick ride with Apollo's sister, overcome my fear, and be able to say I conquered it.

Even if it's a little bit of a lie, it's a step in the right direction.

I open my mouth to respond, but the doorbell interrupts me. It tolls through the house, the deep tone tripping over itself as the person at the door hits it twice.

Artemis heads toward the front door. I go slower. The last time the doorbell rang, a photo was waiting for me. The one where my throat was slit. We never figured out who was behind that, actually. Or, if they did, they didn't tell me.

More nerves transform into snakes coiling in my belly. I wrap my arms around my waist and fight the sudden loathing. I hate being afraid, and I think I hate more that

Artemis isn't. She hasn't gone through anything like this. She strides toward the front of the house, embodying carefree.

Jace meets us there at the same time, his black t-shirt a new addition. His hair sticks up in places, like he ran his hand through it before we arrived. He scowls at her. "Tem."

She grins. "I came over to see our friend."

His gaze ticks to me, then back. "Don't suppose you rang the doorbell?"

"Not necessary when my brother gave me a key... but I did leave the walking gate unlocked." She makes a face. "Sorry."

My mind—and Jace's, I'm sure—jump to conclusions. He points to the hall we just came from, pulling the gun from the side table. He takes Artemis' bag and stuffs it into her arms.

"Go."

The bell rings again, and I jump. "You don't think—"

"I'm going to find out, no matter what I think." He narrows his eyes. "*Go.*"

Artemis takes my hand and tugs me away. We get out of sight, and I dig my heels in. A mischievous grin creeps across her lips, and she stops pulling. We both crouch mostly out of sight, craning around the corner to catch a glimpse.

Jace has the gun in his right hand. He opens the right door, which keeps his gun concealed. His stance is relaxed, and the tension running through his body is subtle. For a moment, Artemis and I can't hear anything. The only thing I can see is his broad back, tall in the doorway.

"Are you telling me she's not in there?"

I gasp.

Artemis grabs for me, but I'm already running. I knock into Jace and come face to face with my parents.

Both of them.

My throat closes, and I launch myself at them. Dad's irritated expression melts to relief, and Mom lets out a shuddering breath. Her lips press into my hair. My parents hold me tightly, and I hug them back just as strong.

Questions bubble up, and I somehow suppress the urge to blurt them all out. How did they find me? Why are they here? What do they know?

"Kora?"

I glance back at Jace, who has the door open wider. Artemis stands a few feet behind him. His gun is gone, presumably tucked away.

I swallow and release them. "Mom, Dad, this is Jace. Jace, my parents."

"Rachel," Mom introduces, extending her hand.

Jace shakes it.

"Kenneth Sinclair." Dad steps up next, his movements jerky when their hands grip each other.

"We should move this inside," Jace says. "Tem, waters?"

Artemis rolls her eyes and nods, dropping her purse and heading back to the kitchen. Jace leads my parents inside, into the front parlor. The same space the sheriff occupied when he came to question us. Me, rather.

The formal space for strangers.

And on some degree, I get it. He doesn't know them. But *I* know them. Hell, they're my parents. We should be bringing them into the kitchen or the den. I almost sit between them, just to get closer, but Jace shoots me a look.

One that says, *Don't you dare.*

Protector mode activated.

They take seats on one of the two couches, and I force

myself to perch on one of the chairs adjacent instead of dropping down beside them. My heart aches for them, and a sudden wave of homesickness.

It's been months since I've seen them.

Weeks since I've talked to them.

Guilt hits me next–how terrible of a daughter am I? All this bad stuff started happening, and instead of asking for help, I hid it from them.

"What are you guys doing here?" I ask.

Jace reclines on the one across from them, spreading his arms along the top of it. I glance from him to them. He wouldn't have called them, right? He seems relaxed, but there's still that tension in his face. Not enough for my parents to detect, but I don't think he's happy about having them in his house.

I swallow and resist the urge to fiddle.

Mom reaches for me and takes my hand. I let her, threading our fingers together.

She leans into me, squeezing gently. "We saw you on the news. And you went radio silent... We were worried. We *are* worried."

The stupid news. "I'm sorry."

"The man, he said you were in the hospital after that house burned down? Why didn't you call us?" Mom's eyebrows rise. "Did you think we'd be mad?"

"Wow, news really made it all the way to Emerald Cove, huh?" My nerves are strangling me.

I force a chuckle and pull away, folding my arms over my stomach. I make sure the brand is tucked out of sight–I haven't been covering it, but I definitely don't need them to see it. That would probably amp up their worry.

My next lie is, "I'm fine."

"You don't look fine." Dad pinches the bridge of his

nose. "I'm sorry, Kora, we thought you were doing well in Sterling Falls. My friend–"

"Friend?" Jace interrupts.

Dad squints in his direction, then turns back to me. "You can come back with us, honey. Do you want to come home?"

Do I...

Do I?

The question is almost impossible to consider. What would happen to the guys if I left? What will happen to me if I stay? What would Cerberus do to me–or them?

"We're worried," Mom says gently. "We called the school, and they said you switched to online. And then we went by your apartment, and it was trashed."

I flinch.

"Kora experienced some difficulties," Jace explains. "I hear that's true for most students who are new to Sterling Falls. There's an adjustment period. It hasn't even been a full semester."

Dad's not buying what Jace is selling. His eyes narrow, and he opens his mouth to finally address him.

Jace rises abruptly. "Kora, a word?"

Artemis reappears with glasses of water. She sets them down on the coffee table, and her brow crinkles when Jace and I both step out of the room. As soon as we're out of sight, he grabs my upper arm and tows me into the kitchen.

My heart pounds. Is this the part where he doesn't let me go back in there? Where he tells me I can't leave Sterling Falls–just in case I thought I could? I'm not going to put up with that behavior. Not right now.

I jerk away from him, putting some distance between us. "What the fuck? You Neanderthal."

"My caveman behavior is about to get a lot fucking

worse if I have to club them over the head." He glowers at me. "Did you call them?"

"Call them?"

He's got to be fucking ridiculous.

I laugh in his face. "I don't even have my fucking cell phone, asshole. How the hell was I going to call them?"

I turn away and close my eyes. Guilt, again. Shame. I *should've* called them. Any normal, sane girl would've called her parents and asked them to bail her out.

But I didn't, and therefore... it's my fault.

"Your phone is on my desk."

I whirl around, only a little shocked to find us chest to chest. He's a grade-A stalker, after all. A looming, quiet, hulking...

"What?"

He smirks. "It kept going off in your room... after. So I put it on silent and left it on the charger in the office."

"The office that none of you use."

He inclines his chin. "I use it sometimes."

"Great, thanks a lot for that information." I step back, but he takes my arm.

His hand slides down, pausing at my wrist. His thumb brushes that damn brand. "Do you want them to know everything?"

Implication: *Do you want them to know all the trauma you went through?*

"No." Big no. Definite no.

"Do you want them to know anything?"

I hesitate, then decide to go with the truth. "No."

The corner of his lips tips up. "We're walking down a

narrow path here, princess. They're going to ask questions you don't want to answer. Something tells me they're not going to take your silence, so you need to lie, and lie well. You know, be convincing about it."

I roll my eyes. "I know how to lie."

He tilts his head. "Do you? To them?"

Fear rattles through me. It isn't so much their reaction to what I've been up to that I'm worried about. I mean, yes, they'll probably be upset that I didn't ask for their help. But these are dangerous people we're talking about. Dangerous people who have no problem killing loose ends.

"I—"

He brushes the brand again, and I shiver.

"Let me do the explaining, then." He stares at me with those cold, ocean-blue eyes of his, and I can't help but think that I'm a sucker.

But I nod anyway, and his hand falls away from my wrist. I lead the way back into the front room. Before I can take a seat on my chair, Jace snags my waist and guides me to sit next to him.

Directly. Next. To. Him.

I let out a hiss of breath, but he just smiles. "Mr. and Mrs. Sinclair."

Dad straightens in his seat.

"Kora has been living here. With me."

I elbow him, but he just keeps smiling. Like a psychopath.

"We're in love," he announces.

Artemis covers her mouth with her hand. Her eyes gleam.

Jesus Christ.

My face is getting hotter by the second.

He pats my leg. "Sorry, babe. I figured we should just be

upfront with them. Someone broke into her apartment a few weeks ago–that's why her apartment looks as it does. Luckily, she wasn't home. But she was afraid, and we were already going steady for the past few months. So, I asked her to move in with me."

Dad's face–well, it would be priceless if I wasn't in the middle of having a panic attack. My heart is pounding. And, more than anything, I wish I had taken advantage of our *lesson* earlier to knee Jace in the balls. Hard. Repeatedly.

The last time I dated someone and moved too quickly, his name was Parker Warton and he was emotionally and physically abusive.

My parents know that. In fact, that's probably why it seems like warning sirens are going off in my dad's brain right now. "You're living here? With..."

"Jace." He glances at me, then back to them.

"Are you a student?" Mom asks. "Kora mentioned dating, but..."

"Did she?" Jace's voice is smooth, like he's not the least bit surprised. "Well, you know your daughter better than anyone. She can be modest. Maybe she didn't want to admit how strong her feelings are."

Artemis watches us with huge eyes. Her phone chimes, and she jumps to her feet. She glances at the screen and hurries out of the room without a word.

"Kora, this seems very sudden. You moved in with him?" Dad's attention is solely on me now. Lines appear between his brows, but he's doing his best not to scowl. He can't hide his shock–and dismay? After all, what kind of idiot jumps into this sort of relationship?

The lie I need to sell isn't an easy one. How do I pretend to be in love with Jace, when I'm pretty sure we hate each other's guts? Most of the time anyway.

I manage a wobbly smile and go with a half-truth. "I was afraid you'd be upset."

"We're not... we're just surprised." He grabs one of the waters and drains half of it in two gulps. *Yeah*, he's not upset–and I'm not a redhead.

Mom rubs his knee. It doesn't seem to do much to mollify him.

"How did you know where to find me?"

She frowns. "When you stopped returning my calls and texts, I got worried. You know we had installed that app that shares our locations..."

"You did?"

Jace straightens. "It's on her phone?"

"Yes–"

He rises. "Excuse me for a moment."

And then it's just us.

My parents move at the same time, coming to sit on either side of me. My muscles are so tense, my stomach cramped, but I can't push them away. I missed them. Like, soul-deep ache missing them. And I didn't realize the weight it was putting on my shoulders until this moment.

"Sorry," I whisper.

Mom touches my cheeks. "I'm sorry you thought you had to keep it from us."

"He seems..." Dad's gaze stays on the doorway Jace left from. "He sure does have a lot of tattoos."

I laugh. If that's the most worrisome thing about Jace, I'll take it. "Yeah, he does."

"He's not involved in the gangs, is he?"

Fuck. My focus snaps back to my father. "What?"

How does he know about the gangs? Why would he assume Jace is part of them?

He presses his lips together. After a quick glance at my

mom, he sighs. In a low voice, he says, "Sterling Falls... Kora, I hope you never see the bad parts of this city. I covered some stories here when I was a journalist for the *Emerald Cove Star*. You know journalists—we're bloodthirsty for a good story, for getting ahead. This was long before any promotion, of course. When I was fighting for my career."

I do know journalists. Grew up around them, many of whom Dad considers friends. Or, considered. Before he became their boss. Now he sits behind a desk and figures out which stories are worth telling.

"I've heard the city is cleaning up its act," Mom says. She pats his knee again. "That man the mayor brought on to keep the college district safe seems reasonable. Reputable, even."

She's referring to Cerberus James. Unlike Jace, he has no tattoos. And he has something that my parents' generation seems to respect: gray hair. Like that translates to *experience*.

They both eye me. "You dating Jace doesn't explain how you were at that party. And they spoke of injuries?"

I gulp. "I'm fine. I promise. It was just smoke inhalation. I went to the party with Marley. Jace wasn't involved."

Lie, lie, lie.

Mom looks at me like I've grown three heads. Maybe I'm Pinocchio, and my nose is growing. She purses her lips, and then she brightens. "I spoke to him!"

I grind to a halt. "Huh?"

"Didn't I speak to him on the phone? He seemed quite nice... a little different, though."

Oh god. *Wolfe* spoke to her. Took my phone after I fell on my ass scaring myself. I try to remember what they spoke about, but my mind is blank.

Artemis reappears, saving me from a response. She

shoots me an apologetic look. "I'm so sorry, Kora. My brother is here with his friend to take me home."

I stiffen.

Shit.

The two guys who I *actually* have a sexual relationship with are here?

Mom will see right through me, if she doesn't already. Thank god for Artemis' quick thinking.

"Oh, well, it was good to see you. Thanks for stopping by." I stand and go over to her, unsure if I should hug her or something. Am I a hugging sort of friend? I don't hug Marley, but I'm not sure if that's because of me or because of her. I never hugged Parker in public, either.

She makes the decision for me, wrapping her arms around my shoulders. "We'll do this again sometime. Without any interruptions." Her expression says, *And we're definitely sneaking out next time.*

Hell, that would've solved all my problems... or created more, if my parents discovered Jace here without me. Who knows what he would've said to them?

I smile. "Perfect."

"Nice to meet you, Mr. and Mrs. Sinclair!" She waves and books it for the garage door.

It's opening, male voices calling out, but they're quickly silenced. I stand frozen when Wolfe comes around the corner. His eyes are wild, and he locks on to me.

And breathes.

The air whooshes out of him.

Why? Was he worried? About me?

Too many questions and no space to ask them.

My heart gives a painful thump, and I shake my head as subtly as possible. His eyes narrow, and he takes a step forward. My eyes go wide, and he pauses. Tilts his head.

Probably trying to make sense of what's going on. But if he speaks, then there's a chance my mom will recognize *his* voice from their brief phone conversation.

That's something I can't explain away, but it would be comical to try. *Oh, him? Yeah, well, he and I are sort of dating. I think. But Jace and I are in love? Yes, right. That is what we just told you.*

"Who is this?" Mom asks.

Wolfe stiffens and cranes around me. I wonder what it must look like, me and two strangers in their front room.

"Wolfe," Artemis calls. "We've got to go."

He ignores her and steps forward again. "You good?"

I roll my eyes and shoo him back the way he came. "Yes, my parents came to visit. I was just explaining that I moved in with my boyfriend, Jace."

His face... oh god, his face is priceless. He sputters, speechless, until Artemis locates him and hauls him away. I can't laugh. I can't freaking even crack a smile because then my parents might realize. So I bite the inside of my cheek and only turn around when I can keep a straight face.

Jace stands next to my parents. He came in through the other door, I guess, and he seems like he's doing his best to not burst out laughing.

The absurdity of this situation.

My parents just seem concerned.

"He seemed awfully familiar toward you," Mom says.

I sigh and flop back into my chair. I wave a hand in the air. "Well, he thinks he has a chance with me."

Their eyes widen.

"She's kidding," Jace says. "He's got no chance."

"Right," Mom murmurs.

Dad glances at his watch. "We're meeting my friend for lunch. Kora, can we take you to dinner?"

And leave the house? Jace can't say no to this. Can't say anything at all, in fact. And he knows it, because a muscle in his jaw tics.

I nod. "Absolutely."

"Good. We'll be back here at six to get you." He rises and kisses my cheek. "Love you, darling."

Mom and I both stand, and she hugs me again. "I'm glad you're okay."

"Me, too. Thanks for coming to check on me. Sorry my phone..." I shrug helplessly.

I walk them slowly to the front door, and I'm hit with another wave of homesickness. Not for *home*, exactly, but for them. I drag my heels a bit and suck my cheek between my teeth.

There is a small part of me that wants them to take me home. As impossible as it is. It's accompanied by my instinct to bury my head in the sand until everything blows over. As if that's an option.

It isn't. It won't ever be an option.

"Who's your friend?" Jace asks my father.

He opens the door for them, and Mom gives me another tight hug before stepping outside. Dad is close on her heels, although he turns once he's past us and appraises Jace.

"No one you'd know," Dad finally says.

My brows furrow, but then it's too late. The lights on their car, parked just beyond the walking gate at the curb, flash. Jace closes the door on them.

We stand in silence for a moment.

Then it hits me that Jace just went *there*. It's not a lie I can just shrug off, it's one I'll have to keep carrying every single time I talk to them. I'll have to either deal with their questions about Jace or lie more.

Just what I didn't want.

"You're an asshole."

Not that he needs me to spell it out for him—I'm pretty sure he recites it to himself in the mirror every morning, just to make sure he doesn't go nice on us.

I plant my hands on my hips. I'm angry enough to hit him, but I don't want to wind up on my back again. The fucker would probably do it, too.

Wolfe storms back in, chased by Artemis. I guess she didn't manage to get him much farther than the door. His face is a mask of fury, and I backpedal. He's not coming for me, though. He strides right up to Jace and decks him.

My hands fly to my mouth at the sickening crunch. I don't know a lot about fighting, but the sounds have always been enough to turn my stomach. Even when my ex...

I shudder.

Jace doesn't retaliate until Wolfe comes at him again. Then Jace shoves his friend away, a scowl pulling down his features. Blood trickles out of one nostril, and he brushes at it with his thumb.

"You get that out of your system?" Jace taunts. "You know there's a time and place for this shit."

Wolfe points in Jace's face. "It's bad enough having to share her with Apollo. But was it your plan all along to just get under her fucking skin and take her away from us?"

I flinch. "He's not—"

"Save it for someone who believes it," Wolfe snaps at me. He roughly pushes his hair back and turns to Jace. "Fuck you."

"Fuck *me*?" He laughs. *Laughs*.

The sound makes my stomach bottom out. But I can't do anything except slowly back away. How do I tell Wolfe that I *don't* want this? That I didn't ask Jace to lie for me?

145

Okay, I did ask for help... But I didn't want him to insert himself into the middle of it.

"You've got a lot bigger problems on your plate than any delusion you have that I'd want Kora." Jace sneers at him. "That's your problem, brother. As far as I'm concerned–"

"Just shut up, both of you," Artemis snaps. She stops beside me and takes my hand. She smooths my fingers between both her palms. "You two couldn't have done this without an audience? You need to work on your people skills. I'm taking Kora out of here."

"Take Apollo–"

Artemis picks up a small statue from the side table and chucks it at Jace. He ducks, and the ceramic explodes against the wall. Pieces fly everywhere.

Everyone goes silent.

"Don't forget who I am." Artemis' voice is downright frozen.

And I don't think I've ever admired someone more.

She keeps my hand in one of hers and tows me out the front door. It swings shut behind us, and we go out the walking gate. Our pace is fast, not giving me time to fret about being outside. She gestures to a cherry-red Audi.

I freeze. "Artemis–"

"Tem."

"Tem," I restart. "If you think this is inconspicuous..."

She laughs and unlocks it, stepping off the sidewalk to get to the driver's side. "We're going to North Falls. If you want to blend in, this is the perfect car."

I don't know about that. I've been to North Falls, to the boardwalk and the beach with Marley and her friends. I can't say I paid a lot of attention to the cars, but it didn't feel *that* rich. I'm pretty sure these cars can cost upward of a hundred thousand dollars.

But what's my other option? Go back inside? Hide in my room? No, thanks.

What the hell, right?

I climb into the passenger seat and buckle in. Last thing I need is for her to hit something and me to be ejected through the windshield.

"Double whammy, huh?" She pulls away from the curb.

"Huh?"

"I mean, you and Jace trying to keep your relationship a secret–I don't blame you for that one, especially since Wolfe and Apollo are..." Tem glances at me and winks. "Can you find my sunglasses? In my purse."

The yellow bag sits on the floor behind her seat. I locate the glasses case fairly easily and pass them to her.

"No, no, they're for you. I've got another pair here." She retrieves another pair from her door, sliding them on. "It'll make you feel less like an outsider. Promise."

I grimace. "Not sure there's a cure for that."

And these have to cost a lot, too. I didn't notice it until now, but she has an air of... richness. That's the only way I can describe it.

"Jace and I aren't in a relationship, by the way." I exhale and put on the glasses. The world darkens, and I let my head fall back against the rest. "He made it up, probably to watch me squirm."

"Huh. Could've fooled me."

"Yeah, no. And I've got the Hell Hounds probably out looking for me." I bolt upright. "We're not going–"

"Relax. They usually stay the fuck out of North Falls because of the guys." She flexes her grip on the wheel. "There's a power dynamic that will make your head spin."

Now that she mentions it... "I don't get it. It seems like any side could just take out the leader of the opposing gang, or they could join forces and kill Jace, Wolfe, or Apollo. Why is there such a... delicate truce?"

"It wasn't always like that. The Titans and Hell Hounds were always feuding–and regular citizens often got trapped in the middle. It was bloody. Sterling Falls was no safer than a war zone."

Wow. "What happened?"

The narrow road we've been traveling on opens up, and we come around a corner into North Falls. Here's a clear difference from downtown, and even the other districts. The houses are larger, the yards more spacious. The cars are nicer. The guys' neighborhood is great, the houses few and far between. And theirs is definitely the most expensive, fortified house.

But this... Lavish. Each and every one.

Like they've all been caught trying to outdo each other.

Tem flicks her blinker on and makes a sharp turn, and suddenly we're crawling through a quiet main street. There's plenty of head-in, diagonally parking in front of the businesses. Some cute shops with expensive-looking mannequins in the windows, a pastry place, some restaurants. Even midday, it's busy here. Tourist season never ends.

I'm still waiting for Tem to answer. But the silence stretches on so long, I force myself to let it go. My curiosity will eventually abate.

"What happened," she finally muses, "was your guys."

My guys. I grip the door handle. "How do you end a decades-long war?"

She lifts her shoulder. "I don't know."

"What?" I twist toward her. "Why not?"

She glances at me. Her face is impassive behind her sunglasses, and I imagine she can't see my wide-eyed expression. I know that they split away from the Hell Hounds to try and make a change. And that didn't work.

But... there's more to the story. More than them controlling the shipping in and out of Sterling Falls. That was what Wolfe explained to me. He barely hinted at the bloodshed it must've taken to wrangle the gangs and end a war. And it must've taken more than just *shipping*. Why did I think it would be so easy?

They've made the gangs afraid of them—or at least come to heel enough to stop fighting. It seems like the sort of thing they'd need an ace up their sleeve to achieve. Something impossible.

Tem doesn't answer me, and my interest deepens. It's an itch I can't reach to scratch.

But, too late, we're pulling into a parking space marked *Reserved*. I have a question on my lips, but she kills the engine and hops out.

I wait a beat, glancing around. Besides this spot, there aren't many available. People on the streets, going in and out of shops... it's busy. Yet, none of them look like they're going to draw a weapon at the sight of *me*. My chest loosens.

I just need to get out of the car.

Artemis waits for me on the curb. When I emerge, the lights of the car flash. Locking me out. Fear flips my stomach, but she doesn't say anything nasty. Or abandon me here. Anything I was afraid of happening... doesn't.

"This is Bow & Arrow." She loops her arm through mine and guides me down the sidewalk, to an impressive building of glass and black stucco. There's no sign declaring it as such, no name written over the nondescript, double-door entrance. Just a symbol–a literal bow and arrow–made of fluorescent tubing that almost blends in with the dark wall.

"What is it?"

"Nightclub and restaurant. Come on, let's get lunch."

"They don't look open."

She laughs. "They're not, but Antonio is here prepping. I'm sure he won't mind."

I narrow my eyes but don't question it when she leads me inside. We enter on a balcony of sorts, with stairs going up to our right and down to our left. I step up to the rail and look out. It's a huge space, broken up by different levels and sections. It's dark, gold-veined marble, glass, silver. It reminds me, oddly enough, of Olympus.

"It's different at night," she says. "It becomes... more."

"More?"

She grins. "You'll just have to come back. What's better than dancing?"

I can think of a few things.

My mortification must be plain to see, because she laughs. She touches my arm and shakes her head. "They won't care if you can't dance, if you just think about your movements with sex on the brain."

Oh my god.

She starts up the stairs, and I follow.

Always following.

One day, I'll lead and people will follow *me*. But that day is not today. We go up and up, past landings that lead into other darkened hallways. It ends in a dimly lit foyer with frosted glass doors that open into a restaurant.

I blink hard at the difference–literally night and day from the club atmosphere downstairs. Down there, no windows, no sunlight. You could dance and drink until sunrise, and you'd never know.

Here, the walls are *all* glass. The bar is made of that same dark marble, the accents gold and silver. Black tablecloths cover the tables. Outside, there's a clear view of the ocean.

"Wow."

"We can sit over here." Artemis points to a cluster of gold wingback chairs. There's a low glass table between them. "I'll be right back."

I wander over, running my fingers over the tabletops as I go. I swallow hard, relishing the ache in my throat. It's subtle enough to ignore, but I need the reminder right now. That I am such a fish out of water. That I still have people looking for me.

That–

Apollo strides through the doors we just came through. My stomach drops when I see who follows him.

Malik. Aka, the right-hand man of Cerberus James.

apollo

I flip the knife in my hand and glare at Malik. I'm mainly here to make sure that Wolfe doesn't do something stupid, but... ah, well. I'm not sure which of us is more likely to go through with an impulse.

Still, I'm taking my job seriously. I'm beside Wolfe, leaning on the hood of his Mercedes. Malik propped his bike up on the kickstand and stands before us with his thumbs hooked in his pockets. The fucking picture of inno-cence—if innocence is a six-foot-something motorcycle club lieutenant.

"We need the girl back," Malik says. "Cerberus won't hurt her. He sees her value."

Wolfe scoffs. "Dad sees her *value*? As, what, a way to control us? No thanks."

Malik narrows his eyes. It's one thing for him and Wolfe to converse over the phone. They can't throttle each other that way. Here, now, I feel like one of them is going to throw a punch at any minute.

And I sure as hell don't need an excuse to fight. I've been itching for it ever since Kora came back. My energy has been higher, my recovery from the gunshot and surgery quicker. She did that for me. Brought me back from Hell, essentially.

Once the doc gives me the all-clear, I'm fighting at Olympus. I usually don't, because hosting has always brought a certain level of enjoyment for me. I like riling up the crowds and egging on the fighters. I like being right there, front and center, when the fight begins and ends.

Wolfe is the only one of us who refuses to fight. He says if he goes there, he'll never come back. Jace and I believe him. He's a dark soul desperately trying to be good. A nearly impossible feat, in our position. But while Jace and I were inducted into the Hell Hounds, Wolfe was born one. His demons go far deeper than ours.

"The heads turned up," Malik says.

Wolfe's jaw tics. He told us this morning that three Hell Hounds had been decapitated. What he didn't mention was that the heads were *missing*. But, judging from his minute reaction, he didn't know.

Jace isn't the only one keeping secrets, then.

"Where?"

Malik frowns at Wolfe.

I keep flipping my blade. It's calming. And a reminder of what happened the last time he saw us together. The handle lands solidly in my palm, and I squeeze it for a moment before sending it into the air again.

"Strung up outside our clubhouse," Malik finally replies.

Bastard.

Wolfe chuckles. "And you want us to send Kora back with you? To *that*?"

"They've been removed." Malik blows out a breath. "Look, I know you're attached to the girl. That's all well and good. But Cerberus has made his orders clear: I return with her, or it's *my* head on the pike. I came to you as a courtesy."

I snort. "As opposed to kidnapping?"

Malik glowers at me. "Don't push me, kid."

"Kid." I elbow Wolfe and push off the car, palming my knife and stowing it. "You believe this asshole?"

Wolfe is silent. Contemplative.

Sometimes I can read his mind. We operate on the same wavelength, Jace and Wolfe and me. But there are occasions when his thoughts take a turn no one can predict.

Like right now.

"Someone pulled Kora out of the fire," Wolfe says. "Was it you?"

Malik shakes his head. "No. We found her at the hospital."

"How?"

"Got an anonymous tip." He sighs. "I can't say more than that. I go where Cerb tells me."

"All for a little glory." My voice is more bitter than I'd like it to be—but fuck it. He betrayed us as much as we betrayed the Hell Hounds. "How's it feel to have your soul stained black?"

He sneers at me. "Not as bad as you might think."

"Enough," Wolfe snaps. "Malik, what are you going to do if we refuse?"

The Hell Hound taps his chin, pretending to consider. He already has a backup plan. He wouldn't be here if he didn't have several. And now it's just a matter of choosing the path of least resistance.

That's how Cerberus operates. Lay out the options, lead them to the one he wants. Give up Kora easily—or have her ripped from us. The tension between us rises, so much so that I inch closer to Wolfe. Suddenly, I'm back in sync with my best friend.

Remember, I'm here to keep him from doing something stupid.

As much as I really, *really* don't want to.

"You can take me to Kora, and I'll bring her to Cerberus. She'll stay with us, but you can see her." Malik's lips press flat for a moment, then he continues, "Or, I'll wait until you're all home, and I'll burn it to the ground with you all inside."

Wolfe stares at him.

"Or maybe I'll slip in through her window and drug her. Carry her out without any of you the wiser, and I won't bring her to the clubhouse. Cerberus will have me take her somewhere you will never find her." He spreads his arms. His jacket parts, revealing the gun at his hip. "My boss is a fan of sedation. Just because she's valuable alive doesn't mean she has to be conscious."

"We know what he's a fan of," Wolfe spits.

"You couldn't keep her safe from the Titans. And look what Kronos did to her. You have my word that she'll be treated fairly if she comes with me today. She follows our rules, she'll be fine."

Great. Kora following the rules? When we found her the first time, she was spying on us—and then later, trying to steal from us. Both aren't exactly traits of a Goody Two-shoes. That's what drew me to her. The wild streak that she desperately tries to hide from the world.

Malik spreads his hands. "Guys. There's a reason I'm meeting with you two first."

And not Jace. Fucking hell. If there's one thing I hate more than anything, it's something coming between the three of us. Although, I think something *did* come between

Wolfe and Jace... judging from his bruised knuckles. He wouldn't say, and now we're here.

I clench my teeth. My friend is just as tense, his fingers twitching at his sides. He folds his arms over his chest, keeping his gaze fixed on the Hell Hound.

"He can't keep her," Wolfe says. "He can talk to her. Today. We'll arrange some sort of... we'll figure it out."

Malik nods slowly. "Sure thing, Wolfe."

"Apollo will go with you to collect her." Wolfe glances at me, then away. There's guilt in his eyes, but he tries to hide it.

I let it roll over me. His guilt. The apology for this call will come later, I'm sure. But not in front of Malik. Not before it's happened.

Wolfe scuffs his foot against the asphalt. "She's at Bow & Arrow with Tem."

My sister will be pissed.

Malik's eyes light up. "Great. Let's go, Apollo."

I roll my eyes. Wolfe grabs my arm, hauling me toward him.

"Don't let her out of your sight for a second," he whispers.

I jerk away, nodding. I'm not a fucking idiot, even with the challenges I'm about to face. I've got to escort Kora into hell and make sure she can survive the trip out again.

A pollo and Malik stop in front of me. I glance around the empty restaurant. Anxiety creates a knot in the center of my chest. They both don't say anything for a long moment. Apollo hadn't seen the outfit I had deemed armor–the white and black, the red lipstick– and now he can't take his eyes off me.

It's Malik who pinches the bridge of his nose. "She can't show up like that."

"Like what?" I ask.

Apollo glances at Malik, his expression flickering toward annoyance. "How do you want her to look?"

"Innocent," Malik snaps.

I rear back. "Why do I need to look innocent?"

I need Tem to come back. Or... I don't know. An escape route. Apollo is here, but next to Malik, it doesn't carry much weight. They came in together.

"We need to see Cerberus," Apollo tells me. Apologetic. Soft.

Everything I don't need him to be right now. What I need is for him to get Malik out of here. Or, better yet, get *me* out of here. There's no way in hell I'm walking back into the Hell Hounds clubhouse.

"No." I glance over my shoulder, searching for an escape route. "Not happening."

Malik grimaces. "You either come with me willingly, or I drug you. Or I wait until your guard drops–"

"There's no need to fucking threaten her." Apollo blocks his view of me, his arms crossing. "She's been through enough at the expense of your boss."

"I don't think I could get much more innocent than barely alive when he showed up at the hospital." I glower at Malik. "And yet, he still kept me unconscious for a week, with a tube down my throat to breathe for me. So, do you think a little lipstick is going to make a big difference?"

The kitchen door swings open. Tem steps out, smiling– until she sees who stands in the restaurant. Her demeanor instantly freezes over.

Malik inclines his chin slightly. "Artemis."

Her eyes narrow. "Malikai."

Oh boy. I shouldn't be surprised that they seem to know each other. Her brother was raised in the Hell Hounds, and Malik probably was, too. That's how Cerberus seems to operate. Induct them young and keep them. So if Apollo had a relationship with his sister, she would've known him.

She's not happy about the intrusion, either.

I'm going to grill her about this later–if there is a later.

"You're not allowed here." She lifts her chin, gaze still cold. It reminds me of Jace for a split second–how chilly he can be when he wants.

Malik shrugs. "I'm here on official business."

"And I'm here to *officially* tell you to get the fuck out." She puts her hand on the bar counter at her side, as if to steady herself. "Apollo."

"We'll be gone in a moment." He glances at his sister. "Sorry, Tem."

Her gaze shutters, and she turns away from him.

"Well?" This from Malik.

I swallow. What choice do I have? "Just to talk?"

His expression doesn't change.

Apollo exhales and takes my hand. "Do you trust me to keep you safe?"

No.

I should.

I want to.

But I can't. Not after Kronos got to us. Not after his men put Apollo on the floor in the hospital.

"Doesn't matter if you trust him or not, Kora. You're coming with us." Malik casts one more look at Tem, then shakes his head. "Let's go."

Apollo takes my upper arm. Betrayal lances through me, and he guides me back the way Tem and I came. Into the dark foyer—a jarring change—and down the steps. Outside, to the waiting car. He helps me in, then slides right in after me.

My eyes burn as I struggle to keep my composure.

I shot a Hell Hound, and neither of them seem concerned that Cerberus wants to *talk* to me? He's probably going to put a bullet in my brain and call it a day. It's what Kronos probably wishes he did before he set the basement on fire.

Will I ever get a break?

The car ride is silent. A slow-building panic constricts my lungs, and I can't seem to get a deep breath in. My chest is tight. I'm covered in cold sweat, and my mind won't stop playing through scenarios.

Bad ones.

I wonder if this time around, I'd be able to tell that I was asleep. Like... if somewhere in my subconscious, I'd know it's a possibility.

They make movies about people in comas who are aware.

It's probably different, though, to be medically induced. To be tied down by drugs instead of something wrong in the brain.

I'm afraid this is about to become my reality. And then I'll miss dinner with my parents because I'll be stuck in a private back room in the hospital. Or, worse, kept asleep by a private doctor under Cerberus' thumb.

The drive seems to take years and no time at all. We pull down the long driveway to the clubhouse. It's so secluded, it guarantees them privacy. Woods surround the property from the front and sides, and a huge wooden fence in the back blocks whatever lurks behind the sprawling clubhouse.

More Hell Hounds than I've ever seen swarm the property. Their bikes are scattered in the lot out front. One of them sees Malik at the wheel and salutes, then emits a loud whistle. Immediately, they clear a path.

I shrink back in my seat.

They stare in the windows at me, and their hate is hot.

They know I killed one of them.

Fear blooms in my chest, all at once hot and ice-cold. Their brows lower, the anger around the car spiking. Cerberus might just want to talk, but it seems like everyone else wants to throttle me. I shrink back and try to advert my eyes.

I don't register their reaction to Apollo until it's too late.

They yank his door open, and hands haul him out. He hits the ground, and immediately three Hell Hounds are on him. Their elbows snap back before cracking down, hitting anything they can find.

I scramble out, nearly falling to get to him.

Someone grabs me and drags me away from the fight.

Well, *fight*. Jesus. A Hell Hound falls back, clutching his nose, but another takes his place. The sharp, metallic scent of blood rises in the air. In a matter of seconds, we're at the edge of a circle of Hell Hounds, with Apollo on the ground in the center.

Getting the life beaten out of him.

I glance back, unsurprised to find Cerberus himself holding my arms. Of course he's here, in the middle of this madness.

I rip free and rush forward, shoving one of the Hell Hounds–albeit, one of the skinnier ones–away from Apollo. He wheels around, fist raised, and balks. Then steps back.

Someone else grunts and falls, and Apollo scrambles to his feet. He punches the last Hell Hound and snatches my wrist.

"Get out," he hisses, urging me toward Malik. His nose is bloody, and there's a cut above his eyebrow.

The big guy stands at the edge of the circle, impassive.

My stomach drops.

Better him than Cerberus, I guess, but–

"Apollo–" I step toward him again.

"Get the fuck out of the circle, Kora." He gives me another push, harder this time, and I stumble away.

As soon as I'm within reach, Malik tows me into his side. His arm wraps around my shoulders, cinching me against him.

This is worse than Olympus. Apollo just had surgery–he shouldn't be fighting. But the more I watch, the more I

163

realize he *isn't* fighting. He's doing the bare minimum to defend himself.

The crowd, everyone except Malik and Cerberus, jeer at Apollo as another two Hell Hounds step into the empty space.

"Why are they doing this?" My voice is strangled and hoarse.

Malik leans down. "He deserted us. They're showing him what happens when a traitor returns to Hell Hound territory."

Oh my god. Nausea rolls through me. The blood, the grunts of pain when a hit lands, the toxic energy–I'm going to be sick.

Wolfe... Wolfe didn't pay this price. Did he? If he did, he never mentioned it. The Hell Hounds let him waltz right in the morning he came to see me.

I open and close my mouth.

And a third Hell Hound joins. Apollo takes a punch to his face, and he falls to the ground. His fingers slide through the dirt, looking for purchase, but he doesn't rise farther than his hands and knees.

One of them kicks him in the stomach.

I shriek, the pain exploding through me like *I'm* the one who took the blow. It feels like I'm swallowing razors with the noise, but I can't stop. I struggle against Malik, but my attempts are futile. I can't tear my gaze away from Apollo, either.

They're going to kill him.

A sob tears past my lips, and my whole body burns. I can't watch, but I can't look away, either. There's a part of me that needs to see every detail. I can't let myself forget who they are and what they'll do to someone who used to be one of them.

Cerberus steps into the circle.

Malik wraps a hand around my mouth, silencing me, and the rest of the Hell Hounds go still, too. The amount of power Cerberus wields is chilling. On some level, I think I had delusions about Jace, Wolfe, and Apollo being this strong. Being able to command this many people. But I have yet to see that. They captivate at Olympus, but they don't control them. They made me disappear, but how much effort went into that? How many strings did they have to pull?

Apollo is curled up on his side, his knees brought up to protect his stomach. His hand is pressed to his abdomen.

"Apollo Madden. Your brothers paid the price for abandonment, but you... you had escaped it." Cerberus holds his hands out wide. It's a performance, but not for Apollo's sake.

It's for the Hell Hounds.

Apollo's eyes open into little slits. Barely. His face is swelling.

Cerberus crouches in front of him. He takes his time looking him over, then reaches out and grips him by the hair. Cerberus rips his head back until Apollo can look Cerberus in the eye.

"This is your penance." A declaration.

What will they do to me when I try to escape? Not for the first time, a claustrophobic feeling holds my limbs hostage. I can't inhale more than a shallow gasp. I need to get out of here. To run as far from the Hell Hounds as I can get.

Sterling Falls is dangerous. The Hell Hounds are dangerous. The Titans have retracted their claws, but it makes me wonder when they're going to strike back—and who will be caught in the middle.

Apollo lets out a hoarse breath.

Why did he come with me? Why *him* and not Wolfe, who has already served his time? Or Jace? Anyone but Apollo, who just went through surgery after getting shot trying to save me from Kronos. If anyone doesn't deserve this, it's him.

Malik's fingers tighten on my face, digging into my cheek. It takes me a moment to realize I'm still making a low noise. I press my lips together, although the vibration of my whimper still lives in my chest.

Cerberus pats Apollo's face and rises. He steps over him, still curled on the ground, and gestures toward me. Malik keeps his hand over my mouth and uses his other hand to guide me roughly forward.

We bypass the Hell Hounds who still glare down at Apollo.

Once we're clear of them, they resume their onslaught. Their angry grunts, exertion taking their anger out on *Apollo*, is all I can hear. I fight against Malik, but his grip is iron. I'm caught. Helpless.

Damn Jace for not actually showing me how to get out of a move like this. What had he said? *Stop panicking and use your brain. Where can you reach? What's vulnerable?*

Hard to think that any part of this giant man is vulnerable–but still. Groin, eyes, throat. Weaknesses every man has.

Okay, well... here goes nothing.

The clubhouse looms in front of us. If I go inside–without Apollo–I'm never coming out. That thought might be a prediction or fear, but I can't just do *nothing*. Malik jostles me, and I stumble, going down hard on one knee. Without hesitation, I raise my free elbow and jab it as hard as I can at Malik's groin.

Surprise floods me when my hit actually connects, and he lets out a muffled *oomph* as his grip loosens. I hit it again, for good measure, and then shove him away. I jump to my feet and bolt back to Apollo.

The circle reformed, but somehow I worm my way through. I duck between jeering Hell Hounds and finally come to the edge of the circle. There are two in there, beating the shit out of him.

I wish I was as badass as them. I wish I could stomp into the circle and scare them just from my presence. And then that I had the skill to back it up.

As it is, I just have my insane lack of self-preservation.

So I charge into the circle and tackle one of the assholes.

FOURTEEN

kora

The Hell Hound and I hit the ground and roll. I land under him, and he raises his fist. But he stops. Climbs off me with disgust in his eyes. He spits on the ground beside me for good measure.

I'm not sure Cerberus thought it through when he said I was under his protection. He probably thought that he'd be able to keep me under his influence. But then my guys showed up, and I killed his driver, and everything happened too fast for him to change his mind.

The disgust is the spark that ignites my anger.

I don't think I have control of what happens next. Not really.

But I glance from him to Apollo, who is somehow pushing himself up out of the dirt. The weight of his stare is heavy. If he can even see through the blood and swelling. A beat passes, and he rips his attention back to the Hell Hounds in front of him.

Something flashes toward me.

Without a thought, I reach out and catch it.

A folding knife—*Apollo's* folding knife.

I flip it open.

"Pretty cat grew claws, hmm?"

The rational part of my brain shuts off, and suddenly I don't give a fuck that we're surrounded by at least twenty Hell Hounds eager for violence. Now I'm the one craving it, and I don't have time to be afraid of that emotion.

He doesn't expect me to come at him again. And I have two advantages: one, that he probably won't truly hurt me, and two, the knife. Well... the knife might end up being a hindrance, since I've never stabbed anyone before.

I screech like a banshee and swing at him. I get two lucky hits and a swipe of the knife. To my surprise, it connects. Blood wells in a line on his cheek. Not deep enough to maim him, but... I did that.

He comes after me. I yell and jab forward with the knife, and this time it catches his hand. Nope–it goes straight through his palm.

Holy shit.

I stare at him in horror as he yanks his hand off the blade, still in my grip, and shoves me back. Blood drips down his fingers. I just fucking stabbed him.

I'm on a roll–and I don't think it's a good thing. How did I go from shooting someone to stabbing another? I could barely stomach to watch a fight only a few months ago.

Hands catch me, keeping me from falling on my ass. I cast a quick glance back to make sure it isn't someone who will tow me out of the circle again. Apollo sets me on my feet and pats my shoulder. Most of his attention on the Hell Hound who circles around him.

The guy in front of me seems pissed. His teeth bare at the pain, and he balls his injured hand into a fist. More blood drips into the dirt.

I think that whole *don't touch her* thing has worn off for him.

I glance at Apollo. He keeps one hand on my side, probably to keep track of where I am. More could join at any second. Right? Isn't that the point? I adjust my grip on the knife handle, now slick with blood, and hold it out.

"Try me, psycho," I yell at the Hell Hound.

The Hell Hound just shakes his head. His teeth are gritted, and his expression screams *murder*. I step forward, but Apollo's fist balls in my shirt and yanks me back. I shake my head and refuse to scream. We're trapped like this, inching around to keep the enemies in our sights.

"Get out of the circle," Apollo grunts at me.

"Don't be a fucking idiot," I counter.

The Hell Hound I stabbed darts forward, a sneer twisting his features. I swipe at him, and he hops back. Laughing.

The other one rushes forward, and Apollo takes the hit. He stumbles, and now it's *me* who has to grip his shirt to keep him upright.

He hasn't even fucking fought back.

"Apollo," Cerberus calls. "Enough of this."

It takes a second for me to register what he's saying.

What his order really means.

The fight is over. The circle breaks apart, and Apollo reaches around me to fold the blade back up. He keeps it in my hand, curving my fingers over it.

He doesn't look at me when he does it. Doesn't seem to mind when the tip catches his finger. He keeps me half concealed behind him, rotating around.

"I'm not the one fighting," Apollo calls to his former boss. "Those are the rules, aren't they?"

Cerberus smiles. "Indeed."

171

"I will defend her," Apollo continues. "As I'd expect you would."

I find Cerberus on the edge of where the circle was. Only a few linger now, watching to see what happens. My muscles tense, and instinct screams *trap*. It's been warning me of that for a while now, but I've done my best to ignore it. Foolish of me.

The Hell Hound I injured rushes me. Apollo quickly pivots, pushing me behind him. His foot snaps out and connects with the guy's sternum. The Hell Hound lets out a sharp grunt and tumbles backward. He trips and lands flat on his back, groaning.

His wild gaze finds Cerberus, and his fingers spasm on my arm. I want to wrap my arms around him, but I'm afraid of hurting him worse. As it is, I curl my fingers in the back of his shirt.

And touch a gun.

Why didn't he pull it?

Why didn't he use the knife to defend himself?

Cerberus laughs, and the growing tension around us dissipates.

How does he do that?

Too many questions you'll never get answers to, Kora.

"Come inside." Cerberus stops in front of us, and his gaze goes up and down Apollo. Then what he can see of me. "You look like you need a drink. With a straw."

Apollo chokes on a laugh. "Fuck off."

Cerberus tsks. "I thought I taught you better than that. Or is that your own daddy's manners coming through?"

Apollo flinches.

I narrow my eyes. What happened with Apollo's dad? He's never talked about him—and neither has Artemis.

Shame punches me square in the face. In all our interactions, I never asked him about *him*. His past. Any of it.

Wolfe grew up here. He told me a bit about his mom leaving, the diner where his cousin from her side of the family works. I got the smallest glimpse into what made Wolfe... *Wolfe*. But Apollo? Jace? How they came to be with him is a mystery that I didn't bother trying to solve.

Now I need to know.

But... it would seem that *now* is a terrible time to even ask.

The circle breaks up as quickly as the tension. Some guys head inside, others hang out on the porch. Men are strange creatures.

I step up next to Apollo, who can barely stand. He wavers on his feet, his hand pressed to his stomach.

"Did you know this was going to happen?"

He chuckles. His face is swelling and bruised. "I figured, yeah."

"So why did you come and not Wolfe? Or Jace?" I take his arm and put it over my shoulders.

He leans slightly on me, but not much as he probably needs. I'm hit again with the memory of him in that stupid West Falls house, shot and on the verge of death. This is a slightly better situation–no immediate threat of being murdered, I guess–but it haunts me all the same.

"Wolfe wanted me to go with you." He starts walking toward the clubhouse, trailing after Malik and Cerberus.

"Why?"

He smiles. "He's just working through some jealousy issues."

I stop. "What?"

His dark eyes meet mine. "The two of us? Sharing you?

We've got to work it out of our systems somehow. And he doesn't fight his friends."

"He punched Jace," I mutter.

His face lights up as much as it can. "Oh?"

"For lying to my parents and saying he was my boyfriend."

Apollo freezes, then chuckles. He pulls me along again, and we reach the porch. He lets out a pained breath going up the steps, using a rail to help him.

Walking inside is a trap. I know it. I'm betting Apollo knows it, too. And yet, I can't seem to stop this. I ran into the middle of a fight and came out unscathed, if a bit sore. And bitter. Tackling someone isn't as easy as it looks.

And besides the folded knife clenched in my fist, I'm defenseless.

What else is new?

I'm sick of it. Sick of being a pawn to be shuffled across the chessboard, sick of men in this town underestimating me. I consider my list again. Kronos, Brody, Sheriff Bradshaw, Cerberus. I add Malik.

I'd like to see them all burn.

Cerberus chooses a table in the back corner of the room. His Hell Hounds keep clear, occupying other tables, shooting pool in the back room. Low laughter and conversation drifts around us, combining with the smell of cigar smoke and something sour. Like sweat... or sex.

Apollo slowly lowers himself into one of the chairs. He drags the one beside it closer and gestures for me to sit.

I've been to hell and back, I remind myself. I survived an abusive ex. Living for months on almost nothing. Kronos and his abuse. A fire. This meeting, today? This is nothing.

I meet Cerberus' curious gaze.

"You're different," he finally says.

They did just witness me screaming about Apollo, and I still feel the lump in my throat when I thought Apollo was going to be beaten to death, so I have that going for me.

I raise my eyebrow, while he motions to someone behind us. A moment later, a young Hell Hound arrives at the table with a tray full of drinks. He sets one down in front of Cerberus, then serves the rest of us.

Once he's gone, Cerberus takes a sip and sets his glass back down. Still staring.

It's unnerving.

"Most people respond. It's how a conversation continues."

"I wasn't aware you required a response." I reach out and wrap my fingers around the cup in front of me. I'm not particularly inclined to drink whatever's in it, but it grounds me in the present. The past can't reach up and claw me back into my memories.

He smiles. "You're feisty with your man beside you, even looking like... that."

I glance at Apollo. He glowers but says nothing. He appears to be in serious pain, and his hand hasn't left his abdomen. His wound was freshly healed, if only just. His stitches just came out... He could be bleeding inside. Dying right before my eyes all over again.

I force myself to relax and lean back. "I'd like to think I'm feisty with or without him." I flip the knife open and closed under the table. It's slightly different than the sheriff's, and it takes me a couple of blind tries to get it right. "You'd know if you hadn't kept me unconscious for a week. But now, here we are, so... what do you want? Are we going to be honest with each other?"

He drains the rest of his drink and raises the glass. The same Hell Hound comes scurrying over to collect it.

"I like power, Kora. I like being able to snap my fingers and have things happen." He raises his finger, stalling my question. When the young Hell Hound comes over, Cerberus fixates on him. "Donny. Drink that."

The Hell Hound hesitates. His gaze goes from his boss to the amber liquid. Then he brings it to his lips, tips it back, and downs it in one gulp.

"Now crack the glass over Apollo's head."

Apollo doesn't have time to react before Donny smashes the glass down on his temple. His eyes roll back, and he topples off the chair. Donny hops out of the way, avoiding his body, and guilt crosses his expression.

"That's all," Cerberus tells him. Then his focus returns to me.

I stare at him, trying to find words.

On the floor next to our table, Apollo doesn't move.

"Do you see how easy it is to get you alone?"

Well, that's the fucking truth. Some threats, a group of angry followers, and one well-timed hit to the temple. But there has to be a way to make the most of this.

Maybe get some answers for myself.

I spread my arms. "You've got me alone. Now what? Are you going to tell me why you bought me?"

"You want us to be honest with each other." His jaw tics, then the muscle smooths. He lets one corner of his lips curl upward. "Let's do that. Have you been to Sterling Falls before?"

"Um..." I shrug, my eyes narrowing on him. I'm not sure why this is relevant. "I came to look at it before I moved here."

"Tell me why you chose Sterling Falls."

I sit back. "Why?"

He mirrors my movement. Beside him, Malik is stiff as a

board. And suddenly, clear as a bell, I can hear Wolfe's warning to not tell Cerberus anything important. Anything at all, really, but I have to give the man something.

Sorry, Wolfe.

"I got accepted to SFU."

"And you arrived three months early?"

I catch the inside of my cheek in my teeth and bite down. The pain keeps me sharp, keeps the adrenaline going. The last thing I need is to give in and let him know the full truth.

But half-truths can't hurt. Right?

"I wanted to get to know the city."

He nods along. "But then you encountered my son, Jace, and Apollo." He holds up his hand and ticks off fingers as he talks. "They probably told you to forget that night. Then they wanted to make sure you left, so they took away your job. What else did they take from you?"

I narrow my eyes. "It seems you already know."

"A scholarship," he finishes. "A shame."

"For me. A blessing for you, seeing as how that's why we're here."

He smiles, and I don't feel the sinister thoughts behind it. It's like I'm actually amusing him for once. Which is probably not a good thing.

"You and I are in the spotlight now, Kora. I've been asked to cleanse the city–and I will."

You've wedged yourself in the mayor's ear, is probably what happened. And then when *Kronos* left the door open, Cerberus took his chance. He swept through, and now he's taking up space he should never have been able to occupy.

Because somehow, the guys were able to keep the gangs on their own sides of town. Titans in West Falls, Hell Hounds in East Falls. But that line was obliterated the second I showed up in a hospital room with smoke inhalation, pulled from the remnants of a party house three blocks from campus.

Somehow, I became the grenade that blew everything apart.

"I need answers." My nails bite into my palms. "Kronos could've gotten rid of me for not paying my debt. Instead, he went through the trouble of an auction. Where *you* paid a ridiculous price for me. Why? And why keep me sedated for a week? Was I too much of a hassle to deal with awake? Or are pawns easier to shuffle across the board when they're unconscious?"

I somehow remain sitting, but my blood boils. I've abandoned fear. He can do whatever he wants to me— nothing I say will stop him.

So I may as well ask the questions I want answered.

"Who am I to you? To Kronos?"

Malik shifts ever so slightly.

Cerberus ignores it. "The Titans have grown too comfortable in their space. This *truce* my boys forced upon us has to end. That's one of the reasons you're here."

Great. "So... me being here is just to bring them under your control?"

"No. Not just."

I exhale. "Well, great. The little news segment made it to Emerald Cove, by the way. My parents are in town."

He stops. "Parents. What do they do?"

Kronos knew this—but Cerberus doesn't. I can still call up the shock of having him list their names out for me, their occupations. Marley's picture. He used them to get me to obey him. Used threats of harming them, rather.

I can't let Cerberus do the same.

"Dad's an editor for the *Emerald Cove Star*. He decides

178

where the investigative team goes, what they cover..." I hope that's enough to convince him to leave it alone. My own dagger, wrapped in soft words, is still a sharp edge.

He tilts his head, eyeing me, and then abruptly stands. "I expect my son will be here to collect you soon. Until we meet again."

Without another word, he strides away. I crane around and watch him go out the front door, pounding down the steps. The door swings closed behind him. In a matter of seconds, the motorcycles out there all roar to life.

I glance around, trying not to show too much of my confusion. Only Apollo and Malik remain with me. Even the young Hell Hound made his escape.

"He's not... keeping me?"

Malik frowns, seeming just as perplexed by his boss's behavior. "No. He'll call you when he needs you next."

My relief is bittersweet. In some ways, the feeling seems like a trap. Like I shouldn't let myself relax or breathe easy for a moment. Because as soon as I do, something else is going to happen. Something worse. And I'll hate myself for not seeing it coming.

The switch flipped as soon as I mentioned my parents. Why, though? Because they have a certain level of power over me, too?

I suck my lower lip between my teeth and mull that over. I'd love to see my father go toe to toe with Cerberus. Or, better yet, witness what's happening and blast it in his newspaper.

Maybe just the idea of it turned Cerberus off for now. Or the knowledge that I'm *not* as unprotected as I may seem. I have people who care about me.

I get out of my chair and kneel next to Apollo. He's still out cold.

"Sit down, Kora."

I glare at Malik. "Isn't he your friend?"

The Hell Hound's gaze shutters. "He was."

Was. This town, these gangs, all the secrets everyone holds. And the trauma of the past. Sterling Falls isn't just dark–it's a scorch mark on the earth, pretending to be something else. Something alive and clean and happy.

I touch Apollo's cheek. He's still breathing. His chest rises and falls slowly. That Hell Hound really hit him hard, I guess.

So I go back over and take my chair again.

Malik eyes me. "I follow orders."

"Okay."

"Following orders is how you survive in Sterling Falls. It's how you rise. And it'll keep you safe, too." He braces his forearms on the table. "He wants you to meet him? You do it. He asks you a question? Answer it."

"He says jump, I ask how high?" My voice is wry. "I didn't choose this, you know."

Malik rolls his eyes. "You think any of us chose this? You think my parents wanted me to join the Hell Hounds when I was twelve years old? No. They wanted a smart son to get straight A's, get accepted to a nice college, and never fucking look back."

"Didn't quite turn out that way." I can't picture Malik with a family. With parents, maybe siblings. It seems wrong.

"Well, they're six feet under at any rate."

Ah.

"What else?" I'm afraid my prying will make him stop talking, but I need more. More information, more motivation.

"Tell me this, Kora. Do you think we're all gangbangers

looking for our next fix? Or so wrapped up in our leader and his ideals that we're no better than a cult?" He leans even farther forward, coming into my space.

I tilt away, frowning. "I don't know what I think."

"*I* think you're an angry girl with no one to help you funnel that energy."

I jerk farther back, almost falling off my seat.

"It's why you didn't kill Cerberus—you shot his driver. It's why you're still in Sterling Falls. You're angry and you don't know what else to do. Just admit that you're lost and clueless."

"I'm still in Sterling Falls because I have to be here," I snap. "I'm here because I am *not* going back to Emerald Cove, no matter what happens."

He lifts his chin, and I curse myself in my head. *Have to be here*. Sounds a lot more dramatic than I intended. Malik rises and raps his knuckles on the table.

"See you around, angry girl."

Angry girl.

Invisible girl.

Flower.

Chaos.

I press my palms to my eyes. I've only ever wanted to be one person. *Me*. And yet, I'm constantly under siege by people pulling me in opposite directions. Sometimes I feel like being adopted gave me a new identity that I didn't sign up for.

Who was I before that?

And who will I be when I can no longer be Kora Sinclair?

kora

J ace and Wolfe walk into the clubhouse with their guns drawn. They both look ready for a fight, even though it's just Apollo and me here. Wolfe goes into the kitchen and returns with his weapon stowed.

They stop in front of me, both scowling.

Apollo is still on the floor.

And I'm drunk.

Soon after Malik left, I snagged a bottle of tequila–the top-shelf shit–from behind the bar. It managed to erase my caring first. I worried and fretted about Apollo, checking his abdomen–which is a nasty purple color–and feeling his ribs to make sure they weren't broken. Checking his pulse–which stayed steady–and his breathing. Normal. Fine. He seemed like he was sleeping off a bad hangover or an adrenaline crash. His swollen face, minus the bruises, seemed almost peaceful.

But he wouldn't wake up. And I'm without my phone once again.

I'll have to meet my parents soon. They wanted to take me to dinner, and now I'm weaving in my chair. One sip became two, became six... And I like the warm feeling it gives me. It hits my stomach and spreads fire through my chest.

I may have overdone it.

"What happened?" Jace demands.

His hands are on his hips, and he looks like he's *trying* to be imposing. And it's not working. It hasn't worked since he started being nice to me when I couldn't sleep, and when he didn't follow through on his threats to hurt me. His hand around my throat has turned into something I've started dreaming about. I'll take that over nightmares of killing people, though.

Deep down, he's a softy. I know it, but I'm not sure he does.

Who am I to ruin that surprise?

I giggle. It slips out, and I slap my hand over my mouth. Terrible predicament, but funny that he thinks he can just come in and interrogate me about it.

He's the one who threw me to the hounds, after all.

Wolfe crouches next to his friend and tries to rouse him. When shaking his shoulder doesn't work, Wolfe finds a glass of water and dumps it over his head. Apollo lurches upright, groaning. Water droplets roll down his face, soaking the collar of his shirt.

"Kora," Jace prods. "Get up."

Yeah, right. Now they want to rescue me? After I'm so clearly *fine*? It's a little late for a rescue. I've been here over an hour. If Cerberus really wanted to keep me away from them, he could've. If he wanted to kill Apollo, he would've. He had the opportunity.

He had the opportunity to do whatever the fuck he wanted, and it's only a *miracle* that we're still breathing.

I grab the bottle and take another sip. My fingers are

stained in blood, but I've been ignoring that for the last hour. It's on my arms, too. My shirt is stained with Apollo's. I'd give anything to forget my most recent transgression—stabbing a man in the hand.

Ugh. My stomach knots.

The way I figure it, they chose Apollo to escort me here, and they had to know what would happen. If Cerberus was right in his little speech outside, Jace and Wolfe both went through something similar.

So this was the easy way of getting me off their plate—or getting Apollo off mine. I hate that I don't know their motivation. Their reasoning. There's no sense to having their best friend set up to get injured.

Jace hauls me upright, and the room sways. I burst out laughing again, stumbling sideways. I rip free of his hand and face him.

"You're such a blowhard, Jace King. Is Jace your full name? Or is it Jason? Jackoff? Ja—"

"Stop it."

I shake my head and stride away from him. "Fuck you and your macho energy, Jacey. That shit is getting old."

I need to get out of here—*stat*. And presumably without them.

They don't stop me from going outside and teetering down the porch. There's a motorcycle and another car I only vaguely recognize as theirs. I've never seen it driven, though. It's remained in the garage as long as I've known them.

Which hasn't been long, I remind myself.

I keep walking. Right past their fancy vehicles and toward the road. I still have that knife in my hand. The folded one, crusted with blood.

"Kora," Apollo calls weakly. "Come on, where are you going?"

Away. Away, away, away.

What I wouldn't give to be Dorothy from *The Wizard of Oz*, clicking my heels together three times and wishing for home. Then again, Dorothy was so desperate for the place she left. While I don't even know if home is where I want to go. I just want *out*.

Footsteps follow me.

My path isn't straight—I'm sure I'm easy to catch up with. I just don't give a shit. My mind is set. I'll fucking walk. My parents are in town, they can get me away from these assholes.

"Stop," Wolfe says. "Kora."

I have so many things I want to say, but I can't voice any of them.

One of them huffs.

"Okay, I'm calling it," Jace says. "Grab her."

Arms bind around me, pinning mine to my sides. I squeal, the noise bursting out of me, and throw my head back. It doesn't connect. I try to remember what else Jace told me to do, but he's a stupid teacher with stupid teaching skills. He really needs to work on that.

Lips press against my ear. "Sorry, baby."

Wolfe.

I let out a little sigh against my will, but I don't stop struggling. He seems to expect it, because he lifts my feet off the ground. It doesn't matter how much I kick and struggle. His grip is iron. I screech, flinging myself to the side.

In the end, it's pointless. I can't escape him.

He brings me back to the car. Jace opens the passenger

door, standing there with an unreadable expression. Loathing fills me.

Wolfe puts me in the seat, and I practically dive out of it. My fingers touch the gravel before Wolfe has me back up again.

"Just hold her."

Wolfe grunts affirmation and scoops me back up, somehow containing my limbs. This time *he* slides into the car, still wrapped around me like a human octopus.

Jace steps into the opening and pinches my chin. He makes me meet his gaze, and he's just as pissed off as I am. It's like staring into a mirror.

"Sloppy."

I flinch, but he's not done.

"You want to save yourself in situations like this? You want to be big and bad and strong?" He sneers. "Don't get fucking drunk unless you know you're safe. Your movements were weak. Even a teenage boy could've overpowered you."

I jerk my head away, and he lets me go. He slams the door.

I let myself sag against Wolfe.

A second later, his lips are at my ear again. "He's right."

"Fuck off." I squeeze my eyes shut.

"We'll work on it, flower. We can help you become someone they fear."

I have a feeling I *was* someone they feared. Cerberus, anyway. But something I said... erased it. Eradicated the fear.

Made me nothing more than a stupid girl in a city that wants to swallow her whole.

wolfe

Kora's avoiding us, and it has us on edge. Physically, she's here. She's on the couch with an IV in her arm, courtesy of our concierge doctor. Sobering up for the dinner with her parents. But mentally, she's anywhere *but* here.

She won't make eye contact. She ignores our questions. Moves away from our touch. Well, my touch. Jace isn't dumb enough to try. I wish I knew what to say to make it better, but I don't know what *is* better.

I want to know what the fuck my father did to get in her head.

Apollo had to go back to the hospital. Our doc was worried about internal bleeding and didn't want to risk it. He practically forced Apollo to go.

Jace glares at me when I walk into the rarely used office. He's dusted off the desk and opened his laptop. Normally, we'd just hang out in the den. But Kora... and space.

"Well?"

I scoff. "I don't know. She's not talking."

"Uh-huh. Not talking in general, or just not talking to you?"

No freaking clue.

"Malik said the heads turned up at the clubhouse." I look away. I've got the urge to punch something. *Hard.* The city is spiraling out of our control, and we don't seem to be doing anything about it. We're grasping at broken straws. "Not sure if it's connected to anything, or if Kronos is sending a massive warning. They're not talking about it."

Jace grimaces. "Well, see if you can get any more information. Cerberus is already overstepping."

"And we've done shit about it," I remind him. Again. But what are we supposed to do? Burst into the mayor's office and threaten the asshole? We tried that once... didn't work out so well. Cerberus got to him before we could even consider that.

In a lot of ways, my father makes sure we know that he's smarter than us. That he's got more experience. Older and wiser—all that crap. He takes joy in rubbing it in our faces.

We had a lucky break. That's what he thinks. And I'm starting to believe it, too.

I yank my phone out and drop down into the chair across from Jace. I dial and set the phone on the desk, on speaker.

Malik answers quickly.

"What the fuck happened?" I lean forward and brace my elbows on my knees. "What did he say to her?"

Malik laughs.

I raise my gaze to Jace, whose expression is stony. I know that look—it's his *I need to hit something* face. Too bad for him, we're not exactly able to fulfill that need.

"You serious?" Malik finally asks.

I clear my throat. "What?"

"You're an idiot." The line goes dead.

"He's right."

I twist around. Kora stands in the doorway. She holds a piece of gauze to her arm where the needle was. Did she just yank it out like a heathen? And then her words register.

"Right? You're calling me an idiot?"

She makes a face. "I wish your stupidity was curable, but alas. It's a terminal disease."

Jace scoffs.

Her eyes flick to him, and her brows pull together. She shakes her head slowly. "Are you hell-bent on keeping me here?"

"Yes." He says it savagely, without hesitation.

She nods carefully, then enters the room. She gives me a wide berth and locates her phone on one of the built-in bookshelves. It's been on the charger in here since Kronos abducted her, and we found it... after. She unplugs it and grips it tightly. The screen has a crack, but it's nothing detrimental. She'd still be able to use it.

"By the way." Jace leans back in his chair and folds his arms. "Took that little location tracker off your phone. Since your parents clearly stalk you."

"Great. Perfect. Cut me off from them some more, why don't you?" She eyes us like we might snag her, inching toward the door while keeping us in her line of sight. "And for the record, Cerberus didn't do anything. It was *you*."

She glares at us. Once she reaches her exit, she bolts.

Jace lets out a breath. That interaction hurt him, too? Wouldn't know it from the callous way he talks to her–but he seems to be human sometimes. I don't ask about the tracker on her phone, or her odd reaction.

With her gone, tension bleeds out of the room. I hadn't

even realized it was climbing, but my abs clench. Shit. Whatever he said to her... it's not good.

I just can't figure out what the hell secret my father spilled.

"Maybe he told her about our past," Jace says quietly. "He definitely didn't–"

"I mentioned it." Hinted at the red in our ledger, told her what I thought she should know. But it won't scare her away, not when she knows about it. I wave my hand to dismiss his other idea. Cerberus isn't an idiot–far from it, unfortunately. "If he brought it up, she wouldn't be entirely shocked."

"Then what?"

"Fuck if I know. Malik doesn't seem so inclined to tell us, either."

Jace sighs. "Fine. I've got work to do for Olympus. Check in with Saint and see how preparations are going."

I can only imagine the admin side of Olympus–paying our employees, keeping the lights on–has slipped through the cracks since Kora's arrival. We have a company that handles most of it, but they still require authorization. And attention.

Jace handles it because he's a control freak. Plus, he's decent with numbers and seems to find some sort of comfort in going over the books. More than once, in the beginning, he's caught the people we used trying to pilfer money out.

They disappeared–but that wasn't just on Jace.

I hop up and stride out. I don't know where I'm going until I'm outside Kora's bedroom. The door is closed, but the sound of her moving around comes through.

I clench my jaw and take a step back. *Bad idea, Wolfe.*

And yet, I go forward again and shove her door open. It crashes against the wall, and I storm inside.

Something flies at me and hits me in the face. Cold water splashes everywhere. I catch a glimpse of the plastic cup falling to the floor at my feet. I manage to spot the next thing coming for me, and I duck at the last second. The book hits the door with a jarring crack. It joins the cup on the floor.

I stare at Kora, who yanks another one of those decorative, meaningless books from the shelf and chucks it at me.

This one I catch. Barely.

"Get out of my room." She grabs another book, holding it like a weapon.

I shake my head and stalk toward her. I drop the book I caught on her bed, circling it.

She backs into her bathroom and glares at me. *If looks could kill.* "I mean it. Get away from me."

"No."

She laughs, and I'm shocked at how cold she sounds. When did she become an ice queen? She backs right into the counter, and her eyes go wide at the realization. I hate that the first thought I have is a reminder of how Apollo made her scream in here.

And oh, how it echoes in my mind.

"What did he say to you?" I demand.

She lifts her chin and remains silent.

I box her in. Her breath hitches ever so slightly, but she just grips the counter. Her knuckles go white. She doesn't push me away, though, and I take that for what it is.

Not quite an invitation... but close enough.

I grab her jaw and tilt her head further back. Her gaze drops to my lips and stays there. Her full lips part, her tongue peeking out to wet them. My dick instantly gets hard, pressing against my jeans. Fuck, she's beautiful. And mad. I want to do dirty things to her. But more than that, I want a fight.

"Give me your worst, flower, or else I'll force you to your knees and make you choke on my cock."

She doesn't hesitate to put her palms on my chest and shove. I go back an inch, taking her face with me. She knocks my hand away and pushes me again, with more power this time. I want her angrier than she is. I want her seething hot when I finally fill her.

"Maybe you'd like that," I taunt.

She glowers. No. She *glows*. Beautiful hellion. Her face is getting redder. "You don't know shit. And if you put your dick anywhere near my mouth, I'm biting it off."

I smirk, half tempted to follow through on *my* threat to see if she'd follow through on hers. I want the violence of it. The blood aspect.

But she decides for me. To bring her worst, I guess. She grabs me by the waistband and yanks me into her, and I lower my head so we're nose to nose.

Close enough to kiss.

"Was it your goal to have your best friend beaten to within an inch of his life?" She raises her eyebrows, daring me to respond.

Roughly, I yank her pants and shove them down her hips. I rip her panties off. The tearing noise is loud against our quiet breaths. She pulls at me, too. My shirt, my jeans. We're suddenly frantic with the movement, shedding our clothes. They pile around us until we're naked and glaring at each other.

My non-answer is answer enough.

The violence thrums under my skin. I spin her around and kick her legs wide, then slam into her in one go. She's slick, making it easy, and I bite back a groan.

Immediately, her cunt clenches around me. She feels too fucking good. I grit my teeth against the sensation. She moans, her head falling forward. I see her in the mirror—all of her. Her dark-red hair, her bare breasts. The pain she tried to keep shuttered—and failed to hide.

Fuck. The word echoes in my head.

I pull back and thrust into her, not holding back. I can't. I won't. Her body is a trap I'd gladly walk into. Her pussy calls to me like a siren luring me to my death.

A happy death, I'd bet.

She lets out another noise. I reach for her, wrapping my fingers around her throat. I pull her up and put my lips to her ear. She's a beauty, trussed up with her legs spread for me. Her cheeks are pink. Her breasts bounce every time I move against her.

"Look at yourself as I fuck you," I order.

Her gaze lifts, meeting mine in the mirror. I push inside her again, slower this time. I stare at her as I do. My movements are more controlled. But I shift and roll my hips, hitting a new spot, and her eyes lose focus.

I pull out.

She sags forward, barely catching herself on the counter, before she seems to come back to herself. She whips around, and I take control. I lean down and capture her nipple in my mouth, rolling the bud between my teeth. Her fingers slide into my hair and tug. She wants to redirect me.

Nope.

My dick is made of steel as I move away from her

nipple, refreshing the marks that had lost their color over the past few days. I take the perverse pleasure in knowing that this bathroom is no longer Apollo's.

She reaches between us and wraps her fingers around my cock. She twists, pumping slowly and squeezing the head and sliding her fist back down. It's almost bruising. Definitely punishing. It feels too good. Her other hand stays in my hair, trying to control where my mouth goes.

I raise my head and smirk at her, and her grip slips away. She eyes me. I lift her onto the edge of the counter and grab her thighs, spreading them for me. Before I plunge back into her, I can't resist leaning down and licking her clit.

Her moan is long and low, and she continues to make faint noises as I suck the sensitive bundle of nerves in my mouth. I release it and graze her outer lip with my teeth, and her thighs tremble.

But she refuses to speak. To say my name or anything else.

I bite her again, the other side, and her body jolts.

I bring her right to the edge of orgasm, then back off.

My gaze tempts her to say something–anything. I've been adamant about her coming first. Always. But this isn't regular sex. This is hate-filled. Aggressive. I want to leave bruises on her skin, and I want her to do the same to me.

She seems to get the message, because she snaps forward and grabs my jaw. Instead of kissing me, she turns my head and bites my cheek.

Fuck. It hurts. She clamps down and pulls, and pain sluices through my lust. It amplifies it, too. My body is too hot, too frayed.

When she releases me, I stare at her for too long. And

then I shake my head slowly, my cheek pulsing. Damn if the pain doesn't make me harder.

"You'll pay for that."

She lifts her chin and echoes my earlier words. "Bring your worst, Wolfe."

kora

My pussy is on fire. Every inch of me aches for Wolfe to finish this, but I'd also love nothing more than to leave him with nothing.

I just don't have enough self-control to walk away.

He grips my thighs and spreads my legs again, running his finger through my center. The sensation pricks like electricity, and I stare into his eyes. They've been red, but now they're just green. Green and angry.

He slams back into me, hard enough that my whole body slides backward. He fills me so completely it almost hurts. I lock my ankles around him when he pulls me back toward him.

We lock eyes.

And we stay like that as he rams into me over and over. Our skin dampens with sweat, and my ache grows. I need to climax. Right fucking now. I lift my hips and meet his thrusts, reaching out and grabbing his neck. I pull him to me and press my lips to his.

He immediately sucks my lower lip, raking his teeth against it. I whimper and press closer. I shouldn't be enjoying this. I shouldn't want him to touch me, because this isn't doing anything to alleviate my anger. It's just a way to *show* him how angry I am–and, apparently, how angry he is, too.

He's been this way since I came back to them. With fury locked under his skin.

I want it out.

I rake my nails down his back, like I can unleash his demons this way. And all the while, his cock strokes inside me.

His hand slips between us, and his finger finds my clit. I bite his lip harder than I should, and his blood fills my mouth. His tongue invades me, sharing the taste. He strokes harder, thrusts harder. Our skin slaps together.

My orgasm comes from a long way off, steamrolling my senses. I arch my back, gasping, and his movements turn frantic. I clench at his cock, even as he pounds through it. It prolongs my own climax. And then he goes still, buried inside me, and he comes with a ragged groan.

I've never been a willing participant in this kind of sex before. When my ex hate-fucked me, it was cold, clinical even, afterward. Leaving me alone with my mess of emotions and questioning what the hell happened.

But Wolfe is burning hot against me, and his arms wrap around me. He keeps me locked against him, unable to move even if I wanted to. My arms are locked around his neck, our lips barely touching. We both gasped and breathed against each other through our releases, and now we're motionless.

He shifts slightly, his cock still inside me. He's invaded every part of me.

Maybe it's because of this that I say what's on my mind. I pull back slightly to see his green eyes.

"Did you think it would give you a better chance to have Apollo out of the way? To give your father something else so he'd..." I swallow, imagining the worst. That he and his father orchestrated this to get me away from Apollo, or to... I don't know. It's a selfish thought, but the only one that makes sense. "Jace doesn't give a shit about me. *You*, though. You know your father, you know the Hell Hounds. What he'd do—"

Fuck it. I already asked, but I don't think he understood how much I need an answer from him. "Did you send Apollo to the Hell Hounds knowing he'd be targeted?"

Wolfe's expression softens.

Not what I expected—not from someone who I would presume guilty.

"Kora. *No.*" He brushes hair away from my face. "If I wanted Apollo out of the way, I would've sent him to my father without you."

There's another thing.

"You didn't give me a choice." My voice cracks. "Malik and Apollo came in and demanded I go with them. Why didn't I get a say in whether I wanted to go?"

"Baby, none of us have a choice right now." He captures my lips again, slower this time.

The kiss fills me with a delicious, unfurling heat. And comfort—the most surprising part of all. When I'm pissed, when I'm scared. Exhausted.

He draws back too soon. "We're all caught in a tide that we can't swim out of, and we're just hoping the wave doesn't carry us into the rocks."

I swallow.

He steps back, his cock sliding out of me. For a moment, I let that sudden empty feeling sustain me, and I wait for him to leave. Instead, he turns on the shower. He closes the glass door and leans against the wall. It takes a few minutes for the water to heat, for steam to billow out. All the while, Wolfe watches me. I don't know if I want to escape it, exactly, but he seems to be peeling away my layers with his eyes.

He's always had that ability. Masks or no, his gaze goes straight to my soul.

I wish I could do that, but for most of my life, I've had it easy. I was adopted, I had parents who wanted and cherished me. They couldn't give me everything, but they gave me what they could. Safety, love. Happiness.

That might be the detriment. My downfall.

Where Wolfe is all hard edges, forged from a sadistic father and a mother who abandoned him, I'm soft. Pliable. My birth parents don't exist in my memories.

If I didn't have flashes of my time at the group home, St. Theresa's, and going through the courts to be officially a Sinclair, I don't know if I would've guessed I was anything different.

And then I'm right back in the car with Jace, pulling the trigger. The echo of it, the closeness of my kill. I murdered someone less than forty-eight hours ago, and Wolfe is still looking at me like I'm valuable.

"You *are* valuable."

Did I speak out loud? I bite my lip.

He crosses his arms. I'm still partially on the counter, the edge digging into my ass. My legs are open. There's a few feet of space between us, but I don't know how to ask for him to come closer. Or if that's even what I really want.

I grip the ledge on either side of my hips and look away.

"Sterling Falls is going to strip away my softness." My fear comes out quietly. Timid.

"Good."

My gaze flicks back to Wolfe.

"*Good*, Kora. You can't be soft here. You can't flinch. Sometimes you *don't* flinch, but that's a matter for another day. What battles you pick. What fear you give in to." He lifts one shoulder. "This city has filed many into dust. And some, it's carved into weapons. I think it's up to you what you become."

He gestures to the shower. "I suggest you hop in before I kneel between those pretty legs of yours and see what other secrets I can get you to admit."

Steam swirls between us. And yet... maybe I want a reason to give him more of my soul. One confession at a time.

So I lift myself higher on the counter and part my thighs wider.

He straightens off the wall. His arms fall to his sides, and his hands flex into fists. Like he's trying to control himself.

Laughable, after what we just went through. There's a bite mark blooming into view on his cheek, blood on our tongues. I have the sudden urge to pepper him with my marks, to cover him completely. I wonder if that's how he feels, too. Reddish hickeys along my throat, down to my breasts.

He steps between my legs and steals a kiss from my lips. It's rough and tender, and he cups the back of my head gently. And then it's over—but *he's* not done. He lowers himself, holding my thighs open, and stares at my core.

I've never wanted to close my legs more.

"You're a masterpiece." He glances up at my face, then back down. "I never thought I'd find someone I wanted to worship before, but you... you're the goddess who is easily worth it."

I touch his chin, pulling his face back up. My cheeks burn. "I'm not Persephone."

"You can't shed her just like I can't shed my demons." He kisses my palm. "And just because the legends say Hades tricked her, kept her captive... doesn't mean that version is entirely true."

He leans forward and sucks one of my outer lips into his mouth. His teeth tease it, ghosting closer to my center. When he finally does give my clit attention, two fingers pushing into me, it doesn't take long at all for another orgasm to wash over me.

He rises and kisses me again, his mouth tasting like... *me*. And him.

"Fuck it," he says against my mouth, sliding back into me. I lock my legs around him and kiss him back with everything I have. My heartbeat drums in my ears.

I hold on to his shoulder as he pounds against me. All I can focus on is him—until cool air hits my skin. His, too, judging by the way his muscles tense. But he doesn't stop, he just lifts his head.

My gaze goes over his shoulder.

Jace stands in the doorway, his expression impassive. He seems tense. "Guess you two kissed and made up."

I watch him watch us. My embarrassment is on the floor—Wolfe covers most of me anyway. And I seem to have a twisted set of morals. Because I want him to watch Wolfe and me, if only to drive him nuts.

He watched from the shadows while Apollo and Wolfe played me like an instrument. Now, he's coming into the open about it. Maybe he's admitting his jealousy to himself.

"Fuck off," Wolfe grunts.

"I'm enjoying the show." Jace folds his arms and leans

against the doorframe. He doesn't *seem* like he's enjoying it. He looks... mad. His jaw tics, but he doesn't move.

He seems set on torturing himself, I suppose.

Wolfe rotates his hips, and my eyes roll back. My body is too sensitive, too attuned to his every movement. And Jace's gaze on us is too much to bear... in a good way.

You're still pissed at him.

Well, maybe that's why. Because he's unable to touch me, and I'm about to climax again. His cock is hard, straining against his jeans. But he doesn't move from the doorway. I force myself to look at him again. To hold his gaze, even if it's killing me.

He's pissed, too.

Wolfe's hand slips between us, his fingers finding my clit. His lips brush my ear. "You like his eyes on you, flower? You're wetter."

His thrusts hit harder. Angrier. No doubt Wolfe doesn't want to share me. Not now, when I've unraveled so thoroughly in his hands.

Yeah, I'm ruining this.

Jace is ruining this, too.

I lock my ankles around Wolfe and lean back. My head falls back, too, and I close my eyes. I'm on the edge of coming for a third time.

Wolfe slows. Painstakingly. His fingers on my clit move away, ghosting up my side. He cups my breast, his thumb sweeping over my nipple.

"Tell me what you're thinking, flower."

My lips part. "I'm thinking..."

Another thrust, and my eyes flutter. I raise my head and focus on Jace. He's in the same spot, but he seems significantly more uncomfortable. He makes no move to relieve himself. He's doing his best impression of an angry statue and seems unable to tear himself away.

"I need to come," I say, instead of the challenge on the tip of my tongue.

In this moment, I don't want to beat Jace. I don't want to cause any more pain.

"Fuck." My brow lowers, and I reach between me and Wolfe. Jace's gaze flicks down to where my hand is traveling, and I'd like to think he can imagine what I'm doing. His glare isn't strong enough to x-ray through Wolfe's hips.

I stroke my clit. Wolfe pounds into me again and again. And it isn't until Jace's eyes come back up to mine that pleasure erupts through me.

My head tips back, the orgasm too intense to even think about holding his stare. Wolfe growls, his teeth catching my throat again.

When I open my eyes, Jace is gone.

But there's a note stuck to the door in his place.

Your parents are downstairs.

kora

I wring out my wet hair and eye Wolfe, who has taken up residency on my bed. He looks like a shirtless supermodel, showing off his abs in low-slung gray sweatpants. They don't hide anything–they especially didn't when I walked out of my bedroom with just a towel wrapped around me.

It would be a sin for him to leave the house in those.

He's behaving, though, and keeping his hands to himself. I feel as wrung out as my hair. Jace is downstairs with my parents, who arrived annoyingly early. Who shows up an *hour* before dinner? Did they think I'd be sitting around waiting for them?

"Just tell them what you want, nothing more," Wolfe advises. "They saw you with my dad on the news, so I'm sure they'll have questions..."

"They asked their questions." My voice is wooden. Since they assured me I'm safe, we're continuing on with our plan to go out to dinner. Somewhere. At this point, I'll go anywhere to get away from the guys for an evening. My backup plan, which would've sucked, was to eat in.

I hold up a shirt, and Wolfe wrinkles his nose.

"What's wrong with this one?"

"It's a grandma sweater."

Ugh. I picked it because it had a better chance of covering the freaking hickeys everywhere. I sigh and toss it back into the closet.

"That white one was nice. Sharp."

And now it's in the trash, covered in Apollo's blood.

I cock my head. "You want me to dress sharp?"

He reclines, his arms braced behind his head. "I want you to dress how you want to feel. Are you someone who wears grandma sweaters and lets the city crumble her?"

I turn away. "It's just dinner. With my parents."

"Exactly."

"I should dress how they expect."

He huffs. "Do they steamroll you? Do they think you're meek? Now's the perfect time to show them that you are fine. Hell, that you're excelling."

I'm not, though. I'm afraid I'm on the edge of a cliff, and the wind isn't in my favor.

How long will it take for the nightmares to come back? Last night, I slept–but it was the first time I felt safe in a long time. I didn't so much sleep as I crashed, both from exhaustion and orgasms. I can't do that every night.

"My parents..." I shrug. "They were proud of me when I got the scholarship. And supportive of me coming here. When everything started going downhill, I couldn't tell them. So I'm afraid that they're going to judge me based off of where I am *now*, without knowing how I got here."

He sits up. "Kora."

"I told Jace I didn't want them to know anything," I whisper. "And that's still true. So as far as they know, they think my place was ransacked and I moved in with my boyfriend."

"So, dress like you're in love and happy." His lips quirk. "Sell the lie."

Right. Sell the lie.

I can do that.

I duck back into the closet. After a minute of staring at my options, I pull out black leather pants and retrieve my combat boots. There are blouses I would wear to school—the grandma sweaters, as Wolfe called one—and then there are some tops more fitting for Olympus and the like. Sexier stuff that the guys stocked for me.

Something between those two extremes would work.

Finally, I pick out a silk, teal-blue blouse. It buttons up the front, and the sleeves are three-quarter length. I fasten on the tan leather cuff to hide the hourglass brand, paint on makeup —including painstakingly color-matching concealer to my throat—and brush out my hair. I braid pieces away from my face, clipping them back in a half-up, half-down style.

There.

Wolfe nods when I come out of the closet. My attention zooms in on the bite mark on his cheek, and I wince.

He touches it. "Don't you dare make that face." He examines it in the mirror, then turns back to me. "I like it."

"You like it," I repeat. Forgive me if I sound dubious.

"I'll wear whatever mark you want to give me with pride." He winks and comes closer, pressing a kiss to my temple. "Now go make the most of dinner with your parents. It isn't every day that you have people so worried, they drive an hour and track your phone just to make sure you're okay."

I snort. When he puts it like that...

"What if I mess up?"

"How?"

I shrug. "If I tell them something I shouldn't."

He eyes me, then motions to the door. "Go find out."

A lump fills my throat, and I can't seem to swallow around it. I swipe on dark lipstick, blotting it on a piece of tissue, and leave without a backward glance. I guess, when it comes down to it, I can't rely on Wolfe to give me advice about my own parents. He doesn't know them, and he doesn't really know me, either. Not their version, anyway.

I find them in the front room. They've never been impatient, and the same holds true now. They sit on the couch together, quietly conversing. Wine glasses sit on the coffee table, nearly empty. Their time in this house is coming to an end.

I glance at my phone, at the time. Five minutes till six.

"Hi," I call.

They both stand, wide smiles on their faces. They seem older than they did when I left home. Mom has fine wrinkles around her eyes. Time has not been kind to them–or maybe it's me. Maybe I'm seeing them as new people.

I circle the table and hug both of them, closing my eyes for a moment.

"You guys were early." I keep my tone light. I don't need to accuse them five seconds after walking into the room, but really. Why did they show up so early?

"We were in the neighborhood," Mom says. "We didn't have a problem waiting."

Great.

"Ready to go?" Dad picks up his coat and folds it over his arm. "We've got reservations at Antonio's."

"I'll drive." Jace enters the room with his keys dangling from his fingertips.

I gape at him.

His hair is brushed back, showing some semblance of self-care. Under his leather jacket is a white, collared shirt. Dark jeans. He even shaved, although I have a feeling the scruff will be back in no time.

He looks *nice*. And that is unacceptable.

No way in hell is he crashing dinner with my parents. It was bad enough that he told them we were dating. In love. Living together.

My stomach knots, and I narrow my eyes at him. Trying to tell him to fuck off without actually saying it.

"We're looking forward to getting to know Jace better," Mom says in my ear.

Can she sense my panic?

"Oh?" The word comes out strangled.

She chuckles. "Don't worry, we won't interrogate him."

"*You* might not, but Dad's a journalist at heart." Inquisitions are second nature to him. Actually... this could be fun. See how far my father can push Jace with his questions before my 'boyfriend' snaps.

I chuckle. "On second thought..."

"Devious girl." Mom mirrors my grin.

Jace breezes past us, not even sparing me a glance. Dad trails him, with Mom and I taking the rear.

I link my arm with hers. "How's work?"

"Oh, it's fine. We're approaching tax season, doing a lot of preliminary work. You know the deal." We follow the men into the garage.

Jace stops at the baby-blue convertible. "What do you think, Ken? Care to take her for a spin?"

I scoff. "Do you think—"

Dad glances at his wife. "Well—"

"You and Rachel can take it. Kora and I will follow." Jace

tucks his hands in the pockets of his leather jacket. He seems more relaxed than I've seen him before. Much more than he should be… given the circumstances.

But then my father is lifting the key from Jace's hand, and my mom presses a kiss to my temple.

"He's always wanted a convertible," she confesses in my ear. "He's worming his way into your father's good graces."

They climb in and pull out, and Jace turns to me. The easy expression falls away.

I resist the urge to hit him. How can one person be so insufferable?

"What are you doing?"

"It's called charming the parents, princess." He hands me a helmet, smirking.

I swallow thickly. He can't be serious.

"I'm not getting on your bike." I drop the helmet and glare at him. There are a million other cars in this giant garage. We could take any of them. But his freaking motor-cycle? No.

Jace shrugs. "Okay, I'll go to dinner without you. I'm sure they have many embarrassing stories to tell me. Fasci-nating things about their daughter they're just dying to share with her soon-to-be fiancé."

I gasp and smack him before I can think twice about it.

He snatches my wrist as soon as I make contact and yanks me toward him. I stumble and crash into his chest. He twists my arm behind my back, keeping me against him, and lifts his other hand. I flinch when his fingers brush my temple, but all he does is sweep my hair back and tuck it behind my ear.

His eyes are burning, and I almost miss the chill.

Until he leans in and opens his big fat mouth. "Put the damn helmet on and get on the bike."

Then I just want to hit him again. Bastard.

I jerk free and pick up the helmet. "Do you feel a speck of remorse for your actions?"

"Not around you." He leaves me to struggle, climbing on his bike and turning over the engine.

I fumble with the clasp under my chin for too long, finally clicking it and letting out an exasperated sigh. Apollo had helped me with it–but, on the other hand, I don't want Jace anywhere near my throat.

I climb on the back of the bike and grip the little straps behind me.

He glances back and taps my thigh.

"I'm good."

He lifts one shoulder. The bike shoots forward, then slams to a stop. I slide down the leather and collide with his back. My bones rattle with the force of it, but... message received, I guess.

Asshole.

He manually takes my arms and wraps them around his front. Maybe it's just my imagination, but he seems smug. Of course.

My parents are gone, the gate open. We fly through it and out onto the road. Our weight shifts with the bike into the curve, and he only guns it faster. Cold wind streams past me, tearing at my blouse. I should've taken a jacket, but it's too late now. My skin pricks, chilling me to the core.

By the time we slow, my teeth chatter. I can't feel my fingers, but I am assuming they're still clutching Jace's abdomen. Otherwise, I'd probably have slipped from the back of the bike and shattered on the ground.

We roll to a stop outside a restaurant in North Falls. He moves into a tight parking space, and the motorcycle goes quiet. I can't move except for the shivers racking through my body. Like I've lost control of my muscles.

I didn't think winter was so close, but tonight is unusually cold.

Obviously, I'm paying for it.

"Kora."

My jaw won't loosen enough for me to speak, and we sit immobile for a long moment. Then he's climbing off, somehow leaving me in place, and shucking his helmet and jacket. The warm leather touches my arms as he guides my frozen limbs through the sleeves. He pulls off my helmet carefully, hanging it on the handle.

"You should've said something."

"Always an accusation with you, huh?" I mumble.

His laugh is hoarse. "Jesus, you're freezing."

"You drive like a maniac." But the warmth is working. God, that was a terrible experience. And we have to get back on the bike? I'd rather take a cab.

"I drive just fine."

I shrug off his touch and swing my leg over. I feel better once my feet are on the concrete. More stable. I step away from him quickly and slip the jacket off.

He stops me. "Keep it. What kind of guy would I be if I let my girlfriend walk into a restaurant shaking like a leaf?"

I scowl. "Some lie you got us into."

He takes my hand and leads me forcibly down the street, toward the restaurant's entrance. A valet stands at a kiosk, and his spine snaps straighter when he sees us. Or, more aptly, when he sees Jace.

"Mr. King," he says. "Your party arrived a few minutes ago in your convertible."

"Service on the house for them, Marc. Make up an excuse about a promotion if they ask."

He nods, and Jace pulls me inside.

I, however, am flabbergasted. How many pies does he have his grimy fingers in anyway?

"Please don't tell me you own this restaurant."

He glances down at me, the corner of his lip twitching upward and then smoothing. "Fine, I won't."

Oh my god. "Did you pick this place? Suggest it to them or something?"

"No, actually. But I made a call when they told me where they had reservations."

I look around. Antonio's is rather small, the whole place giving off a dark and cozy vibe. Expensive, too. The patrons are in their best cocktail attire, and it seems we've found where the upper crust of the city dines.

Why my parents would want to eat here is anyone's guess.

"They can't afford this." I dig my heels in, bringing us to a stop. "You can't let them pay for all of us, which they would. Dad's tricky and he'll slip the waiter his card when he gets up to go to the bathroom or something. He won't think twice about it, but what does an average party of four spend? Three hundred bucks?"

"More like five." He sighs. "They're not going to pay, Kora. It's fine."

I let out a breath, and it sounds an awfully lot like his sigh. "I'm not mimicking you. For the record."

"Noted."

"I will pretend to be nice to you for the duration of the dinner."

He smirks. "I figured."

"And you...?"

"If I wanted you to suffer, I could've let you tackle their

questions alone." He resumes walking, and I scramble to catch up.

The tables are arranged around a raised platform in the center of the room. A polished baby grand piano sits on it, a dim spotlight illuminating the raised back. A pianist steps up and begins to play.

We head to the back corner of the room, to the booths. The corner has a rounded booth, and my parents sit on one side. The keys to Jace's convertible sit on the table next to my father.

"Left you in the dust there," Dad says.

I slide into the booth, and Jace follows. I shrug off his jacket and set it beside me. "You've always been a speed demon."

He grins. "Indeed. So, kiddo, how's school going? The whole online thing?"

"Oh, um, it's been fine. Just still adjusting..."

"Your mother and I were thinking about our own college experience. If you're dead set on being virtual, then perhaps you should save some rent money and come home."

"Kora is happy in Sterling Falls," Jace says. "And we were talking about her going back in-person at the start of the next semester."

I glance at him, then focus on the water glass in front of me. It takes everything in me to not react with surprise. I'd love nothing more than to get back on track and return to school. It's been filed in my mind under *Pipe Dream* for the last few months. Yet, I can't tell if he's lying, and it nags at me like an itch I can't reach.

I wish I could read his mind. I also wish we didn't have to do this.

"How did you meet Jace?"

I raise my eyes to meet Mom's inquisitive gaze. This is where I need to come up with something creative, because answering with Olympus isn't going to cut it. But my mind is blank.

Panic surges through me. If this part of the story crumbles, then it all does.

"We met on campus," Jace says. "I was dropping off a package for the university president and quite literally crashed into Kora. It was love at first hit."

My face heats. Jesus, what a story. Love at first hit. "Actually, I crashed into him. I wasn't paying attention."

"Typical Kora." My mom has a big smile on her face. "Always has her nose in her phone or a book. What was it this time?"

"Phone," I say at the same time Jace says, "Book."

I elbow him. Probably harder than I need to, but this seems like the one time I'll get away with it without him throwing a hissy fit. He lets out an oomph as my elbow connects with his ribs.

"It was my phone. Because it went flying."

To my utter shock, he just nods along with me. "You're right."

Are pigs flying? Did he just say I was *right*? I need to immortalize this moment.

"You should be more careful." Mom shakes her head, still grinning. "But it seems like a happy mistake."

"She begged me to go out with her." Jace radiates smug, asshole energy. Not sure if my parents pick up on it, but I do. "It was pretty cute."

I pull at my collar. "I did not."

This whole conversation is killing me.

A waitress arrives at the table and takes our drink orders—a bottle of wine for my parents, some cocktail for me, and a Jack and Coke for Jace. I don't even open my mouth, Jace just orders for all of us after a quick wine consultation with the waitress. My parents don't seem especially bothered that I'm taking up drinking, or that Jace took control of their order. And I might need the liquid courage to get through our meal... although so soon after being drunk? Maybe not the best idea.

"You work at the *Emerald Cove Star*, Ken?"

My father nods emphatically. "Worked my way up there from a small-time journalist, and now I am the editor for our investigative section." He goes on about some of his team, which operates as a sort of spotlight and produces longer, usually breaking news stories. Scandals, crimes that have gone unreported, corporate corruption. When he starts using his hands to describe some of the latest articles his team has produced, I sit back in my seat.

He has a way of making people feel comfortable. And while I'm not entirely sure Jace is buying it, he isn't starting an interrogation of his own. He sits back, too, and puts his arm over my shoulders. I shouldn't be surprised when he pulls me into him.

His warmth envelops me, and we stay like that as Dad talks. I even find myself leaning slightly into him. But it's pretend, so it's *fine*.

Our drinks arrive, and the yellow-and-red drink is placed in front of me. I eye it, then him. When I try to straighten up, his grip tightens.

I put my hand on his thigh and squeeze. "What is this again?"

"Tequila Sunrise." His eyes gleam.

My stomach turns. Tequila. *Great*. Pretty sure I can still taste the tequila from the clubhouse in the back of my throat.

Asshole, I try to transmit through my gaze.

He just smiles wider.

"So, Kora. How was meeting the mayor?" Dad asks.

Now I do straighten, letting Jace's arm fall away. "It was interesting. I didn't know I was going until I was there. Sort of a surprise thing..." That's probably the most truthful thing I've said in their company.

"I've met him a few times. Interesting is a good word to describe that man. Seems he serves a few different masters." Dad sips his wine and turns his attention to Jace. "Isn't that right, son?"

Jace bristles. "Not sure I understand your implication."

"Just that it seems pieces have been shuffled rather quickly in the past few weeks. The online schooling, her moving in, the party and fire... her introduction to the mayor. And Cerberus James."

Mom's brows furrow, and she gives him a weird look. "Do you know something?"

Dad shakes his head and slams his glass down. His gaze doesn't leave my face. "I have half a mind to drag you home, Kora. I'm not sure you understand what you're involved in."

My mouth opens and shuts. I don't know how to answer him. Part of me has wanted that from the jump–the smarter side of me. Another voice in my head screams that I can't leave. That I've made this my new home, with the guys, and I'm determined to fix things.

But I'm saved from a response when Jace's hand lands on my thigh under the table.

"You'd have every right to do that." He shrugs, deceptively calm. His fingers twitch. "But you have to know that distance doesn't stop some people."

My stomach swoops. Dear lord, Jace is threatening him. It's subtle, but it's there. Going back to Emerald Cove won't stop Cerberus—and something tells me it won't stop Jace, either. Not when he puts his mind to something.

And he's put his mind to me.

I just wish I knew why. I wish I knew what made *me* so... alluring. Worth their attention. Because from my point of view, I'm just a girl who tried to attend Sterling Falls University and saw something I shouldn't. That *something* was never even mentioned again. Never mind that I have no idea who they killed or where the body went.

So it's something else entirely?

They glare at each other.

"Well," Mom says. "This has been enlightening. Kora?"

I wince.

"Are you all right, honey?"

A genuine, heartfelt question. And my soul nearly cracks in half because of it.

This is why I didn't want them to come. This is why I pretended everything was okay. Because they've already seen me at my worst, placating Parker. Folding myself over to become something that didn't aggravate him, didn't ruffle any feathers. He had them fooled until they learned what he was doing to me... and by then, it was too late.

I glance from my mom to my dad and steel myself. I can't go with the full truth, but I can give them part of it. "I trust Jace."

Mom sucks in a breath, and she reads my expression. We wait in silence for a moment, and then she nods. "Good enough for me."

Dad isn't as easily swayed. "Where are your parents?"

Jace doesn't move for a long moment. Just his finger, circling the lip of his glass. Like he has to contemplate what to say to such a question.

It should be an easy one, but I never thought to ask.

Something must've happened to put him with the Hell Hounds. And Apollo's family, too. I've only got insight into Wolfe's family. His mother who left, the intensity of his father.

"Dad was a deadbeat," Jace finally says.

Was. My heart aches.

"And your mother?" Dad is relentless.

Jace lifts one shoulder, then leans toward me. I let him pull me back into him, but my emotions are twisting. Confusion with... something else. Worse or better, I can't tell. It's the same feeling I got when he would hold my hand to help keep the nightmares away. Hopeful when I have no right to be.

"She's dead, too." He meets Dad's gaze. "I'm not telling you more than that. I don't talk about my past to strangers."

I suck my lower lip between my teeth. His fingers dig into my shoulder and then relax, pulsing in some sort of a weird massage. It doesn't calm me—if anything, it makes everything inside me riot harder.

"Enough," I say softly. I lift my drink and gulp down a few mouthfuls. The tequila taste is barely there, covered by orange juice and grenadine. Thank god, because after this afternoon, I'm not sure I want to ever taste straight tequila again. "I trust Jace. I'm not in danger. No one is hurting me or keeping me here. I like Sterling Falls. I..."

How to explain?

I lean forward and brace my elbows on the table. "The city terrified me at first. It was a lot to take in, and yes, I got a glimpse of the underbelly. But it's grown on me. Every aspect of it. So, even if you wanted to take me out of here, I wouldn't go. Because Sterling Falls has become my home."

If you asked me three months ago about if I should stay

or leave, I don't know what I would've said. I fought like hell to stay in Sterling Falls, and I'd be dumb to leave it now. It would be akin to giving up.

Right?

"If you're sure," Mom says. "But you can change your mind..."

If Jace wasn't sitting next to me, perhaps I would've agreed with her silent request.

But he is, and we're sitting in a restaurant he owns, and I want to know more about his deadbeat dead father, and his dead mother, and everything that happened between then and now. The curiosity in my chest burns bright, worsening by the second.

Is he an only child?

Did he grow up in Sterling Falls?

What did his dad do to acquire the title deadbeat?

Who is Jace King, and where did he come from?

So I don't respond to my mother. I ignore her question, the wrinkle in her brow, and let Jace order my food. I sip my tequila drink and concentrate on the warmth spreading through my body. And I ignore the fact that I'm picking Sterling Falls over home and my parents and safety.

But, as Jace pointed out... distance doesn't make us safer.

Only conquering the villains will do that.

J ace manages to thwart my father's attempt to pay the
bill. Dad's annoyed but thankful, probably pissed to
be put in the position of having to actually show grat-
itude for the man his daughter is... in love with? Infat-
uated with? Living with. At least the last is the truth.

The food was delicious, and we all passed on dessert
with our hands on our stomachs. Unfortunately. I saw the
menu, and I have been known to have a wicked sweet
tooth. We'll just have to come back, I guess. Or get ice
cream later. Apollo has a sweet tooth, too, and there's
bound to be something around the house.

When we all walk outside, it isn't Jace's baby-blue
convertible waiting for my parents. It's their car. I squint at
it and wonder who brought it over... and who's lurking. I
glance around but don't immediately spot anyone.

Mom and Dad both turn to Jace, but he just shrugs.
"Kora and I aren't heading home. I figured this was more
convenient for all of us."

I pull Jace's jacket sleeves down over my hands and bite
my tongue. He insisted on holding it open for me to slip my

227

arms through, then spun me and took his time zipping it closed. But I'm warm, minus my neck and face. Jace doesn't seem bothered by the sudden chill, either.

"Well. Kora, we're going to come back in a few weekends. Check in on you, maybe spend some more time here." Dad gives me a look. The kind that says, speak now if you want a way out of this situation.

But I don't, so I just hug him and press a kiss to his cheek, saying nothing. Then Mom, who wraps me in a tight hug and kisses my temple.

Jace and I watch them get in their car and pull away from the curb.

He looks down at me and hums.

"What?" I demand.

"That wasn't bad. Pleasant, even." He heads down the street.

I chase after him, flabbergasted. "Pleasant? You verbally sparred with my father—"

"It's not like he threatened to kill me or anything."

"Whose parents threatened to kill you?" I ask under my breath.

He's walking so freaking fast. I hurry to keep up, but his long strides are nearly too much for me. We go a block, down a little hill, and the ocean comes into view at the end of the street. Is he taking me to the beach?

Nothing quite so romantic about walking in the sand with a guy who forced me to pretend to be his girlfriend. When it's cold enough that the tips of my ears are slowly freezing.

I'd sooner expect him to drown me in the waves than hold my hand.

Neither happens, though. We go around the corner of a building, and I stop short at the sight across the street.

The outside of Bow & Arrow is buzzing with people.

So many people.

The sign, nothing more than an icon of a bow and arrow, is lit up in neon on the side of the club. The front door Artemis took me through is open, and two men in black button-up shirts stand next to a red velvet cord. A line extends down the street and around the corner.

"Really?"

"Tem wanted you to see it in all its glory," Jace mutters.

I smile.

"And she wanted to make sure you were in one piece," he adds. "She doesn't trust my word for it."

Ah, yes. Because the last time she saw me, I was being dragged away nicely by Apollo and Malik. The latter of whom she doesn't seem too fond.

I stop and look down at my outfit, mostly hidden under the leather jacket. Who wears silk collared shirts to a nightclub? Not cool people, that's for sure. "I'm not dressed..."

He turns to face me, his gaze sweeping up and down my body. Slowly. Heat crawls across my face. He unzips the jacket and pushes it open, then unbuttons the top of my blouse. It exposes some black lace of my bra, to which I let out a squeak of surprise. He ignores it and fluffs out my hair. He releases the band holding pieces of my twisted braids back and carefully untangles the braids. He brings it all forward, over my shoulders.

"Where'd your septum piercing go?"

I touch my nose, then flip the horseshoe shape down. I prefer rings, but this is easy when I want it conceal it. Like when I have dinner with my parents.

"Better," he grunts.

"All you did was make me in danger of flashing people."

I grimace and pull at the silk. The bra is pretty, and seeing it wouldn't be the biggest travesty.

He smirks. "I'm sure it'll be fine."

I think for a second that he might do something else. Take my hand or touch my hair again. But he just shakes his head slightly and makes his way to the front door.

"The line—"

"You honestly think I'm a wait-in-line sort of person?"

I press my lips together.

The two bouncers spot me and Jace, and one immediately unclips the rope barrier. He gives us a quick nod, and then we're in, striding through the foyer and out onto the balcony that goes up to the restaurant and down to the club.

Jace turns to me suddenly and helps me take his jacket off. He folds it over his arm, giving me an unreadable look. I turn away, taking in Bow & Arrow now that it's come to life.

The lights strobe, illuminating the dancing bodies on the dance floor. The DJ on his platform is dancing behind gold lights that shoot down from the ceiling in little bars, essentially caging him in with lights. There are other platforms with dancing men or women, barely dressed, similarly encased in light-cages. They move sensually to the beat, and it takes me a second to tear my gaze away from them.

Jace leads me past the groups of half-moon booths to another set of stairs. No VIP section, no formal greeting. We're suddenly on the same level as most of the crowd, and I don't know what to do with myself. The music is so loud, it's hard not to let it guide my movements.

Did he bring me here to let loose?

For once, I give myself permission to have fun.

I step into the crowd, not waiting for Jace's permission.

The dancing crowd immediately welcomes me into the fold, effectively separating me from him. I shift, slipping past couples and groups of girls until I'm toward the center. And there I let my head fall back and my arms drift up. I finally let go and *dance*. My heart beats wildly, matching the familiar song remixes.

Hands touch my hips, and I knock them away. I spin to face whoever it was, but no one's there. I inch closer to a group of girls, joining their little circle. In no universe would we ever be friends—they scream the sort of popular that I've never been able to achieve—but one of them nods and smiles at me.

"Saw that creep!" she says in my ear. "Girls have to stick together."

Better than the alternative, for sure.

The song fades into the next, and they let out little screams of excitement. A guy comes up to one of the girls and steals her away, saying something in her ear and moving with her. She gives her friends a smile as she goes. Then another. And soon, my bubble of protection is gone again.

More hands on my hips, this time I don't just knock them off. I pivot quickly and shove.

Wolfe catches my wrists, his eyes wide with surprise. Then lust. I read it clearly in the way he looks at me. He reels me in and holds me close, immediately moving back with the beat. His hands slip down my sides, settling on my hips. I just look at him.

"Dance with me," he says in my ear.

"I don't dance."

He laughs and catches my earlobe in his teeth. White-hot lust rips through me, and I tip my head to the side. His lips move down, over my makeup-covered throat. His thigh slips between my legs, and we start to dance.

As I said—impossible not to. Even if I just lied about not dancing.

"I watched you," he says. "Before I joined you, I was up above, at the railing. But fuck, you're so beautiful. I'm sure every guy wants you. I have half a mind to lay public claim to you right this minute."

A rush goes through me. I don't doubt the sincerity behind his words.

"Is that a compliment?" I narrow my eyes. "I don't want anyone else touching me. Not some sleazebag who thinks he can just come up behind me and—"

"Hey, did someone do that?" Wolfe's finger taps under my chin, bringing my face up. "Do I need to kill someone?"

Funny thing is, he would absolutely be okay killing someone for being inappropriate. I guess it might not be funny, but it does make me smile. It's a nice twist of events to have someone care to that extreme.

"Yeah, but I didn't see who it was." I shrug. "It was over too fast."

Still bothers me, though. Obviously.

His gaze darkens. "No one will get away with that. If it happens again, you fucking punch them in the throat, then let me deal with them."

I swallow.

He catches the movement and leans forward, pressing his lips to mine. In a split second, it goes from a normal kiss to scorching. Our mouths open, sliding against each other, and our dancing slows. He pulls me closer, until his thigh is nestled tighter between my legs. Every move creates friction between us.

It's just not enough. Instead, I pull away. I step back,

too, and take his hand. I lead him farther toward the DJ, then give him my back.

He steps up behind me, and we sway like that. My back rests against his chest. He takes more of my weight, letting me lean on him. I tip my head back and eye the upper levels.

Wolfe was up there—is that where Jace retreated to?

Always watching, never participating.

And just when I thought we were getting somewhere.

Something buzzes against my ass, and it takes me a second to realize it's Wolfe's phone. I'm not sure if he feels it, because he doesn't have any problem ignoring it. I slip my hand into his pocket and retrieve it, swiping it open.

A text from Jace. *Stop fucking around and get up here.*

Hurt radiates through me, and I shove the phone back at Wolfe. Fucking around? There are a million ways to interpret it, but the first and strongest way is that he thinks Wolfe is fucking around *with me*. When he should apparently be doing something more important.

Leave me to dance on my own while Jace and Wolfe do whatever fucking business they have going on.

Understanding dawns on me. I'm the cover. The guise.

Is Jace trying to pull something off under our noses? After all, he used Tem as an excuse to get me here. Or maybe she knows, and she's in on it. She's a fighter at Olympus. She was there the day I showed up, before I stole the mask. She could be involved in a lot more than I think. Either way—I don't want to be part of it.

"Kora," Wolfe tries, glancing at the text. "It's not—"

"Save it," I snap.

It isn't him I'm pissed at but Jace. Yet my anger still comes leaking out at the wrong person.

Wrong person, Kora? He's clearly just as involved as Jace.

233

I scoff and slip through the crowd, hurrying in the opposite direction than where I think Jace might be hiding. Away, to a set of stairs beside a bar. I go up a level and almost crash into Marley.

Fucking hell.

kora

"Kora?" Marley stares at me like I have five heads. I can't so much hear her as I can read her lips. "What are you doing here?"

I shift and pull at the hem of my shirt. "Um... dancing."

Behind her are Janet, Erica, and... whatever the third one's name is. They haven't noticed me yet, but all of them have pink cheeks. Either from alcohol or dancing, I can't quite tell. They sway to the music while talk-yelling at each other.

"Oh, cool." Marley steps closer, her voice raised. "I tried calling you a bunch of times. You were on the news."

Everyone and their freaking mother saw that, huh? "Yeah."

"You went AWOL. I was worried."

Accusations, accusations.

"Sorry." I catch a flash of dark hair that looks an awful lot like Artemis. "I've got to go."

"Wait!" She snatches my wrist and keeps me in place. "We should catch up. It's been weeks."

"I know, I just have a lot going on right now."

"Kora, what a surprise." Janet and her goonies surround us. "Did you just get in? You look... Quite sharp."

There's that fucking word again. Her entire existence is grating on my nerves. I resist the urge to bare my teeth. "I've been here a while."

She smiles. "Aww, that's sweet. You arrived before the crowds?"

I pause and debate just telling her the truth—that I have friends in high fucking places. That I don't have to wait in line to get in, because we strolled right past all of them. We probably passed them, even. But none of those things will win me true kindness from her. That ship sailed a long time ago.

"Something like that." I raise my eyebrows. "And did you wait in line for an hour?"

She cups her ear and leans in. "What was that?"

I roll my eyes. "Nothing."

"My dad got us VIP passes," Marley cuts in. She shows me her wristband. "Do you want to come with us? We have a booth upstairs."

Higher up? Jace and Wolfe might not think to check for me there. I'd have no way of getting to the VIP lounge.

"Sure."

Marley digs another band out of her purse and puts it on opposite the leather cuff. I trail them up another flight of stairs and down a dark hallway. The VIP section is quieter. Easier to talk, I suppose. A man checks our wristbands and waves us through. There's a private bar up here, and a few other occupied booths. The room is a half-moon shape, with a wall of glass that gives occupants a view over the dance floors. One of the cages–made of steel bars *and* vertical lights, I now see–floats at eye level. A couple inside it sensually dance, something borderline dry humping than anything else.

I catch up to Marley, who had gotten a bit ahead of me. Janet leads the way with Erica, and the third is between them and Marley and me.

"So, you met up with your dad?"

Marley grins. "Yeah, we had dinner. Actually, I think he said he had business here, so that's how he got the extra passes. He gave me a whole bunch to come back more times."

"Oh, wow." I glance around. "This place..."

"It's cool, right? Janet's friends with the owner."

My eyebrows hike. "Oh?"

"I guess her dad is friends with the guy."

Business. Friends. My skin prickles, and I have to steel myself before I glance over my shoulder. No one is behind us, nothing seems amiss. The music still pulls at me, pulsing through my body. I check out the rest of the room, and my breath stalls in my chest.

Jace lounges in a booth in the corner, a glass of dark liquid in front of him. His legs are kicked out, one arm over the back of the booth. He's so handsome it hurts–an unfair quality for a rude human. He sits across from two men. A woman in clothing that barely covers her chest sits between them, her gaze glued to Jace. She seems like she's their toy–one man has his hand on her thigh, the other twists her hair between his fingers.

Three against one doesn't seem very fair if they're negotiating.

Business. But that's why Wolfe is supposed to be with him, isn't it?

I glance over the balcony and get a good view of the

dancing below. I don't see Wolfe, though. Figures he wouldn't remain after I hurried away.

All at once, I don't want him to find me. I just want to be normal with these pseudo-friends.

I grab Marley's hand, stepping up beside her. "What are we drinking?"

"Paula's getting us martinis. Do you want one?"

I'm pretty sure martinis aren't made of tequila. But damn, I seem to have a penchant lately for putting myself in the line of fire of alcohol. And now I know the third girl's name... again. I should probably commit it to memory, since they seem to keep returning like stains through white paint.

"Yeah, why not," I answer.

"This is our booth. We're going to sit for a minute, then go dancing." Marley sways, a huge grin on her face. She throws her arm around my neck. "I missed you."

"Missed you, too, Mar." Except, she hasn't been at the forefront of my mind. My secrets have. I let out a breath and decide not to tell her that my parents are in town, and everything else that's happened. My body still aches from the past few days' worth of trauma.

"Paula, can you get Kora a drink?"

I take a seat where I can still keep an eye on Jace. The rest of the girls pile in on the other side, scooching so Erica is right beside me in the U-shaped booth. They don't mind that my focus keeps getting pulled toward Jace's table.

I'm transfixed.

Maybe he can feel the weight of my stare, because at one point, he scans the room. I slouch, and his gaze moves past our table without incident.

Until.

Paula returns with an armful of drinks. She slides them

around and pushes one in front of me. "That'll be ten dollars."

I pause, and embarrassment pricks my skin. She doesn't ask anyone else for money, but her flinty gaze stays trained on my face. Absorbing every micro-expression I can't control.

I should've probably thought about *money* before I ordered a drink, right? And underneath the layers of *the guys are taking care of me* is still the hard, cold fact that I don't have two pennies to rub together.

Fucking hell, Kora.

"I don't have cash on me, but I'll get it to you. Through Marley."

Janet leans toward us. "It's okay, Kora. Next round can be on you, and we'll be even."

I swallow and nod. I might be able to make my escape before then, because four of them at ten dollars each? Fuck, I don't even have ten dollars, let alone forty.

"Chaos!"

My head whips around, searching the room. I find Artemis quickly.

She wears a short gold dress that shimmers as she walks. Her long dark hair is loose around her shoulders. She nods to the space beside me, and I scooch over to give her room. She sits beside me, throwing her arm around my shoulders and leaning in. She has the sort of commanding energy that I think Janet probably wants to have.

Tem looks around the table, then tugs at the VIP bracelet on my wrist. "How'd you get this?"

I notice her wrists are bare. "Marley's dad. He gave them to her."

She tilts her head. "Interesting. Are these your friends?"

I shift, but Tem seems to know where my head is.

Somehow. In a smooth move, she rips the band off and crumples it in her hand.

"You don't need this, Kora. Pretty sure they'd kill me if they saw you with that on your wrist." She taps my leather cuff. "It clashes with your outfit, anyway."

"Who are you?" Janet snaps.

Tem smiles, giving me *shark* vibes. "I'm Kora's friend. Who are you?"

"I–" For once, Janet isn't quite sure what to say. What accolades does she have? But then she seems to realize who she's talking to, and her gaze narrows. "I'm friends with the owner. That's why we're here."

"Interesting." Tem leans back in her seat. "Well, whoever gave you those wristbands wants you to be the entertainment. So. Get to it."

I chuckle under my breath. I'm sure Janet would wiggle her ass if there was an incentive behind it, but just because a stranger is telling her to?

Artemis leans forward again and braces her forearms on the table. "Come on. Is this much different than placing a bet at Olympus? It's the same principle. Meant to give you a high. That's why they let the pretty girls into this section for free."

Ah. Seems this place has an underbelly, too. Or...

"What do you mean?" Erica asks. She seems unsure, for once, and cradles her drink with both hands.

"Why do you think you're here? Not to sit at a table. Go dance. Preferably close to one of the guys who actually paid for such a luxury. Or one of the cages, if you want an extra thrill. I could arrange that for you." Artemis waves her hand around, and for the first time I notice the other women in the room are doing exactly that. Flirting. Seducing.

The vibe in this room is darker.

Shouldn't Marley have known this is where she was taking us? Unless they already know, and they're just waiting for me to make a fool of myself. That would be just like Janet, wouldn't it? To orchestrate this?

Janet eyes me, then Artemis. She leans back and crosses her arms. "What about you?"

Artemis snickers. "Because I've paid my dues. Look, do or don't, I don't really give a shit. I'm just saying, that's the point of this section. You could've gone to any of the VIP sections, and you landed on this one."

"So there are other VIP sections that don't..." Erica glares at Janet. "Why did you pick this one, Janet?"

Janet winces. Still, she makes it look delicate. "I got turned around."

"Because you've been here before," I finish. "With the owner."

Artemis glances at me again, then leans back with a wide smile stretching her dark lips. "Where's he? Janet, did you say?"

She shrugs. "Working, I'd guess."

"At his club." Tem laughs. "Which is *here*. You'd think if you were friends, you wouldn't have ended up with those wristbands. Or he would've escorted you to a nicer VIP lounge..."

Except they didn't come from Janet—they came from Marley. I bite my tongue on that one, not wanting to embarrass my friend. Janet deserves the negative energy anyway.

Janet turns away from Artemis and focuses on me. "I think it's time for another round of drinks, don't you?"

Mine is still three-quarters full. I swallow carefully, unable to voice my objections. You know what would voice its objection? My empty bank account. I don't even have my wallet on me–a motorcycle ride will do that to a girl. I've got nothing.

And she *knows* it.

She smiles. "Or..."

I narrow my eyes.

"A little dare." She follows it with a raise of her eyebrow. It's clear she thinks I won't do whatever the dare is–and she doesn't offer up what it would be, either.

Although I can guess.

"Janet," Marley hisses.

Artemis chuckles and taps her fingers on the table.

"Things just got interesting. You're living up to your namesake." Her words are said under her breath, just for me.

Chaos. That's what she calls me.

And for the first time, I feel like I actually have a friend at the table.

I don't know Artemis very well–she's probably the most mysterious person I've met outside of the guys. But she doesn't undercut me. Or lie.

I think if she knew I was uncomfortable with foul-mouthed bitches *daring* me to do something stupid, she'd put an end to it. But as it is, I know where it's going, and a challenge flares inside me.

You know what? If this is a setup? I will just burn in embarrassment later. In private.

May as well prove Janet wrong. I'm not whatever the fuck she thinks I am.

"Why not?" I answer, finally.

Artemis nods. Marley lets out a squeak of surprise. No doubt she thought I'd back out before the gauntlet was even thrown into the sand. Or that I'd run away... I don't know. I've been her meek friend since forever. Quiet, unassuming. Parker just ground me down more. It made everything worse.

I'm forcing my way out of my shell, and it feels good.

"Go dance in front of one of the guys like your friend wants us to do, and I'll buy the round you're supposed to." Janet's expression turns sharp. "You've got to put some effort into it, though. If you half-ass it..."

I roll my eyes. Inside, though, my nerves have crackled to life, little lightning bolts shooting around my body.

"She should go for the hottest guy in the room," Erica adds. "To make it worth *our* while."

"To see him reject you," Paula adds. "No offense, Kora, you're just a bit... plain."

Artemis snorts and scans the room. "The guy in the dark-blue shirt?"

My stomach twists as the girls follow her gaze. Even Marley. Hell, this could be her brand of fun now. I can't help but let her betrayal slip through my ribs and pierce my heart. It hurts. I *want* her to shut her friends up, but she doesn't. She, along with Janet, Erica, and Paula, locate the man Artemis indicates.

"No." Janet wrinkles her nose. She takes a minute to peruse the room, and I can tell the moment she finds the one. Her lips curl up. "Got it. *Him.* Dark hair. Tattoos. White collared shirt."

The one with the scowl. The one who slid his jacket over my shoulders, who lied to my parents about our predicament. Who confuses me. Who *irritates* me.

Of course it's Jace. It was always going to be him.

Isn't that the reason I agreed in the first place?

kora

I pretend to consider Janet's dare, twisting my lips.

Jace is alone at the table now, staring down at his phone. Wolfe never showed. Never helped him with whatever business they had, probably because the latter was too busy trying to hunt me down.

I nod and nudge Tem to let me out.

She stands, then takes my seat. "Good luck, Chaos."

Jace doesn't look up until I'm right in front of him. I run my fingers across the table and pick up his drink, lifting it to my lips. He doesn't make a move to stop me. In fact, there's a dare in his eyes, too.

I toss back the drink, letting the alcohol burn a path down my throat. It pools like fire in my stomach, spreading quickly. Faint hints of smoke and caramel linger on my tongue.

I slam the glass down and tip my head back. My hair slips off my shoulders, exposing my throat. Here, the way he unbuttoned my shirt does me favors. I know my skin is exposed down to the lace of my bra between my breasts, a narrow strip of pale skin that is meant to tempt him into doing something wicked.

The alcohol is getting to me. First the tequila, now this.

His eyes on me hurt in a way I don't expect. Like razors slicing through my skin. The music pulses, and I make sure he's watching me when I slide my hands up my sides. My fingers tangle in my hair. My hips sway to the beat.

His eyes narrow.

My smile is wicked when I slink closer to him still.

He pivots, his legs now in the open, and I step between them. Something foreign has come over me. Jace pushes my buttons, but I need to hit all of his. Until he's as tortured by this as I am.

Why? Why do I care if he looks at me? He's made it clear he doesn't give a shit.

I step closer and run my hand up his arm. His muscles are tense, and he doesn't move an inch. I lean in close, still swaying to the beat. But I think the beat is lost behind the rush of blood through my ears, because I can't hear it anymore. Just my heart pounding, my heavy breathing.

"Poor Jace King," I say in his ear. "All alone at a club filled with women. Why are you pouting in the corner?"

He grips my hips. His thumbs slide under my shirt, and his touch against my bare skin is electric agony. I pull back just far enough to meet his gaze. His cold blue eyes crash into mine.

I've never wanted someone to kiss me more than I do right now.

"Seems I'm not alone anymore." He draws me even closer.

I lose my balance and grip his shoulders. *Not good enough*, I can hear Janet say. A figment of my imagination, maybe, but right nonetheless.

This isn't a show.

"Dance with me." I cover his hands with mine, keeping them on my hips, and step back.

I almost expect him to refuse. To glower, to revert back to the Jace I'm most familiar with. The asshole version who would rather we not touch, not speak if our words aren't barbed.

But then again... I've always got a different version of him in the darkness.

He comes with me, his hands glued to my skin, and I tip my head back to keep my gaze on his face. He towers over me, and I shouldn't be surprised when he just stands there.

"Dance," he orders.

I smirk, but... I do it. Because I want to, I guess, and because I want to see what he'll do.

Nothing exists outside of us and the tension building between us.

Kiss me, I think again. It isn't the first time I've tried to will him to do something, although this might be the first pleasant thing I've thought at him. Not *fuck off*, which is my go-to around Jace.

I dance, and he watches. Touches. His fingers creep higher, under my shirt, as I spin in his arms. I back into him and grind my ass against his groin. He lets out a huff, and then his grip gets firmer. Hand splayed across my abdomen, keeping me pressed to him. His other runs up and cups my throat.

I swallow.

"Like this?" He nips the shell of my ear.

I twist to look over my shoulder at him, but he just guides my head forward again.

Like Parker, pressing my face into the mattress while he

249

did what he wanted with my body. Like the person who rescued me from the fire, forcing me to look away.

I close my eyes and inhale smoke.

No.

He's definitely not Parker. Not even close. But... he can't be the person who pulled me out of that burning basement, right?

He can't be the one who rescued me.

My heart beats faster and faster, running away with panic. I try to remember the rasp of that man's voice. His hands keeping me turned away. Would I have recognized Jace's voice? If he lowered it or disguised it?

If it was Jace, it means he knew where I was. It means he knocked me unconscious and gave me to Cerberus. It means... he let me be kept in a medically induced coma for a *week*. He let everything that happened, *happen*.

I killed someone because I was backed into a corner.

But who put me in that corner to begin with?

"Kora."

I've stopped dancing. Stopped moving. A sudden burst of fear has me immobile, and I need to *snap the fuck out of it.*

Jace is the root of my problems. He's the one who took my scholarship away and didn't do a damn thing to help me get out of my contract with Kronos. Not really. Everything that happened after, like dominos falling, comes from the first time he ripped the rug out from under me.

My movements are wooden when I step out of his grip. He reaches for me, and I flinch.

I fucking flinch like I'm right back in Parker's apartment, or Kronos' office.

And suddenly Wolfe is there, and his fist is smashing into Jace's face.

For a second time that day.

Jace stumbles backward, caught completely off guard for once.

Wolfe follows him. He lands on top of his best friend and punches him again.

And again.

I'm still fucking frozen when Artemis runs past me and shoves Wolfe off Jace. Wolfe staggers to his feet, seeming ready for round two... except his friend put up no resistance. Didn't try to even fend him off. Either way, it's clearly over. Tem stands over Jace, her body radiating fury.

"Not here," she snaps at him. "Get some fucking common sense."

Wolfe stiffens. His gaze goes to me. "What did he do?"

I shake my head slowly. "Nothing."

"Fuck that," Wolfe growls. "You don't flinch without cause. Without memories attached. What did *he do*?"

"Wolfe," Tem tries.

He holds up a hand, stopping her. He steps toward me carefully and touches my chin. The bite mark on his cheek stands out, and I reach up without thinking. I press my thumb into it.

"I forgot," I admit to Wolfe. "I forgot that Jace is the one who put me in this position."

"This one?" He looks up and down my body.

"The one where I'm in Sterling Falls under your father's thumb." I glance away, ashamed of myself. "I think it's time to go home."

He grunts his affirmation.

I head for the door, ignoring Marley and her cronies. Janet can suck a dick if she thinks I'm acknowledging whatever the fuck just happened.

Wolfe follows.

Artemis... she hesitates, but then her heels click on the stairs, trailing behind us.

"Kora!"

I jerk to a stop and rotate around. The stairwell is dark, all shadows and low lighting. The walls are dark marble with veins of silver and gold.

Jace storms toward us. I plant my fists on my hips, ready to tell him off, but he just plows into me. He tosses me over his shoulder like I weigh nothing and continues down the stairs.

I have a view of his backside, his heels flashing as he hurries down. For a moment, I'm too stunned to do anything. And then I glance up and see Wolfe, eyes wide, and Artemis. Smirking. She winks at me.

Jace doesn't put me down. He moves easily through the crowded hallways outside the VIP section, unbothered by the stares we're garnering. And I just hang there, my face flaming hotter by the second.

Cold air kisses my skin, and then we're outside. We round a corner, and he puts me down. Immediately, he backs me into the wall.

"Give me one reason not to kick your ass," I spit.

There's a weird look in his eye. His cheek is already darkening from the hit he took, but he seems otherwise unruffled. As always. These men are going to be the death of me.

But Jace just raises one eyebrow, still staring me down. "I'd like to see you try."

"I'd like to see you staring up at me from the ground– but I guess Wolfe already took care of that. Winner takes–"

He slams his lips down on mine, cutting me off. Swallowing my words.

My heart stops. My brain stutters around two words.

252

Kissing.

Jace.

I push back into him, increasing the force between us. Rise on my toes, which curl in my shoes. His kiss goes straight through me like liquor, and I'm drunk in seconds. He tastes like the drink I finished, smoke and caramel. Sweet and dangerous. I crave more of it.

He leans into me, winding his fingers through my hair and angling my head. It's possessive and controlling and so completely him.

I make a noise. A whimper in the back of my throat slips out, and that does it.

He yanks himself away and staggers back a few steps. His expression says *I'm* the one who betrayed *him*. Not the other way around.

I touch my lips, unsure if I just imagined that.

It sure as hell is seeming that way.

He shakes his head and faces the street. His shoulders heave.

Holy shit.

My fingers linger on my lips, and I try to wrangle my emotions. Again. Like, what the fuck am I supposed to do with that? Wolfe and I aren't... aren't together. Not officially. And Apollo... Adding Jace is a fucking complication.

One I don't need right now.

My hands shake, and icy wind tears at me. My silk shirt, my hair. It tears at my mental defenses, too, and that just makes me angrier. First thing tomorrow, I'm hunting down a freaking lawyer and seeing what can be done about this contract.

Suppressed anger cramps my stomach. It's hard to take a deep breath, let alone form a sentence. But I do, because I'm sick of remaining pressed to the side of the building like someone Jace can just... use. Kiss and then toss away.

"Take me home." My voice is shockingly steady. I search for his blue car and shove off the wall, heading for it. My knees are weak. "And don't fucking touch me again."

jace

I ruin everything–and I will no doubt ruin Kora.

It's good the princess wants nothing to do with me.

Maybe this will be the final nail in my coffin, and she'll realize how monstrous I am.

Apollo stops outside the office door. He's pale. Still recovering from the kicks to the stomach, I suspect. The hospital ruled out more internal bleeding–he just has some deep bruises to show for his efforts at the Hell Hounds' clubhouse. He's got a bump on his head, too, from where they knocked him unconscious. His face is still swollen, and one hand holds a bag of frozen peas over his eye.

"What are you going to do?" He taps his thigh and waits.

I raise one shoulder. I've been contemplating this very thing since I brought her home. Longer than that, really.

And now, I can taste her on my lips. "I'm going to let her think she's free."

He doesn't like that. His lips twist, and he's silent for a minute. The clock is ticking down. "Then?"

I accept our fate. Mine and hers. And Wolfe's. And Apollo's. I've been bound to them since we left the Hell Hounds, and now I'm adding Kora to the mix. Once she joined us, there was never a possibility of leaving.

I power down my phone and set it on the desk. Apollo has always been patient with me. Understanding. That's why he doesn't blame me for sending him to the clubhouse with Kora. He doesn't blame Wolfe–but he should blame both of us. He should be pissed that we put him in that position. And yet.

There's a chance he won't forgive me for this.

I meet his gaze, but I refuse to give away my plans. Refuse to be the one to break him after all he's sacrificed for us. I settle on cryptic. A hint at what's to come. What I have planned.

What's *been* planned and already kicked into motion.

"And then it'll be too late."

kora

Bang. Something hot splatters across my face.

My eyes fly open, and I shoot upright in bed. My heart is going a mile a minute, and it takes me a long moment to rein in my fear.

I'm safe.

In my bedroom, in the dark, I don't *feel* safe. I feel like someone is about to push me off the edge of a building. I touch my face to reassure myself that there isn't warm blood on my skin. But I don't get it.

My cheeks are wet.

I hop out of bed and scramble into the bathroom, flicking on the light.

Not blood.

Tears.

I scowl at my reflection and rub the salty liquid away with a hand towel. My face is too pale, and the memory of alcohol–just enough to push me into *tipsy* territory–turns my stomach.

In the dream, I held the gun to Wolfe's chest. He was keeping me steady, his hands on my arms, as he goaded me.

This time, though, I gave in and pulled the trigger. Then the blood that jarred me awake.

No time to see if I really killed him in my dream or if I was going to swing around and open fire on anyone else. Dreams are tricky. Subconsciousness plays a big role in that, I think. Memories stacked on fears and hopes.

As it is, I can't go back to sleep.

With a groan, I put socks on and find a sweatshirt. My clock reads two o'clock in the morning. Jace, Wolfe, and I got home from Bow & Arrow at ten-ish, and I immediately went to find Apollo.

He was in bed with a bag of frozen veggies on his face. The lights were on, his attention on the laptop playing a movie on his lap. But when he saw me, he pushed it aside and patted the space next to him.

I went and curled up next to him, but I couldn't speak. Guilt kept me from spilling the events to him–dancing with Wolfe, kissing Jace. And then coming to Apollo. I don't know what I'm going to do if they make me choose between them.

But he didn't pry. He stroked my hair and my back, until I fell asleep.

I vaguely remember Wolfe coming in and picking me up. He carried me back to my own bed and pulled the covers up to my chin. His lips brushed my forehead–and then another kiss from different lips. Apollo's.

I close my eyes now, head bowing. Whatever Apollo had to attend to... he could've left me in his bed. Maybe he could've staved off the nightmares.

We're back to square one, where I'm afraid to sleep alone.

Ridiculous.

I open my door and step into the hall. Once upon a

time, my door would've been locked at night. I somehow earned my freedom to wander. So that's what I do. I take silent steps past Wolfe's and Apollo's rooms, pausing only to listen for movement.

Light spills out from under Wolfe's door.

The imagery of shooting him is too fresh in my mind, so I keep going. Past Apollo's dark room. To the stairs. Down to the first floor. I let my feet guide me without giving it too much thought, and I'm not too surprised when I end up in front of the music room.

I haven't been here since before.

But... *before*, I needed it. The comfort. In a way, it's easy to fall back into the habit of relying on this room. *And Jace.* How could I forget that he's the one who always found me? Sought me out in the darkest point of the night. He'd bring me back to bed, sit with me until I fell asleep. My heart aches.

My fingers graze the doorknob, and I freeze. My brain takes a second to process: first the light that's visible under the door, then the piano.

Someone's playing it.

And since Wolfe is in his room, and I sincerely doubt it's Apollo, that just leaves one culprit: Jace.

My hand falls away from the doorknob, but I don't move.

He plays the keys hesitantly at first. Like he's trying to find his way through an old memory. I stay perfectly still as he goes through it once, missing a note or two, and slowly gains confidence.

The piece he plays is familiar.

I step to the side and carefully turn, sliding down the wall to sit on the floor. I pull my legs up, wrapping my arms around them, and rest my chin on my knee. I close my eyes and let the music wash over me.

Where do I know it from?

It reminds me of a lullaby. The sort children find in music boxes with the twirling ballerinas. The ones meant to hold jewelry or precious items.

The familiarity is comforting.

He plays through it twice more, then switches to something else. A different melody, a minor key. It's haunting. It scratches at something in my brain just out of reach. Maybe from an old movie, or a piece meant for a different instrument.

And then it stops.

I scramble to my feet just as the door opens. He steps into the hall, and his gaze burns right through me. I'm unprepared for the way my heart skips a beat.

One kiss and I can't be normal around him? Is that how it's going to be?

Absolutely not.

"What?" I challenge.

He shakes his head. "Go on."

"What?" Softer. More confused. Go on? Leave?

"Go in. Play the piano. Get it out of your system so I can put you to bed."

Like a child. That's how he means it. Put me to bed. No, thanks.

I shake my head slowly and retreat a step. Nightmares be damned.

Jace be damned. I won't let him push me around like this. Even if there's a dangerous part of me that wants to say, *fuck it*, grab him by the front of his shirt, and slam our lips together.

Not going to happen.

"I can put myself to bed."

He inclines his chin. He's changed out of the white collared shirt into a black cotton t-shirt and checkered pajama pants. His hair is once again messy, and there's a hint of a shadow on his cheeks. The beard is coming back. I can't decide if it makes him hotter or more annoying.

Both, I decide.

"You don't get to boss me around," I add.

"I'm aware that you think that."

"I don't follow your directions."

He frowns. "I'm well aware of that, too."

I narrow my eyes and take another step back. "My legs are cold, so I'm just going to..."

Mistake. His gaze drops to my bare legs, then crawls up my body. My short sleep shorts, the baggy sweatshirt. My hair... well, it might be a nest. I don't actually know. When he takes a step toward me, I can't seem to move.

My heart transforms into a hummingbird with frantic wings.

He reaches for me, lifting a lock of my hair. He twists it between his fingers, but his attention stays trained on my face. I've never wanted someone to touch me more. I've never wanted to run away so badly. But I'm caught in his web, and all I can do is stare at him with wide eyes.

If he crosses that distance, another inch...

He tips his head back, analyzing my reaction through half-lidded eyes. "You enjoyed me kissing you. That's why I did it, you know. Because I see the way you look at me when the others aren't watching. I see everything you want to hide."

Goosebumps break out along my arms. "Sure you do."

"Enough to scare you."

He unnerves me. There's a difference.

"In your dreams, Jace." I'm instantly annoyed again, although I can't tell if it's with him or myself. Why mention dreams at all? He probably knows that *nightmares* are what drove me down here, as they did every other night we crossed paths in the music room.

And anyway, that breaks the spell.

His hand drops.

My breath rushes out, and finally my muscles unlock. I can't deal with any more freaking disappointment tonight. He doesn't stop me from bolting. I hurry all the way back to my room and climb into my bed. My heart pounds.

When I finally, *finally* fall asleep, I don't dream of blood and gunshots.

I dream of that haunting melody and the taste of smoke and caramel.

kora

B ack to hiding.
Sulking.
My phone buzzes on my nightstand, and I lunge for it. Besides sneaking down at an ungodly hour this morning to get coffee and snacks, I haven't left my room.

I mull over what I've learned about Jace. That his father was a deadbeat, and his mom is just plain *dead*. My chest is tight, and it isn't that I'm sympathetic... I think, rather, that I can relate. I don't know how. He doesn't talk about his past with strangers, he said. Is that why I don't know him? And Apollo... all I know is that he has a sister as mysterious as him.

And no one's come knocking. It makes me wonder how long they'll let me stay in here before one of them tries to talk to me. Or lure me out.

They only know the bare minimum that I've offered them, too. Their insight stems from my decision to move to Sterling Falls. The scholarship, school, my abusive ex-boyfriend. In the back of my mind, I consider when he's going to find me. I never mentioned Sterling Falls, or the university, but... I left abruptly. To escape *him*. Parker was the original monster who had me running.

I clear my throat and shove those thoughts away. The caller's number is blocked, but I answer it anyway. I expect Cerberus. Or Malik. Everyone wants something, and Cerberus still considers me *his*. He'll say jump and expect me to ask how high.

"Hello?"

Breathing.

I repeat my greeting, then pull the phone back to look at the screen. It's still lit, the call connected. "Is someone there?"

There's a click, then a deep, garbled voice says, "You should've left Sterling Falls. This is your last warning."

It disconnects.

For a second, I'm confused. The voice sounded like it went through an audio mixer, obscuring any way of being able to identify the caller. Not just their voice, but their gender.

Then it hits me, and I let out a laugh. I toss my phone away. Honestly, what the hell am I supposed to do with that? Be afraid? Ten bucks says it's Janet trying to scare me off. It's clear she doesn't like me. It's not like I'm her biggest fan. This is precisely something she'd do to have Marley all to herself.

Not that I'm doing anything to maintain *that* friendship.

I've got a slew of texts from Marley that I've been too annoyed to answer. I just can't deal with it right now. Her questions, her outrage over how my friend reacted–Artemis, I suppose, at Bow & Arrow–and the thinly veiled hints about my adventures with more than one man. Seems like she recognized Wolfe from that video call a while ago, and I didn't exactly hide the fact that Jace and I know each other.

My last warning. That's implying that Janet's warned me before. Are we counting her bitchy attitude as one?

My phone buzzes again, and I answer too quickly. This number isn't blocked, but I don't care. If it's Janet's idea of a prank, I'm sure she'd want to follow up. See how it landed.

"What is it?" I snap.

"Whoa. Something up?"

It takes me a second to place the voice.

Malik, of course. The first call threw me off, but he's who I really expected.

I let out a sigh and rub my temple. "Nope. Sorry."

"Boss wants to see you."

Great. I'd like to think this is my karma. Steal a mask, shoot a man–I'm getting what's coming to me. Slowly. Painfully.

"I'm going to assume this isn't a request." I need to put on real clothes. And a way out of here. If he wants me to get to the clubhouse, I'm going to need a little help.

"You would assume correctly."

I bite my lip. "I'm not really on speaking terms with the guys right now."

Malik laughs. It goes on for a while, even as I put the phone on speaker in my closet and yank jeans out of a drawer. He just laughs and laughs like he expected this, in some way.

"I'll send a car."

I eye my phone. "How am I supposed to walk out of the house? It's a fortress."

"Ah, so you don't want them to know you're going?"

I scoff. "I'd like to disappear from Sterling Falls completely, but I don't think that's an option."

He pauses. "All you have to do is ask."

Is Malik really offering to get me away from them? They don't want me out of Sterling Falls–they want me to stay right where they can find me. And use me.

"Dress nicely," Malik adds. "I'll come up with a distraction for your guards. Be ready in an hour and wait for my text."

I grimace.

And yet... it has to say something about me that I'd be more willing to go with Malik than spend any more time in this house. Wolfe and I made up, sort of. Apollo didn't do anything wrong. And Jace is... *Jace*. Enough said.

I rub my chest to ease the anxious knot, but it doesn't get better. I trade out my jeans for a blush-colored skirt. The material is thick and soft, and it flows easily when I walk. It hits mid-calf. My wardrobe... I don't quite understand it. That outfit I wore to Olympus? Not them. But half the clothes didn't come from my apartment, and I haven't questioned it. I just sort of assumed that the guys hired someone to get me clothes. Nothing has tags on it, though.

My chest pangs again.

I actually *miss* Olympus. The energy and the masks. The chaos of it all.

Figuring my wardrobe is a mystery for another day, I finish getting ready and stand by my door. I grip my phone tightly, double-checking the screen every few minutes. I twist the knob, making sure I'm not locked in from the outside like the first night I stayed here.

It moves easily under my hand, and I crack the door for good measure.

The hallway is silent.

My phone goes off, and I scramble to unlock it and read the text.

Go to the garden - Malik

At least he signed his name.

The doorbell rings. I wait a moment, then tiptoe down the hall to the staircase. I can hear someone talking at the front door, then another voice joins. I move silently down the stairs and into the room beside the kitchen. From there, it's a straight shot out the door and back to the gardens.

As soon as I'm outside, I book it. It seems less imposing during the day. The sun is setting, but it's easy enough to pick my way back there. And the alarms that once plagued us, the floodlights, don't go off. I duck through the once-grand opening, now hidden from view by ivy-covered walls.

I managed to survive the whole day in my room. I pull my jacket closer around my body, tucking my hands in my pockets. Lesson learned from last time.

Malik sits on the steps of the gazebo.

I stop in front of him and raise my eyebrows. "How'd you get back here? How did you avoid the cameras and... alarms?"

"You forget that I know your guys. I know how they operate." He shrugs. "It's my job to get into the places that people try to keep me away from. A cut cord here, a looped feed there..."

"One part of your job. Another part is kidnapping." I narrow my eyes. "Right?"

He chuckles. "Indeed. Part of my job."

I wave my hand at my outfit. "Is this nice enough?"

"Probably."

"And where are we going?"

He sighs and gestures for me to follow him. He leads me around the side of the gazebo, showing a *hole* in the hedges. It was cut diagonally to be almost invisible when viewing it straight-on. He pulls some of the loose shrubbery away.

I shake my head and step through.

He follows me, and suddenly we're on the other side of Jace's property. We go a few feet, and that hole disappears completely. Clever.

"That's the problem when people rely on nature to defend their space." Malik walks beside me, heading away from the house. There's a barely there path through the woods. "Nature is unpredictable."

"As are people," I point out. Correcting him slightly, again. Nervous habit.

He grunts his acknowledgement.

"What does he want from me?"

Malik pauses, glancing over at me and then away.

"Please tell me," I whisper.

"You're going to dinner with the sheriff."

I stop. Slam on the brakes. Malik keeps going another few feet before he realizes I'm not with him. And I have half a mind to rush back to the house. The *sheriff*? No fucking way. "He was with Kronos after I was abducted. Now he's doing deals with the Hell Hounds? Why the fuck–"

"He seems to have taken an interest in you. The invisible girl, he called you." Malik squints at me. "We all heard the rumors from Kronos, and the Titan's peculiar interest in you. Most people who default on a loan with him end up dead."

"So Cerberus is content to let Bradshaw–"

Malik's lips flatten. A clear indication that, however nice he might be, he's Cerberus' right-hand man.

Can't trust any of them.

"What Cerberus does is none of your business. Who he loans you out to is none of your goddamn business. Come on–you can't be late." He jerks his head toward the path.

Loaning me out. It makes me wonder what Cerberus is getting in return.

Malik leads me to a side street, where his car awaits. I don't ask questions and climb into the passenger seat. My nerves are thrumming, and I fiddle with the cuff on my wrist. I don't want to know how he distracted the guys, or when that hole in the hedge came to be. Especially since I was out there alone, at night, not too long ago.

We pull up to a restaurant on the outskirts of the college district. We're close to the heart of the city, where the university and academy sit, and the age group for this area is much closer to me than I'm used to.

I guess I figured we'd be going somewhere... low-key.

Not so much.

He climbs out and opens my door, extending his hand to help me out. I take it. My knees shake, and I *hate* that reaction. Where did my sullen indifference go? I had such a lock on it when I used to deal with Kronos. Back before I knew what real consequences were.

I've grown into my fear.

But eventually maybe I'll grow out of it.

Sheriff Bradshaw waits in the lobby. He wears a charcoal-gray suit and crisp white shirt. It's perfectly tailored to his tall, muscular frame. No tie. His beard is trimmed close to his jaw, and his orange-red hair is short on the sides. Long on top. Pieces fall over his forehead.

If I wasn't wary of him, I'd think he was attractive.

"Ms. Sinclair." He holds out his arm.

I tilt my head. Malik left me at the door, so I stand in front of him alone. Who is he today? Villain, savior, or lackey? And who is he when he's not the sheriff? The sudden urge to push him off guard urges my next question.

"Are you married, Bradshaw?"

He laughs. "Nathan."

I tilt my head.

"My first name is Nathan." He offers his arm again. "Our table awaits."

Reluctantly, I take his arm and let him lead me through the restaurant. We have a table in the middle, surrounded by others. Busy. A lot of people nod hello to the sheriff, smile, offer their congratulations for the mayor's accommodation.

Whatever. I don't know what they're talking about, and I'm not sure it matters anyway.

He pushes my chair in as I sit, then circles and takes his own seat. I shrug out of my jacket and tilt my head.

I have the distinct impression of dining with a shark. *Two can play that game.*

"You didn't answer my question."

Nathan Bradshaw lifts his left hand, showing me the barren ring finger. "I'm not married. Or dating."

"Hmm." I smooth my hands along my thighs. "I'll admit, I'm surprised you wanted to see me." *Lie.* I'm disgusted that he's forcing me to have dinner with him and using Cerberus to make it happen.

He smiles.

"What happened to Kronos?"

That drops his smile real fast. "He's away, licking his wounds. Cerberus picked a hell of a time to stage an attack, that's for sure."

My heartbeat quickens. "Attack?"

"Going after the mayor," the sheriff explains. "And the neutral zone. It's bold, but he only got away with it because Kronos failed to kill you."

I gulp. "He had plenty of chances."

"And yet, when it came down to it, he failed." His jaw tics. "Or do you think something else kept you alive?"

"I'm alive because someone–"

Bradshaw's eyes gleam. "Oh, yes. *That*. It's been on my mind for a while, trying to work out who might have pulled you out of the fire. Do you know?"

I lean back and open my mouth. The waiter appears with water, and I close my mouth again. *Saved by the bell.* We stare at each other in silence until he's done, and the sheriff orders us a bottle of wine.

Wine I will certainly not be drinking.

I can't answer who pulled me out of the fire. My instinct says its Jace, and I can't betray him like that. Not without talking to him first... and we're not really on speaking terms. He'd probably bullshit his way out of it anyway.

Instead of lying or admitting the truth, I counter with, "Whose side are you–"

A man appears at our table. "Sheriff. Good to see you."

The sheriff's eyebrow rises, then smooths. That's the only annoyance he shows before he rises, shaking the newcomer's hand. "Alex. Didn't think you'd be around tonight."

"I had plans with my girlfriend, but her dad is in the hospital." The man shrugs, his expression rueful. "Davis and I are meeting in an hour to discuss a new proposal, and this place has the best shrimp scampi."

Bradshaw nods. "You dining alone, then?"

"Unfortunately, yes."

The sheriff pauses. "Well, you're welcome to dine with us." He sweeps his hand in my direction. "Alex, this is Kora Sinclair. Kora, this is Alderman Alex Sterling."

I start to rise, but Alex just shakes his head. "Ladies shouldn't have to stand. Please."

He offers his hand, and I shake it. Alex Sterling. The name sounds... familiar.

Wait a second. "Sterling like, *Sterling Falls*?"

He grins and pulls out the chair between Bradshaw and me. "Yes, actually. My family originally founded this town."

"That's cool." I shift in my seat. My gaze flicks to the sheriff, only to find him completely at ease. I focus back on Alex. "What does an alderman do?"

"It's a fancy title for elected officials on the City Council." He raises his hand, catching our waiter's attention. Once he's ordered a drink, he eyes me again. He seems to be in his mid-thirties, with dark-brown hair and dark eyes.

"With the mayor," I guess.

He chuckles. "We work alongside the mayor on budgets, ordinances, things like that. Rather minimal interaction, luckily. He has questionable taste in friends. Right, Nate?"

Zing. Not the mayor's biggest fan? Openly, too, apparently. And perhaps not the biggest fan of the sheriff...

Bradshaw tips his head to the side. "Whatever you say, Alderman."

"Either way, your council would've had to approve Cerberus James to patrol the college district after that fire, right?" I press my lips together after the last word leaves my mouth. Probably shouldn't have said that.

But Alex just leans back and drums his fingers on the white tablecloth. He glances at Bradshaw. "I like her, Nate. She's quick."

My stomach is in knots. I lean forward, unwilling to drop the issue. "You know he leads a gang, right? You want that sort of man–"

"Kora," Bradshaw warns.

I'm on thin ice. And, somehow, we're getting away from

why he asked me here. Who knows what his ulterior motive is? All I know is that he has one.

And it's about damn time I get one, too. Besides *survive*. I'm *quick* but I'm not being smart. What good is thinking on my feet if I'm not planning a step ahead? Or three steps? Or five?

"Her semester is almost finished," Bradshaw says to Alex. "And after that, she's heading back to Emerald Cove."

Am I? An off-kilter lie, unless the sheriff knows something I don't. Unless he knows when Cerberus is going to relax his grip on me.

Inside information like that... It again forces me to ask myself, *whose side is he on?*

"Are you?" Alex appraises me. "Pity. We need more solid citizens like you around."

I suppress the urge to roll my eyes. "You don't know me."

His smile is predatory for just an instant. A flash of it before the charm takes back over. "I think I've got a pretty good idea. I've heard a lot about you... through the grapevine."

I stare at him as he pushes his chair back and stands.

The waiter returns with his drink, which Alex plucks from the guy's fingers. "It's been a pleasure, Sheriff. Ms. Sinclair. I hope we get to do this again sometime."

And then he just... saunters away.

The sheriff reaches across the table and snags my wrist. He pulls it toward him and quickly unbuckles my wide bracelet.

"What are you doing?" I jerk back, but he holds fast.

The brand is white now, more healed and a lot less angry than it was the first time he saw it. He runs his finger over it, then abruptly releases me. "Remember this brand

279

when you're dealing with men like him." The venom in his voice is surprising.

I withdraw and cradle my wrist against my stomach. Nausea rolls in my stomach.

"You let that happen to me," I say under my breath. "Maybe not directly, but you had the power to shut down the Titans–"

His laugh is hoarse. Disbelieving. "You and I are alike, you know."

I shut up and eye him. I can't believe that we're alike. My eyebrows raise, and I wait for a minute–but he doesn't continue.

"We're not. If I saw you rotting in a cell, I wouldn't leave you there. I wouldn't let you be *sold*." I spit the last word. Am I unreasonably angry? The sheriff has proven to have low morals–and shaky loyalty. That's not me. I'm nothing like him.

He winces, then nods. "Listen, Kora. I asked you to dinner to warn you. Your boys aren't as infallible as you think they are. A drug charge–"

"They're aware," I snap. "The drugs were planted in their Jeep after Kronos hit it and kidnapped me." Jesus, is he for real?

The sheriff just shakes his head. "Cerberus wants Sterling Falls. Pretend it's me he's going to lock away, pretend it's Jace or Wolfe or Apollo, whoever you're sleeping with this week. But sooner or later, he's going to take away everything you care about–and then he'll be free to take the rest." He shakes his head. "I don't believe you want that to happen."

I bristle. Of course I don't–but what power do I have?

His gaze drops to my wrist again. "That's a testament to what you went through."

"I know."

"Then why do you hide it?"

Because it's embarrassing. Because if people see it, they'll think I'm with Kronos and the Titans. That association is the last thing I want.

"Kora Sinclair?" The waiter stops by our table, glancing quickly at the sheriff before back to me. "You have a phone call at the front desk."

I raise my eyebrow at Bradshaw, but he just in clines his chin.

I sigh and stand, following the waiter back to the front. I cast one look back at the sheriff, unsurprised that his eyes are locked on me. I have a feeling our dinner has ended before it began.

kora

He hands me a cordless phone. For some reason, I'm terrified that it's Cerberus. Like he's going to say, *sorry, sold you again*. And then a black bag will be put over my head, or some monster will drug me, and away I'll go.

I steel myself when I put the phone to my ear and say hello.

"Hey, Chaos."

Relieve sweeps through me at Tem's cheerful voice.

"What kind of mischief did you find yourself in?"

I choke back a laugh. "You mean going to dinner with the sheriff isn't a normal thing?"

She scoffs. "Come outside."

"What?"

"Outside. You remember my car, don't you?"

The cherry-red Audi? Impossible to forget. I don't need much more prompting than that. Walking away from Bradshaw, I assumed the worst—but this is so much better. I end the call and wink at the waiter, then stride outside. My jacket is forgotten at the table, but whatever.

Tem's car is easy to find–but it isn't her who leans against the passenger door.

Nyx grins at me. Dark sunglasses on top of her head keep her hair out of her face. With an oversized black fur– fake, I hope–jacket and dark-washed skinny jeans, paired with black ankle boots that have a wicked stiletto heel on them, she looks like a movie star. And I *am* a little starstruck by her for a moment.

I can't forget seeing her fight Tem. Then seeing her later at the cliffs with her boyfriend. She's likable. Nice, even. But utterly intimidating.

"Hey, stranger," she greets me. "You got your guys in a little bit of a tizzy."

I quirk my lips, then shiver. It's officially *cold*. She steps aside and opens the door, revealing Tem in the driver's seat.

Tem waves at me. "Quick! Before you let all the heat out."

Nyx laughs and slips into the back seat. I take the front and slam the door shut, immediately leaning forward to hold my fingers in front of the heat.

"Coat, Kora? It's freezing out."

"With Bradshaw at the table." I lean back and roll my head to the side, giving Tem a once-over.

She's dressed to kill, too. Gold leather pants, a cropped white top, and a brown leather jacket that hangs open. She glances over at me as she pulls onto the road. "Apollo called a search party to hunt you down."

"You know what? I'm not even surprised by that. But I've been gone an hour, tops."

"What happened?"

Nyx leans forward. "Don't get us wrong, we're glad to have spotted you through the window. Was that the alderman you were sitting with, too?"

I meet her gaze. "Alex Sterling? Are you familiar with him?"

She shrugs. "All I know is that he was elected about a year ago. People were excited that he was a Sterling, although there were some rumors... I don't know. A lot was going on at the time. I think I even voted for him."

"He's got some weird fixation on cleaning the town up," Tem mutters. "He runs a lot of campaigns for removing the gangs–but who does the mayor end up turning to after that fire? Cerberus. It's ironic."

I glance around. We're on the road that goes toward East Falls, riding along the cliffs. It was off this road that I met Nyx. And, if I'm not mistaken, this will lead us to Olympus.

Oh, shit. "It's Friday."

Tem grins and nudges me. "Didn't think you'd want to miss this."

"Are we going to Olympus?" Interest pricks at my skin. It feels like an eternity since I went there. "Are you fighting?"

"Neither of us this time," Nyx answers. "Saint is hosting."

I sit up straighter. "Wait. Really?"

"Apollo is on restricted duty until further notice." Tem flexes her grip on the steering wheel. "Damn Malik and his Hell Hounds."

Guilt punches me in the gut. I take it on as my fault, even when it's not. The blame rests with Wolfe and Jace. Or, more appropriately, with the Hell Hounds. Still, I blurt out, "Tem, I'm so sorry–"

"Don't be." She pats my knee. "My brother knew what he was getting into when he took you there."

Nyx chuckles. "This town would be better off run by a woman."

"Damn straight." Artemis grins. "We know how to get shit done without starting wars."

I allow myself a small smile, even though it doesn't seem like the way of things will be changing anytime soon.

We arrive at Olympus in no time. There aren't a lot of cars—in fact, there's only a few. Tem parks closest to the cliffs and twists in her seat, so both Nyx and I are in her sights. Nyx opens a cooler wedged on the floor behind the driver's seat, and she hands her friend a can of beer.

"Want one?" She offers me a can.

I hesitate, then take it. The aluminum is cold, and I shiver again.

Tem snorts and turns up the heat.

I crack my can, and the three of us knock them together. I can't say I'm the biggest fan of beer—one might argue that I don't have much experience drinking in general, except for the few times this week that I've got my hands on tequila—but after I get over the initial taste, it isn't too bad.

"So... Saint is hosting." I shift, feeling awkward.

This is why I don't do social situations.

"He helps out with Olympus when they need him." Nyx props her foot up. "His first true love is art. He designed their costumes and masks. He owns a tattoo shop. I've been trying to convince Tem to get one forever." She reaches forward and pokes her. "A cute little bow and arrow or something? A deer skull?"

"A bow and—"

Realization hits me. As a self-proclaimed Greek mythology lover, I sure do have a lot to learn. *Artemis*. Goddess of the hunt. A freaking bow and arrow is practically her call sign.

I smack my forehead. "The club?"

Artemis has the decency to blush. "Guilty. I was able to afford the down payment from fighting at Olympus, and it took a few years to really get it to a place I wanted. But yeah. She's all mine."

Wow. And last night, Janet bragged about knowing the owner—a guy—in front of Tem and me. I burst out laughing, tipping my head back. Of course she lied. And she probably knew it, felt insecure, and felt the need to have someone call and tell me to leave Sterling Falls.

"What about you?" I swivel to face Nyx. "What's your secret?"

She wrinkles her nose. "To life?"

I shrug.

She takes a moment to think about it, then takes another swig of beer. "I took a leap and chased a thrill. And I was rewarded for it."

Tem snorts. "She jumped off a cliff with Saint after the opening night of Olympus. She was part of the first group of fighters invited to participate."

"An underdog, Jace called me." She flashes me a smile. "He learned his lesson after that."

"Yeah, because she took down Hercules. You might remember him as the big guy who challenged Jace."

"She was too busy stealing the mask," Nyx points out.

My face heats. "Desperate times."

My fingers automatically go to my wrist, and I freeze. The sheriff still has my damn cuff. He probably left it sitting on the table for anyone to take. But now, I have a weird sensation of being naked in a crowded room, with all eyes on me.

They both catch the shift.

"Hey, it's okay." Nyx gestures to my wrist. "Fuck Kronos.

No one's going to look at that and see you as someone who is on his side. But..."

I raise my eyebrows. "But what?"

She lifts a shoulder. "We could fix it. If you wanted. I'm totally an advocate of rocking your battle wounds, so to speak, but–"

"Thank you." My heart swells, then the feeling bursts. "I just... haven't accepted it. I should, right? Before I go and turn it into something new."

Artemis smiles. "Hey, you ever go to therapy?"

I snort. "Court mandated up until I was eighteen."

"So you're like, together. Mentally." Nyx eyes me.

"Hell no. Therapy didn't tell me to get out of my abusive relationship. It didn't help me conquer my fear instead of running away." I shake my head, fighting a frown. "I'm a runner. It's practically confirmed."

"Oh, come on." Artemis nudges me. "It had to do some good, right?"

"Well, yeah. I guess it helped me accept that my parents love me." Ugh, emotions. I was a fragile kid, always wondering if they were going to ship me back to St. Theresa's. After all, my biological parents did that. They had me and then gave me up.

It forced me to try and be perfect. And when I *wasn't*, as was inevitable for a kid, I would have a meltdown. Here I am, years later, trying to be perfect still. Not falling apart, not fragile, not emotional.

"I killed someone."

Artemis and Nyx both pause. With good reason. Who just admits to murder?

Nyx reaches out and grips my forearm. It's reassuring. She doesn't ask any questions, just offers the silent comfort.

"I don't know why I just told you that." My voice comes

out hoarse. "It was a few days ago, and that's something therapy definitely did *not* prepare me for. Coping with... that."

"Was it necessary?" Nyx asks.

My head jerks up and down, and I take a gulp of the beer. The warmth is starting to seep through my limbs. Not enough to make me feel better about my situation. *Was it necessary?* I certainly thought so at the time. But I can't decide if my guilt is suddenly pushing back on it, so I tell them the details. How I took Jace's gun and pointed it first at Cerberus, then ultimately shot his driver. The blood, the sound.

We don't speak for a long moment.

"It was," Nyx says quietly. "Who knows where they were going to take you? It was survival, and you took it into your own hands. You know what? Good for you."

"My brother has killed for me." Tem exhales. "He rescued me after our dick father sold me off and left a trail of blood behind us."

Oh, shit. Sold off? "When?"

"I was fifteen." She glances away. "I didn't want to make your confession about me. But we've all done things that we're ashamed of—even if our survival depended on it. I've done unspeakable things, Kora. You trying to survive is admirable."

"You, too." I try to picture what sort of situation Apollo would've had to rescue her from. What sort of monster buys a fifteen-year-old girl?

I shudder.

What kind of monster *sells* a fifteen-year-old girl?

"Rest easy, Kora." Nyx's hand is still on my arm, and she squeezes gently. "You're not alone."

I blink rapidly, trying not to tear up. "Where were you guys four months ago?"

Tem laughs, but it's sad. "You've got us now. Come on, it looks like the show is about to begin."

My phone vibrates in my lap, and I automatically swipe to read it.

Ice flashes through me at the words on the screen.

Tomorrow at the clubhouse - Malik

I drop my phone in the cupholder. Just because they think they can rule my life doesn't mean I have to let it ruin my night.

kora

T he Olympus doors swing open, admitting the first few people in line. I'm surprised at how many people are here already, clamoring to get inside. Their masks are in place, and I inhale deeply as we walk toward the entrance. I didn't realize how much I missed this.

I've been baptized by violence—it shouldn't surprise me that I've begun to crave it. Yet it does, like a new favorite flavor. The first time I was here, I could barely look at the fighters. I don't know how I'm going to react now, but something tells me I'll have a different reaction.

"Ready?" Nyx asks. She hands me a mask.

I chuckle. It's flowers. Real ones, of course. Their fragrance sticks in my nose. Blood-red roses frame the eyes, petals scattered in a sweeping motion that's similar to the raven masks. It reminds me of Ares and his blood-red eyes.

"Who put you up to this?"

She winks and practically confirms it–Wolfe had something to do with it.

I shake my head and slip it on. It's comfortable, with

silk ties that Nyx helps secure for me. Immediately, I feel myself slip into a new role. It's different from before. Maybe because I know what to expect, I know *who* to expect. A surprising confidence straightens my spine.

We approach the doors. Artemis has a gold mask with horns that seem much too similar to Apollo's to be coincidence. His deer skull mask leaps to the forefront of my mind.

Nyx wears the stars across half her face. The material is pitch-black with pockets of little reflective pieces spread across it. It covers one eye, her nose, and curves away from her dark-red lips. I'm not sure it's much of a disguise—but then again, she's not going for that. Everyone knows who she is from the tattoos and her stature.

Impossible to miss, with or without a mask.

The man at the door wears a snake mask. It seems like the full snake is right there on his face, curling over his forehead, his nose. The tail runs down his jaw. It's inky-black, the scales defined and gleaming.

I shudder.

Snakes are *not* my thing.

Nyx and Tem walk on either side of me, keeping me from veering toward the back of the line. I suppose they don't have to, but the thought of skipping past them all makes my skin crawl. Still, we keep going up the steps until we're right in front of the door.

His gaze flicks from Tem to Nyx, then me.

"What's up, Ky?" Tem winks at him. "They should get you more clothes."

I was so focused on the mask, I didn't notice his open black shirt. The bottom, tucked into his black pants, is the only thing keeping it somewhat together. His abs look oiled in the low light.

He chuckles and tips his head toward the opening. "Have fun, ladies."

We enter, and I take another breath. Incense. Flowers. Where the foyer was once cold, there are now blooms along one of the walls. Gold half-moon-shaped pots holding flowering plants. Ivy drapes down, little aerial roots holding on to the marble.

"Wow."

"A transformation," Tem says. "It was due."

I glance around the rest of Olympus. Up the stairs, the statue that captivated my attention is different. It's still the same man in his forlorn posture, but the black-and-gold paint that dripped down him has now been joined by flecks of silver. Like starlight. And the gold crown that perched, at an angle, on his head? Replaced with a circlet of roses.

Chills break out through my body.

"Why, though?"

Artemis glances at me and squeezes my hand. "Isn't it obvious?"

"No." I'm whispering.

We stop close to the stairs, and more people are carefully filling in around us.

"You," Nyx says.

Impossible.

"What do you think happened when Persephone went to the underworld?" I shake my head. "Do you think she had any say over it, or was she just serving time? Tricked to live half the year with a monster."

"I think she loved him." Artemis steps in front of me and grips my shoulders. "I think she ate that pomegranate willingly, because she was sick and tired of the life she lived before them."

295

"Him," I correct, my eyes narrowing. But my heart picks up speed, regardless.

She nods and releases me.

Nyx sheds her fur jacket. She motions to Artemis, who does the same. Under Nyx's black fur coat is a glittering silver handkerchief of a shirt. It's a halter top, and the back is held together by dainty silver ribbons. It's impressive and insane and shows off her beautiful tattoos.

She catches me gawking and grins. "I know. It isn't often that Saint has the stage and has to deal with me as the distraction. Usually it's the other way around."

I laugh.

She heads away from us, slipping easily through the crowd. They part for her. She's tall, and I keep my gaze on her dark hair until she disappears behind someone taller than her.

"Kora," Artemis whispers.

A hush falls over the crowd.

I follow her gaze, and my heart seizes. Wolfe—*Ares*—storms down the steps. His focus is already pinned on me. Open white shirt, tucked into his pants similar to the door-man. Red streaks across his chest, dripping from his jaw like someone cut his throat. His mask is such a dark red, it's almost black. His abs ripple as he strides toward me.

The crowd doesn't just part—they stumble out of his way, making an opening directly to me.

I stand tall, but my lungs are tight. I snuck out, and I can practically feel his anger from here.

He doesn't stop until he's in my space. His hands wrap around my throat, his thumbs urging me to lift my face. And when his lips crash into mine, I don't fight it.

I've never felt anything more right.

He nips my lip, drawing blood. He's catching my quick pulse in his fingers. I grip his wrists and kiss him back.

Fuck, I want him.

His tongue slips into my mouth. He tastes me, invades me, tilts my head to get deeper. My lips feel rough and swollen when he finally lifts away.

His red eyes burn into me.

All at once, I'm aware that we're surrounded by people. My cheeks heat, and he drops his hands from my neck. I catch his wrist, turning his hands palm up, and glare. They're red—and so is my neck now, I imagine.

"Bastard," I whisper.

He doesn't answer, just sweeps his thumb across my cheek. My gaze falls, and only then do I realize he has a rose pinned to his breast pocket. I swallow sharply. And then he's gone. Turning his back on me, he disappears down one of the halls and out of sight.

"Sometimes I think this isn't Olympus–this is Hell," I whisper. I touch my lips.

Artemis chuckles under her breath. "Nyx is going to be pissed that she missed the show. Damn, that was fucking hot."

Nyx weaves back toward us, her eyes wide. "What did I miss?"

"Ares kissing the life back into Kora," Tem supplies.

"He didn't." My protest falls on deaf ears as Tem relays what happened. I just stare at the statue and try to figure out when I infected them enough to change *Olympus* for me.

But then the crowd quiets again, so suddenly I hadn't realized their murmurs had resumed. Some still cast curious glances at me, but it's easier to ignore them than I would've thought. I carry Ares' handprint on my throat. When have they ever seen such a display?

Saint comes down the stairs, approaching from the left wing, and I realize I haven't seen him at Olympus before. He might've been around when Nyx fought–the night I stole the mask–but I was a little distracted.

His tattoos are on display. In the flickering light, it almost looks like they're moving.

He wears a white collared shirt, the sleeves rolled up to his elbows, and light canvas pants. His mask is gold, and it takes me a minute to realize the plain part that covers his eyes, forehead, and bridge of his nose gives way to a pair of wings that sweep back from his temples.

Hermes. The messenger of the gods.

The staff he holds is also gold, with two snakes intertwining, twisting around the pole above his grip. They're poised to bite each other. Another pair of wings decorates the very top of the staff.

Nyx breathes out a little sigh. Her eyes are fastened on him–and his gaze, after sweeping the area, lands on her. And sticks.

"Welcome to Olympus." His voice is lighter than Apollo's, but he still commands the room. Easily. "I'm Hermes, your host for the night." He explains the rules, the fighters. *The Chosen*, he calls them. And again, I have to wonder *how*. What do these people do to get into Olympus as a fighter? To even have a chance at a favor from the guys?

"Hades has been challenged," he says, "and Hades is answering."

The crowd around us bursts into cheers.

"Unexpected," Artemis whispers to me. "He didn't say anything about it."

I nod carefully. The thought of Jace fighting, oddly, creates a knot in my stomach.

"Let the games begin." Then Saint reaches into his pocket, and he throws something down on the step below him. With a *crack*, smoke erupts upward. The same dramatics I saw of Apollo. Seems they all have a flair for it. And when the smoke clears, he's gone.

"I love when he does that." Nyx links her arm with mine. "Come on, let's get a good view up close."

"Like..."

She leads me down the hall, avoiding the stairs. We're one of the first people into the large room with the raised platform. The sand that opponents squared off on before is gone, replaced with tan mats.

The first fight, Hermes announces a white-masked woman who goes by Hestia. She wears a tight white long-sleeve shirt and leggings. Her feet are bare, and her white-blonde hair is plaited. She faces off against Perseus, a lean man with dark-blond hair and a scowl. His black fabric mask is wide, obscuring most of his features.

"She's been training with me for the last few years," Nyx says in my ear. "She looks like a nice, pleasant girl until she unleashes her crazy on you."

Sure enough, she puts up a good fight. Literally. Blood drips from her nose onto her chest, but she just smiles at Perseus. They collide again and again.

This time, the violence of it doesn't turn my stomach. I find myself watching Hestia's movements. How her gaze flicks to his legs or arms a split second before he moves them.

I lean toward Tem. "How can she anticipate him?"

Artemis snorts. "Because they've been sleeping together

299

for six months. They aren't usually unlucky enough to get paired together."

"She looks like she's enjoying it," Nyx points out.

"Do you enjoy sparring with Saint?"

Nyx laughs. "Only in the bedroom."

"I'd fight who I was dating." Artemis nudges me. "Like, win the fight or don't bother asking me out, bitch."

I snort. "You got any contenders?"

"Not a one."

Nyx eyes her, but it's brief. Searching. I open my mouth to ask, but Perseus lands a nasty punch to the side of Hestia's head.

She goes down, and the crowd goes nuts. I fidget with my hands, willing her to get up. In my mind, she's me. The innocent all in white, up against seemingly impossible odds.

In the end, though, Hermes springs back onto the platform and declares Perseus the winner. And it feels like I'm the one left lying on the mat this time.

"Do you know who Hades is fighting?" I've been itching to ask.

We've seen three fights now, each one bloodier than the last. The crowd roars for it, frantic every time one pulls ahead and the end looms. It's intoxicating and exhausting all at once.

"No idea," Tem answers.

Saint–*Hermes*–eyes Nyx again. In the interlude, music plays. She swings her hips, pointing at him, and he smirks at her.

"They're so cute, they make me want to vomit." Artemis sticks her finger in her mouth.

I chuckle. I rotate, taking in the rest of the room. The people surrounding us haven't so much as touched us, and I think that's probably due to the red handprints around my throat. When I asked Artemis how noticeable they were, she just laughed and shook her head.

So, yeah. Maybe Ares staking his claim in front of everyone is a blessing.

My eyes meet someone's on the balcony to my left. Ice

shoots down my spine. I turn and squint, but the person is already turning away. Slipping between a girl and guy and out of sight.

What the fuck?

"Hades," Hermes introduces, just as the lights flicker out.

I jump.

Artemis grabs my hand and squeezes. "It'll be okay."

That's not why.

A spotlight appears, and it feels like déjà vu to see him standing there. Plain dark mask, shirtless. He stands motionless, his arms loose at his sides. Last time, he had the skull painted on his face. Now... he seems more human. And I can't for the life of me understand *why*. What's different about tonight?

Whether he knows I'm here or not, he seems determined not to look in my direction.

Hermes' laugh gives me chills. "And I will apologize– both to Hades and to you. His challenger asked to remain anonymous... to further his chance of Hades agreeing."

Hades inclines his chin.

"Are you ready to meet his challenger?" Hermes throws his arms wide, asking all of us.

And we respond. The whole place goes crazy with cheering, yelling, screaming. We're all strung up by Hermes' question.

I do want to know. I want to see this fight more than anything. *He likes to toy with them*, a fighter told me. When I missed Hades' fight to steal his mask.

Bummer.

Now, anticipation licks at me.

The lights flicker again, and then the doors to the fight- ers' corridor booms open. I crane around, trying to see who approaches. The yelling intensifies, it grows in my ears until I'm sure the sound will be embedded in my brain long after I leave here.

Nyx flinches. It's the only indication I get that something's wrong.

The people blocking my view shift just as Ares steps up onto the platform.

Artemis gasps and grips my forearm. "He doesn't fight."

I can't stop staring. He pulls his shirt off and drops it to the mat, then kicks it away. He's glaring at Hades like he wants to kill him.

This is my fault. It has to be.

Hermes shifts, stepping between them. He says something to Hades, but I'm too busy fighting my way forward. We're already as close as we can get, but it isn't enough. I can't let him go through with this.

I seek out Jace behind the black mask. His cold eyes skate over me, ignoring me completely.

Hell. Maybe he wants this just as much as Wolfe.

"Kora, *stop*." Artemis yanks me backward, and suddenly Nyx is with her, helping to keep me from doing something stupid. "They probably need to work this out one way or another, don't they? Better here, than..."

Than somewhere that won't stop them from actually killing each other?

I growl my frustration, but I stay silent. All I can do is watch.

Hermes leaves them alone on the platform. They circle each other warily. Hades has shed his arrogance—at least, it seems it. His swagger is still there, but it's forced. He wasn't acting confident before, he just *was*. Now, it's a show.

Ares acts first. He moves fast, driving forward and into

Hades. He shows no fear for himself, no sign that he needs to protect his face, his torso. He just goes at Hades.

And Hades lets him. In an instant, they're down on the mat. Ares straddles Hades and punches his face once, twice.

Hades doesn't fight back.

I let out a yell and renew my struggle against the girls. As much as I loathe Jace for what he's put me through, this is too much. This is Wolfe out of control.

Hades' breaking point comes before I can do anything. He throws Ares off of him, and the latter hits the mat on his side. They both rise, and Hades wipes the blood from his mouth with the back of his hand.

He spits and smiles at his friend. "Best you got?"

Ares scowls. "Fight back, you fucker."

Hades just lifts one shoulder. He moves to the left, circling the platform, and stops right in front of us. His back is to me—but Ares has the perfect view.

And Hades uses me as a distraction. He sees it the second Ares registers where I am in the crowd. He kicks at Ares, catching him in the stomach, and then they're both back in it. Locked together, kicking and yanking at each other.

A switch flips in Ares. Where he once had control, now it slips away like it was never there to begin with. He's a demon shaking loose his restraints.

Those red contacts—I wonder if he wears them because he's afraid of seeing the world in shades of red. If he wears them to face his fears every time they dress as the gods.

No one is immortal. Not even here.

"Shit," Artemis mutters.

She saw it, too, as Ares circles and lets us glimpse his dead expression.

Hades hops on the balls of his feet, still grinning. Still

loose, despite the hits he's taken to his face and torso. They're both bleeding, both not walking as easily. But it's Ares who charges Hades again, dodging Hades' counter attack, and gets him in a chokehold. They fall backward, Ares locking Hades down with his legs, and his arm around Hades' throat.

Seconds pass as they struggle.

Ares looks checked out. His eyes are unfocused.

Hades is... stubborn. Until his eyes roll back and his body goes limp.

Still, Ares doesn't release him.

I scream. Not because I think it'll do any good or because I'm upset about Jace losing a fucking fight for once. Because I feel helpless like this. Because they put me in a position to watch Ares lose himself in darkness.

I kick at Artemis, connecting with her shin, and her grip on my arm loosens. I shove Nyx away and scramble up onto the platform.

Front-row view to the violence.

I fall to my knees beside Hades and cup Ares' cheeks. His arms are shaking with how hard he's gripping.

"Baby, you've got to let him go." I slap his cheek lightly, trying to get him to focus on me. To come back from wherever he's spiraled. "Come back to me. Let him go."

And I just know I'll be following him into the darkness. I would pull him out if he'd let me.

"You're killing him. Wolfe. *Please.*"

That gets him.

His eyes refocus, finding mine, and immediately his grip slackens. He shoves Hades away and staggers to his feet, then spins in a slow circle.

After a few seconds, Hades coughs and sucks in a deep breath.

I stare at Ares from my position on my knees. We match, him and I. From his red eyes to my red hair, to the outfits we wear.

But the role I'm playing isn't supposed to be his. No matter how close we get, there's always going to be *that*. Persephone always belonged to someone else.

I glance at Hades, who has climbed to his feet. Hermes helps him stand. Shakily, I rise, too.

"Why?" I ask Ares.

I wish *his* mask would allow him to be more truthful. He says he can look into my eyes—and probably a lot of other people in here—and see who I am. And I wish like hell that I could do that to him, but all I see right now is anger and regret.

"Let's take this outside," Hermes says pointedly. "Or better yet, to his rooms."

I nod once and follow Ares out. Hermes and Hades take up the rear, trailing us into the dim hallway. The doors close behind us, and then the door to Hades' room closes us in, as well.

I pull my mask down. The ties catch it, let it dangle around my neck, and I move away from them. Or else I'll hit them both upside the head, and that probably won't help. But when I turn back, Hermes has left us and it's just those two, staring at *me* like I'm the outsider.

And, yes, I am.

But I'm one of them now, too. They made sure of that.

I march up to Hades. He doesn't move as I pull the mask off his face, dropping it to the floor. And suddenly he's back to being Jace. Still arrogant but quiet. His lip is split, the skin around his eyes darkening. He's got abrasions on his cheeks from the force of Ares' hits, and there's a few reddening marks on his ribs.

He just lifts a brow, like he's curious to see where I'm going to take this. Hell if I know–I didn't have a plan when Wolfe was choking Jace, and I still don't have a plan.

Except for the fact that I *hate* that I'm the one who's come between them.

I spin around and approach Ares. He stands stiffly in the middle of the room, his hands balling into fists and then splaying. Over and over, like that's the only way his anger can escape. Through his poor, bruised knuckles.

There's more to this. More to him than the fury rattling against his skin. There's agony underneath it all, and remorse, and deep down is the guy I'm falling for.

I move more carefully with him. I reach up and untie the mask, and it slips down his front between us. I cup his cheeks and direct his gaze to me.

"Take your contacts out," I order softly.

He doesn't balk at that. He removes them with surprising accuracy–for someone without a mirror, anyway–and lets them join the mask on the floor. He's still brimming with energy. I imagine it crackling just out of sight–lightning waiting to strike. And I shiver, because I want some of that. I want his anger and passion and *everything* that he has to give.

"Wolfe." Reaffirming his name. Reaffirming that he's here with me, not still on that platform. Not fighting whatever demons he saw in Jace's place.

Speaking of...

I face Jace head-on. "Why the hell did you fight him?"

He shrugs. "Seemed like he needed to get something off his chest."

"*Seems like* you're just looking for trouble," I mumble.

Jace crosses his arms. "What's the favor, Wolfe?"

I blink. "What?"

"He won. A favor." Jace enunciates like I'm deaf.

"Kora," Wolfe says. He's moved away, to the couch. He beckons to me.

I go. Of course I go. And when I'm close enough, he pulls me down to straddle his lap. He lifts my skirt, arranging it around us, and meets my gaze. I crave this contact. To know that he's not lost to me.

"You saved Jace's life," he says under his breath.

I tremble. "I know."

"Thought you hated him?"

"I'm still leaning that way. Doesn't mean I want you to kill your best friend."

Wolfe leans forward and runs his nose up my throat. The move is unexpected, and I go completely still. His hands inch up my sides, slipping under my shirt. His lips touch the corner of my jaw, inching toward my ear, and I tip my head to give him access.

"You went somewhere dark."

His teeth drag across my earlobe. "I'm still somewhere dark, flower. I don't have any light in me. But fighting him in front of people is better than the alternative."

"And you fought him because..."

"Because he's ruining you." Wolfe suddenly grips the back of my neck, anticipating my withdrawal. He keeps me close, and his gaze flits to Jace. "He's ruining everything."

Is that why they fought?

He shifts his hips, and his hard cock presses into my panties. Perfectly aligned, except for our clothes. His free hand slips under my skirt and undoes his pants. He tugs my panties aside, and I shift a little.

I don't want Jace to ruin everything–not me, either–and I open my mouth to tell him so. But Wolfe's fingers spasm on my neck, and the words die in my throat.

His gaze goes to Jace. "You like to watch, don't you, Jace? But if you touch her against her will again…"

He thrusts into me.

My head automatically falls back. He fills me completely, and a groan slips past my lips. He surges up under me, hitting a spot deep inside that sends a fluttering feeling through my abdomen. I grip Wolfe's shoulders and meet his hard gaze.

"It wasn't against my will," I breathe.

He stills, and that hand around my neck slips forward. His thumb brushes the corner of my jaw. Every move sheds little flakes of red paint between us.

"Say that again."

"I…" God. This is the truth I couldn't admit to Jace last night, but I need to voice it now. "I've been wanting him to kiss me."

Since he was caught watching–more than once. Since every time he aggravates me, I wish it would end in him hate-fucking me. That's a deep thought I haven't even admitted to myself. Since we danced.

Wolfe's gaze shutters, then his eyes flick to Jace. "Well?"

"Well, what?"

Wolfe directs my face in his direction. "Show her what you think of *that*."

I eye Jace. He stands almost awkwardly in the middle of the room. He's strung tighter than a bow. My chest fills with butterflies when Jace takes a step toward us. Then another. Wolfe has stopped moving inside me, and I can't seem to take a deep enough breath. My heart is going to burst.

Wolfe releases my neck, and Jace immediately takes it. His fingers wind through my hair, forcing me to lean back.

"Are you going to kiss me?" Better than to beg for it.

For a second, I wonder if he's going to actually make me say it. *Please, Jace, kiss me.* It's on the tip of my tongue.

He watches me. His eyes roam all over my face, taking in everything. I don't know why this situation is turning me on so much. My body is on fire, but all I want is for Wolfe to start moving again, and for Jace to kiss me.

I might die if I don't get that.

And then he does.

Kiss me, that is. He comes down, and our lips brush, and then there's no helping me.

Wolfe groans and rolls his hips, and the friction turns me on even more.

Fuck, what the hell am I doing? Kissing one guy while another is inside me? But I wouldn't change this—and part of me is grateful that Wolfe pushed the issue.

Jace nips my lower lip until my mouth opens, and his tongue tastes me. His hand squeezes on my throat, and my breath stutters.

"She likes that," Wolfe murmurs. His fingers slip into my panties, through my wetness. He pinches my clit, and I jump.

Jace tears his lips away and moves to my cheek. He breathes in sharply, holding my head still. I can't keep my eyes open as Wolfe continues his assault on my clit, and the lazy way he thrusts up into me.

Jace pulls my shirt off. I lift my arms, letting him toss it behind him, and he puts a knee on the couch. He's fixated on my chest. My nipples pebble, showing through the thin bra, and he immediately removes that, too.

He leans forward and takes one in his mouth.

I meet Wolfe's eyes, and he grins at me. His hand moves up, rolling my other nipple in his finger.

It's too much.

"I'm going to come," I pant. I squirm on Wolfe's lap. "Guys."

"Shh," Wolfe whispers. "We've got you."

"I know." I hold on to him tighter.

Jace's teeth graze my breast, and then he pulls away. Abruptly. He shoves his pants down and reveals his thick cock.

I mean, holy shit. I now understand his arrogance–he's been walking around with a monster between his legs. *Fuck me twice.* Wolfe is packing. He's got a pretty dick, if we're being honest. But Jace's makes my cunt clench.

He grips his length and tugs, jerking himself off with steady, quick strokes. I can't take my eyes off it, even as my pleasure builds higher and higher. I'm just an instrument that Wolfe plays with skill.

All at once, the intensity in me crests. I come wordlessly, my muscles tightening. My eyes shut on their own, and my head falls back.

Wolfe circles his hips and then lets out a grunt. He slams up into me, pulling me down by my hips to meet him. He finally stops, fully seated inside me, and he comes with a groan. His cock pulses, and I can't stop my muscles from clenching at him again.

"Kora," Jace says. "Look at me."

I don't have a snippy remark. I turn my head and see his eyes first, then drop down to where he's still jacking himself off.

"Open your mouth."

A thrill rushes down my spine. Wolfe's fingers tighten on my hips, but I do what he says.

Because I want to see this through.

He steps closer. Before he can stop me, I lean forward and lick the tip. He lets out a hiss of breath. That's the only warning I get before ropes of milky cum spill out. It coats my tongue, fills my mouth. It spills down my chin.

Fuck. It's dirty and hot, and I shouldn't be attracted to this, but I am.

Jace's thumb presses on my lower lip, opening my mouth wider. His gaze is pitch-black, those eyes so fucking full of fire that I don't know what to do with it.

We're going to burn. I just know it.

"Swallow," he orders, eyes on my mouth.

I do. And I like the taste of him.

That's the most worrying part of all.

wolfe

Fuck, fuck, fuck.

Let's make a list of things I didn't plan on happening:

Fighting Jace. In fact, we had a pact. An agreement. *I don't fight.* Period. And the reason is very clear to see: I almost killed him. I would've if Kora wasn't there. She might be the only person who could've stopped me. The only one besides Apollo... and Jace. But Jace was unconscious, and Apollo is here. Home. Nursing deep bruises...

Which brings me to the second thing. My father's men attacking him.

Did I know it was going to happen? I should've. But I put it out of my mind because I thought Dad would make an exception with Kora there. That he'd agree she deserved some safety.

Ha. Laughable, now that I'm seriously considering it.

She disappears into the house once we're home, the garage door lowering closed behind us. Jace and I sit in silence in his car, and I twitch. "I meant it."

He exhales. "I know."

The *favor*. Such malice behind such a simple concept. Ask, and you shall receive. That was our motto–until the cost became too high. Now, the price is higher as a result.

Basic economics.

Kora might not have caught me *asking* for it, but I did. And Jace agreed, whether he wanted to or not. I asked for *her*.

And then he came on her tongue like a Neanderthal.

"She looked spooked," Jace says.

I glance at him. "When?"

"Before our fight. Before you came out."

"And you just... ignored it?" I scowl. "Of course."

He rolls his eyes. "We have security at Olympus. Nothing would've happened to her. Besides, she was with Nyx and Artemis."

I contemplate that. Sure, I can see his point. But I know for a fact that there are plenty of monsters who would love to see us fall–and my father is just one of them. Nyx and Artemis are great fighters, but even they don't know all the shit we've waded through.

Shit that might be coming back to bite us in the ass.

Spooked. I can clearly picture her wide eyes. The shiver of her skin when she's afraid. The rapid drum of her pulse. And anger once again fills me. I'd love to let go of it. To say goodbye to my quick temper, the insidious thoughts.

Jace is plagued with those, too. The thoughts and memories. He just hides it better.

And that makes it worse.

"You're ridiculous." I hop out of the car. I'm still mad that he kissed her, that he treats her like shit, that he–

A scream dislodges my thoughts.

Kora.

Jace and I burst from the garage and sprint into the

house. She screams again. Upstairs. He lets me go first, bounding up just behind me. I get to her room first and skid to a halt.

She's across the room, by the bathroom. She's changed into sleep clothes, a big sweatshirt that I recognize from my own collection, and shorts. The red paint on her throat that I marked her with is gone. Her slim legs are bare, and she clutches a hand towel against her chest.

Her bed covers are flipped back, revealing a coiled black snake.

A *dead* snake.

Its blood is splattered across the sheets, the head cleanly severed from its body.

Bile turns my stomach, and I hurry to her side. I pull her into my chest, and she sinks into me without hesitating.

My gaze finds Jace.

It can't be a coincidence that this snake looks deceptively similar to the masks our employees at Olympus wore.

I shiver.

For years, we've protected our identity. A handful of people knew we ran Olympus. Cerberus, of course, and some of his higher-ups like Malik. Our employees–each one was thoroughly vetted. Nyx and Saint, Artemis... they're practically family.

"I-is it–"

"Dead," I say into her hair. "Come on, don't look at it."

Where the fuck is Apollo?

I guide her out and try to keep a level head. The reality of the situation sinks in, though, and I'm not sure how I keep myself together. Someone broke into our *house*. And not for the first time. Jace catches my eye.

We're back on the same page. Not that we were ever

really off it–just when it comes to Kora–but the rest of it? We're still solid.

And he nods once, understanding the questions running through my head.

He leads the way into the hall and down to Apollo's room. He opens it without knocking and stops short. He's sound asleep.

Fucker.

"You've got to be kidding me." I release Kora long enough to stalk forward and shake him. We're usually light sleepers, and he *slept through* someone putting a fucking snake in Kora's bed?

Unacceptable.

I have half a mind to beat *his* ass.

But he doesn't wake up.

I shake harder when he doesn't even react. "Apollo. Wake up, bud."

"Wolfe." Kora touches my arm.

I go still, gripping Apollo's arm. He's warm. He's *breathing*. Why the fuck won't he wake up?

She moves around me and lifts a glass. Water, I would've assumed, but at this angle, it looks like there's something distorting it. The thinnest layer of oil across the top. She sniffs it and shrugs. "I'm not a drug expert, but this doesn't seem normal."

"You're saying someone poisoned his water." Jace glances around. "Which he gets from the... tap."

"Or he could've grabbed an old glass," Kora suggests.

He doesn't listen to her, instead turning around and leaving us in Apollo's room. I have half a mind to follow him, just to see where the fuck he's going to investigate. Something crashes downstairs.

Kora sprints past me. I cast one look at Apollo and

groan. I would've had her wait here with his unconscious ass. I guess he'll be okay, seeing as how he's survived the last few hours alone. I shake my head and pat his shoulder.

"We'll get you right as rain, buddy," I assure him.

I find her and Jace in the kitchen. He has all the glasses spread out on the island.

"All of them," he grits out.

"What?"

"They all have that residue on them." He slides me a glass.

I hold it up to the light. Sure enough, it's barely noticeable—but it's there. If we were in a hurry to get a drink, I doubt it would catch our attention.

Jace meets my gaze. I know what he's thinking. And I'm sort of thinking it, too. We're going to have to call in reinforcements on this one. Not the sheriff—I wouldn't trust that fucker to have access to my house—but a team that can sweep this place from top to bottom.

The message is crystal clear: it's not safe here anymore.

And that means Kora needs to go somewhere that can protect her—because we clearly can't do that here.

Fuck, fuck, fuck.

kora

I sit on the floor in the foyer surrounded by my bags. My phone is on top of the one to my left, but the dark screen taunts me. They let in their doctor a few minutes ago, and both guys went upstairs with the doc to check on Apollo.

Snakes freak me out. Granted, my visible reaction to the masks might've given me away, but not a lot of people know that. And I don't think very many would use it against me like that.

Are they calling *me* a snake? Are they saying there's a snake close to me?

Or is it a warning tied to Olympus?

To the guys?

There are too many mysteries to keep track of, and my head spins when I think about the last few months. Maybe I need to channel my father. Become my own sort of investigator and figure this shit out.

With a sigh, I grab my phone and open the notes app.

I write: *Weird Shit*

Okay. So first, there was the culminating incident: I

witnessed Apollo stab someone. I'm pretty sure they were meeting with Cerberus, and it was one of those jobs that they do for him. Which means the guy he killed was a Hell Hound. Although who he was and where they took the body is unknown. And probably unimportant.

Then my scholarship was taken away, as well as my job. Jace's handiwork. Although, having now *met* Jace, I think he could've convinced me a lot harder to leave Sterling Falls without pulling that many strings.

After I got tangled up with Kronos, the guys found me. Then Apollo's motorcycle exploded–which introduced me to the sheriff. At the time, we pinned that on Kronos–but that bastard likes to brag. He never did about that.

Besides, what would be the point of trying to kill me? I was worth money to him at that point.

I rub my brow and keep typing.

Motorcycle explosion - ???

What the hell came next?

That photo. And the outfit I wore in it.

The photo seems like it's the more alarming of the two, because the outfit could've come from anywhere. And, shit. I don't even know what the guys did with the photo. Whoever put it on the doorstep got past their security and gate.

I scrunch my brows. Were there cameras up at that time? I think they came later.

But perhaps whoever did *that* also did *this*. Reasonable assumption? I write it down.

Whoever made the photo had to be at Olympus to take the photo *and* be good at photo manipulation. Or know someone who is.

On a new line, I write, *the sheriff* and leave it at that. There are too many questions around him anyway. Whose side is he on? What does he want? He tried to sneak a listening device into this house, but he later gave me the knife when my life was in danger. He was with Cerberus and the mayor in front of the burnt frat house. And then that weird-as-hell dinner with his cold warning.

My stomach drops. Sure, *he* wasn't successful with the listening device. But what if whoever put him up to it was?

I text Wolfe my theory on a listening device, my hands shaking as I type.

Oh. And I still don't know who pulled me out of the fire. I should really confront Jace about it, but I'm afraid of what he might say. Lies... or the truth.

Next, the Jeep and the drugs. Still unresolved.

I suck my lower lip between my teeth, worrying at the skin. The phone call seemed inconsequential, but with the snake in my bed... I don't know. It could still be nothing, but Janet would've had to tell someone to call me. I add it to my list.

And finally, the person I thought I saw at Olympus.

The doorbell rings, and I flinch.

Wolfe comes down and glances at me, then away. I want to ask how Apollo is–the doctor has been up there for a while–but the words won't come. A muscle in his jaw tics, but he doesn't speak. He opens the front door and steps aside, letting Malik in.

I really don't want to go with him.

My bags are packed to leave with Malik. For my protection, Jace argued. Because they can't keep me safe here, not when they can't even protect themselves.

Bullshit.

That suffocating feeling is back. It sticks in my throat, making it hard to swallow. To breathe. Malik stops in front of me and raises an eyebrow.

I scowl at him and push to my feet. "Give me a second."

I head upstairs and peek in Apollo's room. He's resting at an incline, the doctor checking his pulse. His eyes are still closed, but he doesn't look any the worse for wear. He has an IV drip with a clear bag of liquid hanging from his bedpost. And the doc doesn't seem overly concerned.

Yet, Jace isn't up here.

I continue my search and find him outside. He runs his fingers through his hair, seemingly unaware that I'm here. But then he glances over his shoulder, and the corner of his lip tips down.

Great start.

"I can't go with him." I fold my arms over my chest. "I'll have to resort to drastic measures."

He grunts.

"I'm serious. What's the point of any of this if you just shove me back into the arms of Cerberus James? We never found out why he paid so much money–"

"I know why he paid so much."

My teeth clack shut.

"What do you want, Kora? You want to stay with your boyfriends?" He glowers at me. "You think a little action will bend us to your will? You should've left Sterling Falls when you had the chance."

"You're not the first to tell me that today," I snap.

"Oh yeah, princess? Who else?"

I shift. "I don't know. But that's not the point."

"Right." He rolls his eyes. "So, back to it."

Back to why I want to stay *here*?

A few months ago, it was Kronos and his threats against my family that kept me in Sterling Falls. But now, I can't imagine leaving the beautiful, dark town. I want to be normal here. I want to go back to school and actually graduate. I want the light parts of the city, not just the bleak spots.

But maybe the city doesn't want me.

"Jace, *please*." My gaze drops to my feet.

"You want me to do something about this? You want me to save you from Cerberus James?"

I step up beside him and glower in his direction. "He can control me, and I hate it. You of all people should know *exactly* how I feel about it."

His lips flatten. A moment passes before he nods once and turns on his heel. I cast one last glance around the backyard, then follow him inside.

"I'm coming with you," Jace says to Malik.

Wolfe's eyebrows hike. "Oh?"

They have a silent conversation, and Wolfe's jaw tenses. Then he comes to me. He presses a kiss to my cheek. "You'll be okay."

I shake my head. Last time he said that...

"Come along, Kora." Jace's keys jingle in his grip. Malik leaves from the front door, and I once again trail Jace. This time to the garage, to the convertible. The top is up, at least. I slide into the passenger seat.

We ride in silence behind Malik's car. Looks like he was considerate of the bags I was going to be hauling with me, and he chose something bigger than a bike.

In no time, we arrive at the Hell Hounds' clubhouse. Cerberus waits for us inside, and his lips twitch when he sees Jace come in after me.

"What a surprise," he calls. "Come. Sit."

Jace lays his hand on my shoulder, stopping me from approaching. He shakes his head. "Let's talk in your office."

"Business? It's after hours." Cerberus lifts the glass in front of him. "I've been drinking."

"I don't know when you're not," Jace replies.

The older man chuckles. Hell Hounds are scattered around the large room, minding their own business. Some cast intrigued looks in our direction, but the murmur of conversation never ceases. Finally, Cerberus nods. "Okay, fine."

"She's not privy to our conversation."

I stiffen.

Cerberus grins. "Ah, I see. Malik, stay with Kora. Jace and I will return." His gaze flicks to me. "Make yourself comfortable."

Great. Suddenly, trusting Jace to get me out of here seems like a terrible idea.

"What are you drinking?" Malik asks me.

I shake my head and head to the bar. One of the younger Hell Hounds mans it, but half his attention is on the movie playing on the television mounted above the shelves of liquor.

"Jesus, Donny," Malik snaps, banging his hand on the bar. "Can you pretend to be working?"

The young guy spins around. He's the same one who hit Apollo with the glass.

I narrow my eyes at him, and he has the good grace to seem sheepish.

"Beer," Malik says. "And change the channel to the goddamn news or something."

Donny scrambles to obey. He slides two bottles our way, the tops popped off, then locates the remote. The eighties movie flips to a news anchor relaying something about the college. The subtitles scroll along the bottom, but I watch halfheartedly. I'm more worried about my current predicament than whatever mess SFU has got itself into.

I glance at the door Jace and Cerberus disappeared

through, and my stomach swoops. The whole situation with Cerberus has been fucking strange. He treats me with kid gloves ninety percent of the time—the other ten percent, he's threatening to knock me out by way of horse tranquilizers.

Well, maybe not that way. But a heavy sedative at the least. The memory of the prick of the needle and burn of the drug in my neck is hard to shake. Especially here.

But Jace has never handled me like that. I mean, yes, he deals with me. And he puts up with Wolfe and Apollo and our growing relationships. My cheeks heat at *that* thought. And sometimes he's cruel. Like he doesn't *want* to do it, but obligation drives him.

Why does he feel obligated?

"Holy shit," Malik breathes. "Donny. Volume."

My attention snaps back to the screen, and my heart immediately climbs into my throat. There's a reporter outside Jace's house. In the driveway are two of the sheriff's cars and a black SUV. The cop cars are lit up, the blue, white, and red lights flashing slowly.

Donny finally gets the volume up, and the reporter's voice comes through loud and clear.

"...word that the men behind a massive drug ring in Sterling Falls have been discovered. The Sterling Falls Drug Enforcement Agency has been keeping a tight lid on their investigation, but new details have come to light. And we received early word that they're ready to make arrests."

Behind her, the front doors open. The gates are already open wide, although one is off its hinges. Forced open, then.

A man in a suit exits first, followed by a younger man dressed the same way. I squint and lean forward, my heart in my throat. The second man looks familiar—but it isn't until they zoom in that my heart *does* stop. And then lurch. My whole body has a violent, immediate reaction.

"No, no, no." I stand and back away like it's *me* he's arresting.

"Kora?"

"This can't be happening." I grip my hair, but my eyes are glued to the screen.

Wolfe comes next. His hands are behind his back, and the sheriff follows right behind. He grips Wolfe's bicep and practically shoves him down the steps ahead of him. Then Apollo, with another cop behind him. He's led in a similar manner, although his movements are sluggish. *Still drugged*.

But my eyes can't stop going back to the suited men. To the painfully familiar one. He stands with his hands in his pockets, and everything about him is the same. The way he brushes his hair, his posture. His expression–blurry on camera now but unmistakable. *Gleeful.*

Parker Warton.

The abusive ex who drove me to leave Emerald Cove in the first place.

"Kora," Malik snaps. "What the fuck is going on?"

I shake my head and storm toward the back room. Jace will fix this.

The door opens, and Jace meets me in the hallway. He sees my expression and stops dead, confusion pulling his brows together.

"What happened?" he barks.

"Wolfe and Apollo–"

My phone buzzes, and my heart skips. Maybe Wolfe or Apollo will tell me that this is all a mistake. But it isn't them. It's a text from a blocked number.

See? You should've left while you had the chance.

Its meaning is clear. I caused this.

Words won't form in my mouth for a long moment, and I struggle to say it. All of it. That they've been arrested, that it's my fault, that somehow my ex found us. Was it from being on the news with the mayor? It reached my parents—why wouldn't it reach Parker?

I've been a massive idiot.

I should've protected myself. Fought harder for my face to be kept out of the public eye.

Jace grips my shoulders. His confusion melts into concern. "Whatever it is, it's okay. Just breathe."

Breathe? Yeah, right.

I take a deep breath as directed. Jace has strings to pull. Connections. He can get Wolfe and Apollo out of this… bogus drug charge. Right?

"We have a solution."

"But—"

"Kora." He gives me a *look*, and I press my lips together. "Just listen. For the next two minutes, keep your goddamn mouth shut."

"Jace—"

He covers my mouth with his hand. "Don't you trust me, Sinclair?"

"Asshole," I say against his palm. It's muffled, but I think he gets the idea.

He slowly removes his hand, and I decide that he can fucking wait to find out that his two best friends were just arrested. Clearly, he's not going to let me talk anyway, and this just serves him right. Although the idea of waiting pangs in my chest.

We go into the office, where Cerberus stands behind a desk. "Kora Sinclair. Do you or do you not want to remove me as the holder of this contract over you?"

I gulp. Jace said to stay silent, so...

Cerberus chuckles and turns his focus to Jace. "She listens to you better than she ever listened to me."

He shrugs. "She likes me better."

Cerberus grins. "That she does. Still, for the record, I'll need a verbal response. Kora?"

"Yes." I clear my throat and repeat it louder.

"All right, I accept your terms." Cerberus taps the papers. "Sign here."

I stiffen. Jace's hand touches my back, pushing me forward. I scan the paper on the desk. It's a contract, flipped open to the last page. Cerberus has already signed on the line above.

"Let's make your freedom official," Jace says in my ear.

Something twists in my gut.

A warning that this is the exact opposite of what I want.

"Sign it, or we'll start unpacking your bags in my guest room," Cerberus snaps. "I've about had it with these boys running you all over town. If you want things to stay as they are..."

I shake off my doubt and pick up the pen. My palms are sweating. My mother would yell at me for not reading the contract, but we don't have time for that. We need to go help Wolfe and Apollo. I scrawl my signature and step back quickly, like it's going to immediately bite me for it.

Jace nods and steps up beside me, adding his signature to the list.

My heart stops. "Why are you signing that?"

He glances over his shoulder at me, his expression unreadable.

Don't you trust me, Sinclair? A trap. A motherfucking trap that I just waltzed right into.

Kora Sinclair, you did NOT just sign that stupid

fucking contract over to Jace. A siren plays in my head, the sort of warning sound before the bombs begin to drop.

Did I really just fall for that? Am I the world's biggest sucker?

"No," I whisper.

Because where Cerberus can be bribed, Jace wouldn't. And whether or not he wants me gone is beside the point. When would I ever be able to get out of this?

My pulse thunders in my ears, and I grit my teeth to stop from screaming.

Control. He's always wanted control.

Now he has it.

Cerberus takes a seat behind his desk and leans back in it, grinning at me. "Happy now, girl? You're out from under my thumb."

"Out of the pan and into the fire." My face is hot, and I can't even look at Jace.

He doesn't seem to have a problem looking at me, though. He leans in and says, "Let's go."

I swallow. "Is that an order?"

Jace pauses and faces me. He runs his fingers down my jaw and pushes my hair off my shoulder. It's oddly menacing, even though my stupid heart takes comfort in it. Like a silent threat and apology rolled into one.

He runs his fingers through my hair and nods slowly. "Yes, Kora, that's an order."

It hits me square in the chest.

This is the end of the road, Kora.

Escape just evaporated like it never existed for me.

Jace spins me around and propels me back toward the main room. Guess he was serious about leaving.

A thought occurs to me, and I dig my heels in. "You

didn't orchestrate the drugs, did you? To get Wolfe and Apollo out of the way?"

He pauses. Turns me back around. "What?"

He can't be serious.

I glare at him. "Wolfe and Apollo were just arrested–"

"You've got to be fucking kidding me. They can't be arrested."

Not a good time to tell him about my ex being behind it, then. I mean, I guess I don't *know* that he was behind it–it's just another gut feeling. I should listen to those more often.

"We saw it on the news. They led them out of the house in cuffs." I hate that I'm relaying this information so easily instead of making him sweat for it. But, on the other hand, I hate that my guys have to spend even a minute in handcuffs.

Jace shakes his head and pulls out his phone. He calls Wolfe first, but it goes straight to voicemail. Then Apollo– same thing.

"Fuck. Come on." He grabs my hand and yanks me forward now, moving faster. He gets ahead of me, dragging me behind him.

We almost reach the main room when it happens.

Boom.

An explosion rocks through the clubhouse, and the whole building gives a violent lurch. Jace and I are thrown backward by the force. It's the weirdest feeling of weight-lessness before I crash back down.

I hit the floor flat on my back. The heat hits me, and my upper body curves to the side. I cover my head with my arm and feel around for Jace with my other, but I can't reach him.

Smoke and dust surge down the hallway, and the whole building keeps trembling like it's suddenly unstable. I can't breathe. The dust covers me, the grit in my eyes, my hair, my nose. The fall knocked the wind out of my lungs, and I lie on my side, choking, until my lungs finally expand.

Dust and smoke fills my mouth, and I cough to expel it. I yank my shirt up over my nose and mouth.

The building lurches again. My ears ache, a familiar high-pitched whine the only thing I can hear for a long moment. I whimper. Something heavy is sprawled across my legs, pinning me down. I lift on my elbow and squint. The world is blurry, but I can make out the person lying across my lower half.

Jace.

He doesn't move. He was in the lead and probably took the brunt of the force. It's pure luck that I'm not unconscious.

I strain to hear anything, to shift him off me. Pain lances up my arm when I try to shove him away, and I immediately stop. I cup my arm, surprised to find pieces of glass embedded in my skin.

What the fuck just happened?

Another noise pierces the ringing in my ears. A rapid *pop, pop, pop.*

My blood goes cold.

Gunfire?

An explosion and gunfire?

I swing my head around and try to discern where the sound is coming from. I push more frantically at Jace, trying not to panic. I'm in such a rush to get free, I don't notice the footsteps behind me until hands grab under my arms and haul me up.

I yell as I slide out from under Jace. I get my feet under me and immediately twist.

A tall man stands in front of me, his dark jacket hood up

over his head. From under it, his dark eyes peer out from behind a snake mask. Unlike the ones from Olympus, this obscures his face in its entirety.

I shiver violently.

His attention goes over my head. He pulls a gun from his hip and yanks me close, then fires twice over my shoulder.

I automatically flinch and hunker down. If he hit his mark, I'm definitely not going to turn around and look. I've seen enough blood in the past few months...

"Always getting yourself in trouble," the man says to me.

Immediately, recognition fills me. Not from his face or any detail in particular.

No, his voice. He's the one that I've wondered about in the back of my mind. The one we should've devoted more time to finding.

The one who rescued me from the fire.

Not Jace. Of course it wasn't. It's *him*, this mysterious stalker.

"You should've left Sterling Falls when you had the chance." He grips my upper arm and tows me back the way he came, confirming that he was the one who texted me.

There's still gunfire from the front of the building. From where the explosion happened.

Did he set it to go off? Or is something bigger happening? My brain is moving in slow motion, but I know I don't want to be dragged out of here without a fight.

I've spent so much time *not* fighting, and that needs to change. Without hesitation, I dig my heels in and throw myself backward. I only have a split second to be surprised that it works, and my arm slips from his grip. Now's my only chance to make sure Jace is okay. I make it to his side and shake his arm.

His eyes open, then go wide.

Fingers wrap in my hair and wrench me back. Pain burns across my scalp as the masked man drags me away from Jace. I scream and kick, sliding along the floor. I hold on to his wrist, trying to lessen the burn of my hair being yanked out, but he's relentless. Until we're a good ways away, and he stops.

His eyes flash behind the mask, and he crouches beside me. "You have a choice right now. Stay here and become caught in yet another web or come with me. Avoid the war with the Titans that's brewing right outside." His gaze lifts, and his finger twitches closer to the trigger. "Your choice, K. What do you think Kronos is going to do when he finds you in here? Or, better yet, what will *you* do when this place is flooded with Hell Hounds and Titans set on killing each other?"

I gulp. War? Parker is in Sterling Falls, too, presumably looking for me. The city is no longer safe. I don't think it's been safe for me for a long time, but it's getting worse.

And Jace... he made this deal with Cerberus behind my back. Trapped me in another corner, with a fate no worse than where I started. I trusted him enough to sign that piece of paper, and it bit me in the ass.

But no matter how guilty I feel, I won't condemn him.

I point back toward Jace. "I'm not leaving without him."

We watch Jace roll and sit up, drawing his weapon smoothly. Before he can raise it, the masked man lifts his own firearm and presses it to my temple.

"Not so fast."

Jace goes still. He eyes us, then carefully stands.

"Toss your weapons." The masked man's voice is all authority.

I'm hyperaware of the muzzle touching my skin. It's hot from use, but I ignore it. I refuse to show fear to this stranger—not when he's clearly been behind more than just this. How did he find me here? How did he rescue me out of the fire?

Jace drops his gun to the floor and kicks it away.

"Ankle," the man sighs. "You think I was born yesterday?"

We step back. Once Jace has removed another, smaller gun, he walks toward us. His hands stay up in surrender, palms facing us. His eyes burn into mine.

I don't know what the hell I just got us into, but it can't be good.

But maybe... maybe we have a chance to escape this if we stick together.

The *pop pop pop* of gunfire is getting louder. There are shouts from outside.

"Move," the masked man orders. "Down the hall."

Jace goes first, walking with a limp. There's blood on the back of his shirt. Did he hit his head, too? It gives his hair a wet look.

The masked man lowers the gun as soon as Jace is ahead of us, but it doesn't stop him from keeping a tight grip on my upper arm. He keeps me next to him as we find the back exit.

Jace shoves the door open and peers outside. "It's clear."

"Red car," the man says.

It takes a second for Jace to find it, but then he nods. We follow him out, our bodies hunched to stay low. There's a row of five cars parked next to each other against the back fence. Jace gets to the red one, standing to the side.

The lights flash, and the trunk opens.

"Get in," the masked man says.

Jace's brow lowers. "You're kidding."

"You can get in, or I can shoot her in the leg and put *her* in it. Your choice."

I flinch.

"Fine, man. Fucking hell." Jace pushes the trunk door open wider and sits on the edge. He puts one foot in, then the other, and slowly lowers himself inside.

"Zip tie your feet. They're in a bag in there."

I make a squeaking noise of protest, but the man doesn't react. He just holds the gun steady, the muzzle trained on my side, and Jace does what he says. Honestly, I'm surprised Jace is even considering doing what the man is asking. But he does it with a stoic expression.

First his ankles, and then he waves the bag at the guy. "Suppose you want me to bind my wrists, too?"

"Yep."

Jace does it slowly, biting the ends and yanking them tight.

"Great." The man strides forward, leaving me temporarily behind, and pulls something from his pocket. I don't see the small black device until it's too late. He leans down and touches it to Jace's arm.

The buzz of the stun gun is loud, like bees, and immediately, Jace's body goes rigid.

He slams the trunk shut and glances at me. "Get in the back seat."

"Over here!" someone yells. "I've got her!"

I turn and see Titans—it has to be Titans—rushing

around the clubhouse. They wear all black and carry clubs, chains, guns.

Fear bleeds through me, and I rush to climb into the car. As soon as the door shuts, the man throws it in drive.

He floors it—toward the fence.

I scream. We crash through the wood, splintered pieces going everywhere. The man doesn't comment, doesn't even remove his mask. We careen through tall grass. The car finally bursts onto a dirt two-track. The headlights barely illuminate far enough ahead of us to see anything.

With shaky hands, I put my seatbelt on. It scrapes against my injured arm, and I bite back a whimper.

Jace is in the trunk.

Wolfe and Apollo are in custody.

My *ex* is back.

I close my eyes and open them, hoping that this is just a really terrible, awful dream. That I'll wake up and it'll be three o'clock in the morning, and I'll wander down to the music room and fiddle with the piano until the adrenaline fades.

But when I open them again, I'm still in the car. The shock and adrenaline are still going strong, keeping me from feeling the worst of my injuries. My eyes are gritty from dust and ash, and it takes me a few seconds of blinking for my vision to clear.

"Where are you taking us?"

My question goes unanswered. I stare out the front windshield and try to predict where we're going, but I've got nothing. Not until we've navigated through the industrial district in South Falls and turn onto the main road out.

I guess he wasn't kidding that I should've left–now he's removing me, himself.

Twenty minutes later, he pulls over onto the side of the

road. There's barely enough room here for a few cars, and the sign says something about no overnight parking.

I shiver in my seat.

Something thumps loudly from the trunk, and I jump.

The man meets my gaze in the rearview mirror, and then he removes his mask.

I gulp, waiting for the familiarity to hit–but there's nothing.

I've never seen him before.

He tosses the snake mask aside and runs his fingers through his dark hair. He's older than I expected. "It's better that you don't recognize me," he says quietly. "Otherwise, this wouldn't have worked."

"Right." I look around. "Are you going to kill me?"

"No."

I nod to myself. "You called me K earlier."

He lifts one shoulder. He hands me a water bottle and a wide plastic container. He motions for my face. "Rinse your eyes out."

I lean forward and do as he says, letting the water run over my eyes and clear away the grit. When I'm done, he gives me a napkin. I dry my face and take a drink. I'm trying not to freak out, but that seems like a pointless endeavor. This panic is sludge, weighing me down.

How much fight do I have left in me?

Headlights precede a car coming from the opposite direction. I expect them to pass, but instead, they turn into the pull-off, facing us, and shut their lights off.

I lean forward. "Did you sell me?"

The man chokes. He turns around and faces me fully, and his gaze takes in everything. Up and down. It isn't in a sexual way, or even a creepy way. Just like someone trying to see *something* that they thought they'd recognize.

But the moment passes, and he shakes his head slightly. He gets out and circles around the car, opening my door. He offers his hand.

This is the guy who knocked me unconscious after saving me from the fire.

Is that what's going to happen to me now?

He wiggles his fingers, and I hesitantly take his hand. He helps me out.

"Kora!"

I turn.

My mother rushes from the other car, hurrying around it. She barely looks at the man at my side and throws her arms around my shoulders.

"Oh my god," I say. "What are you doing here?"

My dad is close behind. He joins the hug, and I don't know whether to cry or laugh.

I thought he was going to kill me. I should say that to them, but I can't.

"Oh, honey." Dad cups my face. "We're so sorry for scaring you. We knew you were in trouble and didn't think you could get out of it on your own."

I step back from their embrace and digest that. "You didn't believe me when I said I wanted to stay."

"That man had influence over you," Dad says. "Come on. Get in the car."

"But–"

"He's in the trunk, Ken."

His friend. The one he was so mysterious about. I still don't have a name, but that, at least, clicks into place. I should've known. Should've put it together sooner.

Dad nods slowly. He puts his arm around my shoulders. "Do what you have to do. But I don't want him coming after her. Never again."

The man's expression remains impassive. Why wouldn't it? He already killed someone tonight–shot them in the hallway without asking any questions. "I'll take care of it."

They shake hands. Dad leads me to the car and sets me into the back seat. He closes me in, and that's when I come to my senses. I can't let that guy *take care of* Jace, like he's a situation and not a person.

A person who hasn't harmed me.

Is he going to kill Jace? Bury him in the woods?

"And the other ones?" Mom asks. Her voice is clear, directed at the man who got us out of the clubhouse.

"Arrested."

Shame burns my cheeks, and I lunge for the door handle.

It doesn't open.

My dad climbs into the driver's seat and cranes around. I'm still yanking at it, to no avail, when he exhales. "It's okay, Kora. We know what kind of influence boys like them can have... and we'll get you sorted."

Sorted.

"Away from here," I finish. "Away from them."

"Yes. We need to keep you safe." Dad puts the car in reverse, and we back away from the man. From Jace. "We'll get you an appointment with your psychiatrist. Stockholm Syndrome. They made you reliant on them. It isn't your fault, Kora. When you're feeling better, you can go to school somewhere else."

"Anywhere else," Mom echoes.

I press my hand to the glass. My heart is breaking, but I don't say another word. I can't fight any more. I didn't let them *Stockholm Syndrome* me into liking them. It wasn't like that at all. But as much as I want to voice it, the words don't come.

We pass the *Leaving Sterling Falls* sign, and I close my eyes.

Going, going...

Gone.

TO BE CONTINUED

in *Rebel*: mybook.to/rebelsf

acknowledgments

Let's take a moment to breathe through that ending, right?

Thank you all SO much for reading (and hopefully enjoying) Fighter! I am obsessed with this world. And, of course, Greek Mythology. I've been dreaming about writing something like this for years.

A big shout out/thank you to my team. Early readers with invaluable advice, and listening to me work through the plot in voice messages (So. Many. Voice. Messages.) — Rebecca, Erica R., and Ari; beta readers, Jolie Vines, Shawna, Clarissa, and Brandy. I appreciate you all so, so much!

To my editors, Emmy Ellis at Studio ENP and Paige Sayer Proofreading, and my wonderful cover designing team, Qamber Designs - thank you for helping me make the best book possible.

Thank you, thank you, thank you!

also by s. massery

Dark Bully Romance

Fallen Royals

#1 Wicked Dreams

#2 Wicked Games

#3 Wicked Promises

#4 Vicious Desire

#5 Cruel Abandon

#6 Wild Fury

Standalone

Brutal Obsession

Mafia Romance

DeSantis Mafia Series

#1 Ruthless Saint

#2 Savage Prince

#3 Stolen Crown

Romantic Suspense

Broken Mercenaries Series

#1 Blood Sky

#2 Angel of Death

#3 Morning Star

about the author

S. Massery is a dark romance author who loves injecting a good dose of suspense into her stories. She lives in Western Massachusetts with her dog, Alice.

Before adventuring into the world of writing, she went to college in Boston and held a wide variety of jobs—including working on a dude ranch in Wyoming (a personal highlight). She has a love affair with coffee and chocolate. When S. Massery isn't writing, she can be found devouring books, playing outside with her dog, or trying to make people smile.

Join her newsletter to stay up to date on new releases: http://smassery.com/newsletter

Made in United States
Orlando, FL
01 August 2024

49813924R00214